HER BROTHER'S KEEPER

SACRED HEARTS MC
BOOK 9

A.J. DOWNEY

COPYRIGHT

Book editing & design by Maggie Kern @ Ms.K Edits

Cover art by Dar Albert at Wicked Smart Designs

DEDICATION

To Sarah Ann Scott-Gillespie, because you are one of my most inspiring readers. The time we got together at Glass City was too short. Thank you for pushing me to broaden my horizons.

PROLOGUE

N ox...

Dude, a week into December and the good ole Wally World was a fucking madhouse. I hated Christmas; it was a family holiday and even though I'd had Rush, Grind, and Archer coming up - when you came up in the system? Thanksgiving? Christmas? Hell, just about every holiday had pretty much been a solid reminder of everything you didn't have and never would. The only reason I was even here was to pick up booze. Trig and Sunshine's wedding had pretty much wiped the club out; we were still waiting on the bulk order to come in. If I was going to have any hope of getting my drink on this weekend, then I had to make a pit stop. I may have hated the corporate bullshit that was Walmart, but I couldn't deny their booze prices were some of the cheapest around here.

"I'm sorry, ma'am, but it says it's declined," the cashier murmured. I gave her another once over while *Joy to the World* grated in my ears over the store's PA system. Fuck, I hated Christmas. I dropped my eyes back to the glowing screen of my smartphone and texted Rush back.

"You must be doing something wrong! I have over six hundred dollars in that account; run it again." I glanced back up from my phone at the bitter, old, trailer-trash bitch in line in front of me. She'd been giving the poor girl behind the register a hell of a time going on five minutes now. I couldn't help myself, I glanced back the girl's way again.

She was a knockout, but you'd never hear me say it out loud because can we say jailbait? The girl couldn't have been much older than sixteen or seventeen. Her long, chestnut hair in a braid over one shoulder looked glossy in the buzzing overhead lights. She didn't wear makeup and she didn't need to, either. She had a natural beauty and surprisingly flawless skin for obviously being a teen.

I watched her key something into the register and incline her head with some serious grace to indicate that the woman should try again. I watched as the checker waited, those wide brown eyes a little too wide, for the predictable outcome.

"I'm sorry, ma'am…" she began, and the woman exploded at her.

"What's the matter with you, are you stupid or something?" I blinked, and the checker tried to stammer out an apology, tried to remain professional and all, but the blonde out of a bottle wasn't having any of it.

"Seriously? You're doing it all wrong, I have money in that account! You're stupid or something." She crossed her arms over her saggy titties in her low-cut leopard print top and I wish like hell I were joking about that. "Get me your manager, you stupid cunt!" the woman demanded and she was screaming at the checkout girl who'd gone completely red in the face, her eyes welling and tears spilling over and that was the point that I'd had enough.

"Yo! Who you calling a cunt you two-bit, crack-headed, trailer park bitch?" I demanded and took a menacing step in her direction. "It's fucking Christmas! Who talks to a kid like that on Christmas? Look at her!" I barked. "There's no reason for you to be nasty to this girl when all she's trying to do is help your skank ass. Now, you're wasting her time, you're wasting my time, and you're wasting all of these people's time," I said flinging an arm back to indicate the jammed checkout line. "Personally, I think that's enough. You damn sure ain't gonna waste her manager's time on top of everyone else you've put out. Now, get the fuck up out of here!"

My explosion set off a round of cheers and applause behind me; the trailer park bitch grabbed her wallet and stuffed it into her rhinestone and fringed black leather purse. She made a noise, tossed her hair that seriously if I had a match, it would have gone up worse than Michael Jackson's hair during that Pepsi commercial disaster. Before she turned on her patent leather heels in her fake ass leather leggings and clipped towards the exit she shrieked at me "Fuck you!" I glared at her the whole damned way, it wasn't below me to whoop her ass. I didn't think that she could technically be classified as a lady, and the club might just let it slide.

And the girl? Well, fuck. The next thing I knew, she was around from behind the register and bawling into the front of my cut, my arms held out as I looked down at the crown of glossy brown hair, wondering what was happening.

"Thank you," she sobbed. "My dad died this morning, and I have to be here, I have to pay the bills and it's just me and my brother now and she was just being so mean, and I couldn't help her, and it's not fair! She was just being so awful and it's like I don't have a dad anymore, why is she being so mean?"

I looked up into the stricken face of the manager standing behind the girl as I patted her shoulder awkwardly. "It's no problem," I said hollowly. "It's gonna be okay." I lied because, I mean, she was just a girl, and damn sure not even old enough to drink. The fuck?

"Maren, sweetheart, why don't you come over here?" her manager called, and I let her go. The checkout girl kept her head bowed and someone else slipped behind the register while her manager took her off to the side. I checked my wallet and paid the new guy at the register for the booze using my card instead of the cash I'd planned on using. I stopped wordlessly in front of the girl and shoved every bit of green I had into her hands.

"I'm sorry for your loss, baby girl," I told her, my heart falling flat on its ass in the middle of my chest. She stared at me, wide-eyed, her mouth hanging open in surprise, but before she could speak, I got myself the fuck out of there. I had not expected that. Just goes to show, be kind always, you never fuckin' know what demons someone's wrestling on any given day. *Fuck.*

1

N **ox...**

"What's eating you?" Rush demanded lightly, kicking my booted feet off the chair I had them propped on, so he could sit down. One look at my face and he shut it, asking without words in the way that we'd always had, *'Are you okay?'*

Truth be told, I didn't know if I was. It was over a week later and I couldn't stop thinking about her, the girl from Walmart who'd lost her dad. I drank some of the Wild Turkey in my glass and sighed heavily. Most of the boys were partied out, and so they weren't here this week. It was quiet for a Saturday night. They happened around here, not very often, but they did.

Dragon, ever fuckin' perceptive that *that* guy was, relocated from his usual table over to ours. Disney and Aaron's conversation stuttering to a stop over at the bar.

"What's going on, Nox?" Dragon asked.

I sucked in a breath and let it out in a big fuckin' sigh, "I stopped in at the Wally World over on Douglas last Friday before church," I said, and Disney and Aaron wandered over from the bar to hear what was up. I frowned to myself, and Dragon arched an eyebrow.

"And?" he prompted.

I sat up and downed the last bit of booze in my glass and told them what'd happened. About the pain-in-the-ass broad and the heartbroken girl behind the till.

"I can't stop thinking about her," I said, and my twin's forehead crushed down into a frown.

"Never seen you like this, Bro."

"It's the weirdest thing, man. I just can't shake it. I mean, to lose your pops right before Christmas? I couldn't imagine."

"We didn't have folks, for any of our Christmases. What *is* there to imagine?" Rush asked, leaning way back in his seat, stretching his arms above his head. I gave him a flat, borderline unfriendly look.

"Maybe it's hitting so close because of Archer and Mel," Disney suggested.

"Meh, could be," I said. Mel was pregnant, due in the first week or so of June. Archer was an instant dad with Noah and all, but this was going to be his first biological kid. Honestly, though, I don't think this had anything to do with my older foster brother. I think it had everything to do with those deep, wide brown eyes, haunting me every time I closed mine.

"You get any information we could use to track her down?" Dragon asked.

I frowned. "Like what?"

"A name is a good start," Data said from his little alcove, leaning back in his chair to look through the open door at me.

"Maren, that's all I got, and that's only because her boss said it."

"Maren who works at the Walmart on Douglas," Data said to himself, tipping forward and pulling himself along his desk over to one of the screens and one of the many keyboards laying on its dark surface.

"That enough to actually get you something?" I asked, kind of incredulous.

"We'll find out," he uttered, voice distant as he clacked across keys, his eyes rooted to one of his screens.

"While he works on that, how do you want we should help?" Dragon asked, and I blinked, falling back in my seat.

"Seems to me she's worried about getting the bills paid, why else would she be working the same day her daddy died?" Rush said.

"Too right," I agreed. "She said it was just her and her brother now, I assume that means he's younger than her."

"Fundraiser and toy run?" Dragon asked.

"We do things like that out here?" Rush asked.

"Been a minute since we had a cause other than Veteran's Affairs, and Trig and Ghost usually head those up. We could do it, though."

Dragon scratched his beard and Data called out, "Got it!"

"Got what?" I asked.

"Obituary," he said and began reading off the screen, "Ronald G. Tracy lost his battle with cancer this past Friday and is survived by his two children, Maren Elizabeth Tracy and Sage Hunter Tracy. Services to be held, blah blah blah, looks like they just went down..." He started muttering to himself, "Yeah, thanks for printing their full names..." His volume went back up as he addressed me again, "I should have an address in a couple of minutes."

"You seriously found all of that out because of her first name and where she works?" I asked.

"No, I found it out because you said the dude died last Friday. I put in 'obituaries' and 'Maren' and got lucky on the first try."

"Didn't say anything about a wife in there, did it?" Dragon asked.

"No, it did not," Data agreed.

"I got the impression that she was on her own with the brother. Couldn't tell you what gave me the vibe that he was younger than her."

"The fact that she said that *she* had to pay the bills?" Disney said.

"Girl must be carrying the weight of the world on her shoulders," Aaron murmured and slicked some of his dark hair back off his forehead. "Poor thing," he added.

"How old d'you think she is?" Rush asked.

"Seventeen," Data called out. "The younger brother is eleven."

Dragon sat back in his seat looking smug while the rest of us sat around shaking our heads.

"What's taking so long to get that address?" I asked sarcastically.

Data came out of his digital kingdom and handed me a printed page with the information. "I was printing it out for you."

I blinked and the guys around me started to laugh; I took it from the lanky brother and sure enough, he had an address.

"I'll be a son of a bitch," I muttered.

"Anything else?" he asked.

"Yeah, remind me to keep as much of my shit off the internet as possible," I muttered.

He shook his head. "That's my job, I do what I can to keep us *all* off the internet."

"Good to know," Rush uttered and took a swig of his beer.

"So what 'cha thinkin'?" Dragon asked me, my gaze lingering on the stark black letters and numbers on the crisp white page.

"I'm thinkin', I have no idea how to put together a fuckin' charity run. Charity wasn't exactly our thing back in Arizona."

Dragon nodded, and Rush piped up, "Man, this jailbait really got under your skin, didn't she?"

"Bro, I couldn't even tell you," I said, and I meant it. I literally could not stop thinking about Maren of the soulful brown eyes. I just couldn't.

"Data, take notes," Dragon rumbled, and Data went back to his little command center.

"Ready when you are, P."

And that's how we ended up spending the rest of our Saturday night. Brainstorming and putting together this last-minute charity ride for Maren Tracy and her little brother. I had no idea how I let myself get into this; but strangely, I didn't regret getting involved, not one bit.

2

M aren…

I was in the kitchen, making lunch for me and my little brother, Sage. It wasn't anything fancy, just sandwiches and some soup. It was cold out, and it just seemed like a grilled cheese sandwiches and tomato soup kind of day. At least, that's what I kept telling myself. Really, we were getting down to the wire money wise and I didn't get paid again until after Christmas. The nice part was, at least I was current on all the bills, thanks to the man in my checkout line the day my dad had died.

He'd crammed nearly four hundred dollars into my hands just before he'd left, and I'd been stunned, staring at his back as he'd walked away, the image of the heart wrapped in barbed wire seared into my memory. *The Sacred Hearts,* his jacket had proclaimed, he was one of them and I'd been confused. I mean, bikers weren't typically nice guys, were they? I thought if they had those patches on their backs that they belonged to a gang or something. Of course, it wasn't like I would ever find out or *know* without ever talking to one of them, right? I'd found the internet as a research option less than helpful for this sort of thing because it seemed that the motorcycling community was just as divided as the rest of the world on the issue.

So, I'd kept an eye out in the intervening week, on my way to and from school, and to and from work. I hadn't encountered anyone with the same club affiliation since; though I wondered if that was due to the cold and the snow. I raised my head from where I was pouring soup into two mugs at the roar of machines out on the street. It sounded like a lot of them. Probably more than I had ever seen in one place.

"Maren! Maren, come quick! They're pulling into our driveway!" Sage called from the living room. I rinsed the grease off my hands in the sink from plating the sandwiches and I hurried out of the kitchen. I stepped quickly through the living room drying my hands on a dish towel wondering for the thousandth time, like every time I heard a motorcycle, if it was him.

Those lightly colored eyes, so pale a gray as to almost not even be there had bored into mine and... I don't know, it was like he'd communicated with me, without having said a word.

"Sage, get back here! Don't go out there!" I frustratingly sighed. My little brother wasn't listening to me, hadn't been listening to me like at all since our dad had died. Like now, he already had the front door open, to a man in black leather on the other side, fist poised to knock. I swallowed hard at his appearance. Black gloves with white skeletal finger bones printed on the backs. He had one of those matte black half helmets on; his eyes indiscernible behind black wraparound sunglasses. The lower half of his face was hidden beneath a bandana, printed much like his gloves with a leering skull that overlaid his face beneath perfectly.

He looked down at Sage and his muffled voice asked, "Is your sister home?"

"Why, you here to kidnap her?" Sage asked. "Because I would totally love that."

"Sage!" I snapped and the man at the door lifted his gaze from my brother, pinning me where I stood halfway from the kitchen, up the hallway, into the living room. Though I couldn't see if it was him, the man from the store, the gaze, even through the dark glasses held the same weight, it stole my breath and I swallowed hard, hoping but not expecting.

Sage looked back over his shoulder at me and rolled his eyes, stepping aside and opening the front door wider so they could see me.

"She's right here," he said.

"Can I help you?" I asked, and the man pulled off his sunglasses with one hand and the bandana down off his face with the other.

"Do you remember me?" he asked, and it *was* him, standing on my doorstep.

"Yes, of course. What can I do for you?" I asked, ghosting timidly up to the open door, blasted by the frigid air outside. More of the bikers were stepping up onto our front porch and I shifted from foot to foot, nervously.

"I'm Nox, and these are my brothers and sisters," he said. "We wanted to come by and wish you a Merry Christmas," he said and unzipped his jacket part way down. He pulled out a long green envelope and held it out to me.

"I... I don't understand," I stuttered.

"Take it," he urged gently and I did, reaching out with trembling fingers. It was full of money. I looked up at him and the shock must have been visible on my face because some of the men and women behind him started to laugh and a couple of the other men gave each other high fives.

I was numb with stunned disbelief. I blinked up at him and said again, "I don't understand."

"Well, sweetheart, all you need to understand is that you made an impression on our boy, Nox, here; and he asked us all to help, and so we did."

I let my gaze drift from the man from my checkout line at work to the man who had spoken. He was much shorter than Nox, who was taller than me by a head, although where Nox was slim, this man was wider with an impressive breadth of shoulders. He was also Hispanic, his coal dark eyes sparkling with good feeling, the gray in his beard and the crow's feet fanning out from those dark eyes placing him at quite a bit older than my strange benefactor... maybe a good thirty years or more older.

"How did you know where I lived?" I asked and the older man gave me a crooked grin.

"We have our ways," he said and held out his hand. "I'm Dragon, the president of this here chapter."

"Maren, Maren Tracy," I said giving his gloved hand a light shake. "I honestly don't know what to say, um... I uh... would you like to come in?" I asked, which didn't feel like the right thing to say to a bunch of bikers, but it did feel like the right thing to say to anyone who had just handed you an envelope full of money saying 'Merry Christmas' on your doorstep on the eve before Christmas Eve.

"Nox and I would love to." the older man, Dragon, said before turning back and calling out, "All o' you fuckers make a line and start passing it forward!"

I blinked, but a cheer went up, and the next thing I knew, wrapped gifts were being passed forward and I was staring at Nox who had this ghost of a mischievous smile on his face.

"I don't understand..." I uttered again, and he put a gloved hand on my shoulder and smiled. "You don't have to, just let us do something nice for you and the boy," he said jerking his chin in Sage's direction who was exclaiming over the packages invading our living room.

I looked over to the empty hospice bed that was supposed to be picked up two days after Christmas and felt my eyes well up.

"Why are you doing this?" I asked, and Nox smiled even bigger.

"Because I think you may have forgotten there's good people in the world and that good things happen too."

I stared up at him and I think this is what people meant when they said someone was shocked because it was like I couldn't move and I couldn't speak. I was just speechless, and so incredibly numbed by everything that had happened to us lately.

"Thank you," I murmured watching the bed and couch fill up in the small space, figuring that the last thing I wanted to do was say 'no' when I'd had no hope of getting Sage anything for Christmas this year. Just seeing him lit up and smiling was worth it.

"Hey, it's okay. You know, a lot of us get it," Nox said, low and sympathetic as I dashed at the tears gathering on my lashes. I didn't want to cry, but how could I not?

"I don't know why you would do this for me, I mean you don't even know me!"

"Tell you the truth, I don't know either, but that's okay, too. Sometimes people are put in your path for a reason, it's just on you if you answer the call or not."

He confounded me, confused me, and at the same time, delighted me with the smile he'd put on my brother's face. I stared at him with gratitude and hugged him tightly like I had in the store.

"Thank you, so, so, much. I didn't think I was going to be able to do it, but maybe I can, thanks to you."

He patted my shoulder awkwardly and chuckled. "Maybe here's to the start of a new friendship," he said and I pulled back to see him eyeing my brother, Sage, who was looking at all of the leather-clad men with adoration.

I didn't quite know what to think right that minute about that, but I couldn't deny that it sounded appealing. I was curious about this guy.

"I'm sorry, I just finished fixing us lunch, and I want Sage to eat it before it gets cold," I said giving my head a little shake, trying to wake up from this dream that wasn't a dream at all, but totally real. "I um, I could try to fix enough for everyone, it's just grilled cheese and tomato soup…"

"Thank you kindly," Dragon said, smiling brightly, "but we've got to ride before it snows again."

"Oh, I completely understand, I really don't know how to thank all of you."

"It's no problem," Nox said and he pulled off one of his gloves to fish in the sideways slanted outside pocket on his jacket beneath the leather vest that he wore over it. He pulled out a business card and handed it to me.

"You call if you need anything," he murmured. "Okay?"

I looked down at the card, *Landon Fisher LMP* was written on it, and it was just a plain white business card, with blocked blue letters on it. I didn't know what an LMP was, but I could Google it and the business name on the upper lefthand corner.

"Okay," I agreed and nodded.

"My cell's on the back, and I mean it, if you need help with anything here around the house, a fix or whatever, I'm pretty sure me or one of my brothers will know how to do it. Hopefully, that takes a little more of the pressure off." I flicked my gaze from the card in my hand up to his face and he winked at me, pulling his glove back on.

"I really don't know what to say," I said. I'd already said thank you, but all of this went so far beyond a mere 'thank you' and he was right, knowing I could reach out if something went nuts in the house really did take some of the fear of living in the house alone, just me and Sage.

Even when my father was near the end, he was still a comforting presence to me. I was doing everything before, but he was still the adult, you know? Still smart, still the planner and thinking ahead for just about every eventuality. He'd tried so hard to hold on until I was eighteen, which was just three months away, but when he realized he couldn't, he'd signed the paperwork readily while he was still alive, emancipating me. As far as the courts were concerned, I was a legal adult and capable of caring for Sage.

We'd still been supplied a state social worker with the Department of Children's Health Services to oversee that I could and would take care of Sage but even there I'd been lucky. Pamela Swanson had been working with me for a while and she'd become a good ally. Raising an eleven-year-old boy who was angry and hurt and just didn't understand what was at stake was harder than you could imagine.

"I mean it, Maren. Call me if you need anything," Nox murmured and I shuddered, coming up out of my deep, dark, thoughts like a swimmer coming up for air. I stared, wide-eyed while my brain tried to catch up.

"Y'know, Maren's a pretty name," Dragon remarked, before tipping three fingers to the red bandana covering his forehead like he was tipping a hat and stepping back out my front door. I smiled and gave a nod to accept the compliment he'd given me. Nox followed his president back out the door.

"Thank you all, so much!" I called out to the large group and another cheer went up before the roar of motorcycles being kicked to life drowned them out. Sage stood next to me grinning and I put an arm around his shoulders. He shrugged me off with an annoyed glare and I sighed inwardly.

I watched Nox and his brothers ride off, his sisters paired off and riding on the bikes behind the other men and wondered even more about them all. I was still confused. I mean, bikers were outlaws, weren't they? Thieves and drug dealers and almost like modern day asphalt pirates.

I looked down at the envelope of money in my hand and closed the front door saying to my brother, "Sage, go eat your dinner before it gets cold."

"No way! I want to open some of these."

"No, you can wait until Christmas."

"Yeah, but Dad is dead, who is gonna stop me? You?"

I arched an eyebrow at my brother and counted to ten inside my head. "Sage, he was my father, too. Now go eat your dinner before it gets cold. We're sticking to family tradition. This Christmas is no different from any others. One on Christmas eve, the rest on Christmas morning."

Sage rolled his eyes and my temper frayed even further. I crossed my arms, pulling my cardigan closer around me. The door standing open for as long as it had, had sufficiently chilled the house and I couldn't afford to turn up the heat. Or at least I couldn't a minute ago. *You're still going to have to make the money in the envelope stretch as far as possible,* I told myself.

Out loud I said, "Roll your eyes at me again, Sage, see what it gets you."

He gave me a dirty look. "You're not *Mom,* Maren," he sniped at me, but he was moving in the direction of the kitchen now.

"You're right, I'm not, but I am all you've got a little brother. We're all each other has left," I murmured, but I was talking to myself; Sage was already sitting at the kitchen counter eating his soup. I shoved the envelope in my back pocket and considered the business card again, turning it over.

I mean it. Anything, it read, and below that, was his cell phone number as promised. The fresh ache of the loss of our dad throbbed anew in the center of my chest. I wanted so badly not to feel so alone like I did, to have someone that I could talk to about this who was grown up enough to understand.

None of my classmates did, and for that, I was more than a little jealous. Gone were my days where the worst thing I had to worry about was what outfit I was going to wear to the Friday night football game. Hello days of being responsible for a terminally ill parent and obstinate preteen brother. Except I would give anything to still be responsible for a terminally ill dad, rather than simply responsible for everything that came after.

His funeral had already been carried out, but I still needed to pick up his urn from the funeral home. The handwritten text on the back of the business card blurred as my eyes welled up with tears. I slid it into my back pocket with the envelope and stared at the gifts piled on the sheets and blankets on the couch.

I'd been sleeping down here almost the full last three months of Dad's life. I had my bedroom upstairs, but the first night, after my father had died, when I'd tried to sleep in it, I couldn't bring myself to. I'd tossed and turned and had eventually wound up back down here. I'd lain awake wondering if I'd ever meet the strange and wonderful biker who'd been so kind when that woman had been so awful and now here he was been and gone, delivering more kindness when all I could do was despair over the fact that I couldn't give my brother a Christmas this year.

I wondered briefly if my dad had a hand in that from wherever he was now, the words Nox had uttered about answering a call sticking with me.

"It's not fair, you know?" Sage demanded, calling from the kitchen.

"What's not?" I called back.

"You making me come in here and eat before my food got cold but you're still in there."

"You're right, I'm coming," I called with a sigh, wiping the tears out from under my eyes with my middle fingers.

I took a fortifying breath and went to eat with my little brother who I knew was only acting out lately because he was hurting. He did that, a mean little shit one minute, the next he had to be in whatever room I was, just so he didn't feel lonely. I had to be patient. I had to be strong. I had to be kind. Most importantly, I had to be everything our mom was not. I had to just hold on and be here, no matter how hard it got, because I couldn't leave Sage all alone.

3

N ox...

Bzzt! Bzzt!

I groped for my phone on the nightstand and sucked in a deep breath, squinting at the screen which was damn bright in the dark of my room.

Unknown: Are you awake, by chance?

I blinked, forehead wrinkled and shot back: **who is this?** I had a feeling I knew who it was, but I just wanted to be sure before I blabbed business that didn't belong on a stranger's cell.

Unknown: I'm sorry, it's Maren.

Me: Don't b, and yeah, I'm up. Is everything OK?

While the bouncing dots indicating she was replying did their thing, I took the liberty of adding 'Maren Tracy' to the unknown number's contact info, as well as saving it to my phone. I had a feeling the girl needed a friend. I didn't mind being that for her.

Maren: Yes! I mean, everything is okay with the house and with Sage... I guess I just can't sleep.

Me: I don't blame u girl.

Maren: There was over five thousand dollars in that envelope.

Me: I know.

Maren: Why? I just really can't get my head around it.

Me: I honestly couldn't tell u. Ur situation resonated with me I guess.

Maren: I'm sorry.

Me: Why?

Maren: That means your dad died, right?

Me: Actually no, I never met my dad. I don't know if he's alive or dead.

Maren: Oh, your mom then?

Me: Actually don't know if she's alive or dead either.

Maren: Oh. Then how does my situation compare?

Me: I grew up in foster care with my twin brother and 2 other foster brothers.

Maren: Oh, I'm so sorry. I don't want that for Sage.

Me: That's what got me, I think. When u said u had 2 take care of him. I'd hate to see either of u go into the system. It's not some place u want to be. Trust me.

Maren: I do, believe me, I do; but I wouldn't end up there, my dad signed the papers to emancipate me before he died. Technically I'm a legal adult, but so far I don't feel like one. 😢

Me: Could have fooled me, ur doing pretty okay.

Maren: Now how do you figure that?

Me: House was clean. The boy was fed and taken care of. Power was on, heat was on – means u pay ur bills. Didn't look like there were any drugs, drinking, or partying going on.

Maren: LOL I'm not exactly a party girl.

Me: That's good. See. Ahead of the game already.

Maren: What game?

Me: The one called life. Ur doing good by all accounts.

Maren: I probably shouldn't even be talking to you.

Me: How's that?

Maren: I mean, it's late and I'm probably bothering you.

Me: If u were bothering me I would have said so.

She didn't text back right away, the little dots at the bottom of the screen suspiciously absent, the little message below the blue chat bubble I'd just sent marked 'read' though, so I waited; drifting off some before jolting awake when the phone buzzed against my chest.

Maren: Thank you.

Me: For what?

Maren: For listening. It's been a lot harder than I expected.

Me: Anytime, and I mean that. Ur good, girl. I promise.

Maren: I think I should try to sleep.

Me: OK, keep in touch. I'm here anytime. If I don't answer right away, I promise I'll hit u back as soon as I see it. K?

Maren: Okay, thank you again.

Me: Ur welcome.

I lay awake, hands behind my head, staring at the ceiling of my room and the shadows bouncing across them. There was a naked tree out back of the building, and sometimes, when the moon shone just right, the shadow would be cast across my ceiling from the high window over my bed. When I couldn't sleep, I'd just lay here and count the spaces, or if there was wind or a breeze, like tonight, I'd watch the shadows dance.

I kept playing the text message exchange in my head and let the wheels do a slow grind. She was a sad girl, wearing her grief with some serious grace. That made her stronger than she knew. She was beautiful, but I wasn't thinking with my dick. Not at seventeen to my thirty-six. That just wouldn't be fair to her, so I shelved any notion of anything beyond just friendship and a helping hand right the fuck now.

It was so late that it was early, which made it Christmas Eve. Poor kids, spending their first Christmas as orphans. I was too young to remember my first Christmas without parents, so it'd always been the norm for me. If I had anything resembling real parents, it was Grind and Arch. Shit, if I had to be honest, Arch was the only real responsible one.

I smirked into the dark. I guess that made Archer the 'mom' out of the four of us, because even though the cold bastard hadn't exactly been nurturing growing up, he had been the one to keep us in line, and not with the beatings that Norma Rae and Duncan were used to handing out.

I felt my smirk slide right off my face at the thought of our foster parents. They'd taken on the four of us boys because Norma Rae had known Duncan had a thing for little girls just budding out and hitting puberty. When we'd been coming up, we'd been pulled out of their place once or twice while investigations of this or that went on. Some neighbor turned them in every once in a while. It was too bad, really, that Norma Rae was so smart about it.

Shit, the beatings when we got back though? Fuck me, those weren't so much fun. Neither was having the four of us crammed into one room for the duration of our lives. We weren't kids, or people to those fruitcakes. We were a monthly paycheck, so they could drown themselves in their booze and cigarettes. Grind was the one who kept the four of us fed, all the way back from the time Rush and I first showed up to when we finally got out of that hellhole by aging out of the fuckin' system.

That kid knew how to hustle up some groceries, man. He had dumpster diving at the local supermarket down to a science. Would come home, backpack loaded with barely expired or food that was still good if we got it into the freezer that night. You would be fuckin' amazed at the shit grocery places tossed out. A total fuckin' waste if you ask me. Homeless folks could eat like motherfuckin' kings every night of the week if only that shit was donated. Seriously, there wasn't anything wrong with any of the food Grind came up with.

If it happened to be a week of slim pickings at the supermarket, he would be the first kid in line with a backpack and two reusable grocery bags at the local church's food pantry. He'd give 'em a bullshit name and come home with all sorts of shit from there, too.

If it was one thing Grind knew how to do, it was putting food on the table, and if it was one thing Arch knew how to do, it was taking on some of Grind's beating when Duncan sobered up enough to catch Grind bringing it into the mobile home. Duncan would beat his ass, boy. He liked to freak the fuck out over Grind 'stealing' and when Grind couldn't take any more of the belt, he would say some sort of code or phrase and Arch would jump in and draw fire. At least until Rush and I got old enough to take our share.

I thought about Maren, about her desperate looks in her brother's direction when he'd been smarting off and just generally acting like a little entitled asshole earlier that day. He'd come up sheltered by the love of his sister and probably their dad, too. I don't know how long the dude had been sick but judging by the state of the house on the outside and the living room, it'd been a long damn time. It made me wonder how fast Maren'd had to grow up. How long she'd been holding down the fort, so to speak.

I also wondered where their mom was at, but it was pretty clear, dead or alive or whatever, that she'd been out of the picture for a long, long time. I mean, there weren't but one or two pictures on the walls with her in it, and the ones she was in? Sage was about my nephew Noah's age, if not younger, and Maren no older than six or seven.

I sighed and closed my eyes, but all I could see was a luminous pair of somber brown eyes and that envelope trembling between her fingers as she fought not to cry again. Here was to hoping that things would get a little better for her and her brother. We would just have to see what happened.

4

M aren…

I sat in the wreckage of wrapping paper and boxes and watched Sage work on a wooden Rubik's Cube that had been beautifully crafted and couldn't be anything less than handmade. I'd certainly never seen anything like it. My small treasure-trove sat in front of me and I was speechless once again, it was too much.

The first gift I had opened was a wooden jewelry box that was hand carved with flowering vines. It was a dark, rich wood that I had no name for and when you opened the hinged top, half of it was set up for rings, little rolls of dark blue velvet ready to hold them. The other half was parceled into small, square, divided pockets to hold, I think for post earrings. There were two shallow drawers set into the front of the box, and I figured they were for earrings, necklaces, and bracelets. It was beautiful, and likewise to Sage's Rubik's Cube, handmade.

Next had been a box of high-end chocolates from this place I had always wanted to try called *Soul Fuel*. Almost all the other senior girls stopped there for coffee on the way to school, but I couldn't afford five dollars a day for coffee when I could make it at home. That five dollars added up quickly, and I just couldn't bring myself to do it, even every once in a while; not when there were things like the water, sewer, garbage, and the ever-dreaded electric bill to pay. Plus, there were other bills most kids never had to think about, such as their phone bill, car insurance, gas for the car, food for the fridge and pantry, cable, even though ours was basic, and the internet; which Sage and I lived and died by when it came to school and entertainment.

We were fortunate there was no house payment, still, there was fire insurance and property taxes, and now a looming inheritance tax debt that I didn't even want to think about. There were just so much my classmates took for granted that I could not, and I felt equal parts blessed for the harsh lesson and cursed. While I knew it was setting me up to be stronger and more ahead of things than any of my classmates would ever be, I was cursed to have the veil of safety stripped away so soon. I was cursed to have lost my dad.

Still, with everything money wise that terrified me; that made the next gift all the sweeter. It was a beautiful, hand-written gift certificate done in calligraphy for free coffee of my choice, any drink, any size, every day for one year from *Soul Fuel*.

There were a couple of iTunes' gift cards for both me and Sage, and Sage had received a mountain of gift cards to just about every local movie theater which would be good for him and a friend to go. He also received a brand-new skateboard, and I was grateful that whoever had thought of that gift, had also purchased a helmet, wrist, elbow, and knee guards and a gift certificate to a local sporting goods store for a sturdy pair of shoes.

There was also a basketball and a basketball hoop meant to be mounted on the house above the garage, a note attached to the back with a phone number and to call it when we were ready to have it put up.

I had also received a beautiful necklace and earring set, garnets in an oval shape, leaves at the top, and so delicate I had to put them on right away. They were beautiful, the garnets large and a deep, rich red that complemented my dark hair and eyes, the settings gleaming in that way that said the metal was white gold rather than silver. It was all, just, so much... I didn't know what to do.

I'd saved the last gift in the pile for a reason because it said it was from Nox. I cradled my coffee mug between both hands and stared at the box for a while, debating on what to do about it, more nervous than I should be about what was inside. I tore the paper and found another beautiful wooden box, though this one was quite a bit heavier than the last.

I lifted the little metal hasp on the front and opened it slowly, smiling at the assortment of bath products inside. From bath bombs to bubble bath, scented salts and shower jellies, just about anything I could want or need for a long relaxing soak was there, enough for a month or more of daily use. It was something I could really use to relax, and it was both sweet and thoughtful.

I picked up my phone and sent a text:

Me: Thank you for my gift, I really love it.

I set about picking up the scattered paper and boxes, breaking the latter down for the recycling bin, my phone singing out that I'd received a new text. I bit my lip, surprised at the slight jump of excitement I felt and looked at the screen.

Nox: I thought it might help u relax a little.

Me: It was very thoughtful and very sweet, all of it is just too much.

"These guys are so cool, Maren. Some of this stuff is so awesome!" I smiled over at Sage who was still hard at work on his cube.

"Wow, you have two sides done already. Good job! I could never figure one of those things out."

"Aw, it's easy! Who are you texting?"

"Nox, I wanted to say thank you."

"Tell him thank you from me, too?" he asked and I nodded. It was nice to have my sweet little brother back for the moment.

"Will do, Sage."

"Thanks," he murmured but he was fully absorbed in the toy in his hands again.

Nox: Ur brother like his?

I smiled and tapped out a response.

Me: Very much so. He asked me to tell you 'thank you' and honestly, that's the best gift you and your club have given me this Christmas. He's distracted, he's my brother for the time being. You have no idea what that means to me.

"Sage, I'm going to take some of this stuff out to the garage, okay?"

My brother looked up and asked, "Do you want help?" I blinked and shook my head gently.

"No, I just wanted to let you know where I was going, thank you for the offer, though."

He nodded and said, "I love you, Sis; I'm sorry I couldn't get you anything for Christmas."

"I love you, too, Sage, and you just did. Best Christmas present ever." I sniffed back some tears and stuck my phone into my back pocket, taking the recyclables out to the big blue recycling bin and stuffing it down.

My phone came through with a text, and as soon as I was finished wrestling with the trash, I looked.

Nox: He been giving u a hard time?

Me: Yes and no. I don't think he knows how to deal with the fact

that I'm it. There's no dad here to tell him to listen to his sister. We're both still trying to cope.

Nox: I get u. U doing okay?

Me: Yes and no. The people are coming the day after tomorrow to take the hospice stuff out of here. I think that is going to be hard for me. I think then it will be real.

Nox: U call me if you need anything, okay?

Me: Okay.

The rest of the day was fairly uneventful for both me and Sage. He went up to play games on his console and to take a nap while I did my best to make a real Christmas dinner, which is a lot harder than it sounds when your cooking skills were still starting out. Tradition in our house always called for a Christmas ham; that was something I wasn't entirely familiar with cooking, but I read the label and managed.

Nox: We're watching Christmas movies here at the club, think u and Sage would want to join?

Me: What movies?

Nox: Die Hard and Die Hard 2

Me: I thought you said you were watching Christmas movies.

Nox: What? Those are Christmas movies!

I laughed.

Me: LOL no they aren't! It's a Wonderful Life, Elf, A Christmas Story... THOSE are Christmas movies.

Nox: Die Hard, Die Hard 2, THOSE are Christmas movies too!

Me: I think we're going to have to agree to disagree on that one, and while I wish we could, I just put dinner in the oven so we're going to have to pass. Plus, I think it's snowing again, and I don't want to kill us trying to get there.

Nox: LOL, easy girl. U don't have to make excuses, I get it. It's Christmas, and time for family. Sage is yours, the club is mine. It's cool.

Me: I'm sorry! I didn't mean for it to come out sounding like a bunch of excuses, I really would if I could.

Nox: It's okay, Maren. Ur good. Text me if you get bored, k?

Me: I will, I promise. 😊

I smiled and finished dinner, feeling a little lighter than I had in… God… since I could remember. It was a good day.

5

N ox...

"Is that Jailbait?" Rush asked looking over my shoulder.

"Fuck you, man and yeah, it was Maren saying thank you to everybody for her and Sage's gifts."

"Aww!" Sunshine smiled from Trigger's lap and I smiled back at her. We were all in the media room, about to start *Die Hard*.

"You invite her and the boy over for this?" Dragon asked, taking a pull off his beer from one of the recliners.

"Yeah, she said naw. She's got their dinner in the oven."

"Shit, she's all grown up way too fast, ain't she?" Dragon muttered and shook his head.

"You ain't lyin'," Dray muttered, hugging Everett closer. She dozed against him where they laid on the media room's extra-long couch.

I sighed unhappily and restlessly. I wanted to see her again, wanted to wave a magic wand and dispel the hurt clouding her eyes every time I looked at her, and it was a bit of a bitch to stay put.

We watched the *Die Hard* movies because let's face it, it wasn't Christmas until you watched Hans Gruber take a swan dive off of Nakatomi Plaza. Then, after the four hours or so romp with Bruce Willis, I was pretty much over it and ready for a nap, so I took myself off to my room.

I checked my phone like six times before I fell asleep, but of course, there was nothing on it. I was beginning to wonder, out of the two of us, who was the fucking teenage girl here. My behavior was downright hilarious when you stopped to think about it.

Although the message that pinged my phone and woke me up at two in the morning reminded me otherwise. It screamed out that there was someone seriously hurting and scared in the midst of all of this and all I wanted was to have the right words to make it all better.

Maren: I miss him so much right now. Why did he have to die? Why couldn't it have been me?

I sighed and pictured her curled on her side, cheeks wet with her tears as she stared at the little rectangle of light that was her phone and waited, waited for me to have the answers, but I didn't. Not when it came to death and dying. No one did, really. Growing up the way I did, I wasn't much of a believer in God. Shit, I mean, if he was up there, he was a right fucking asshole letting all of us suffer down here like we were. Letting Maren suffer now… *Of course, if there was no God, then she probably wouldn't have met me when she did, now would she? You wouldn't be compelled to stick around and help her either, now would you?* I argued with myself and resolutely shoved my inner theological debate team off to the side. Right now, this girl, who was in so much pain it made me raw just to see it, was reaching out for a lifeline.

Me: Baby don't talk like that… Ur here because as much of a dick as he is, God doesn't give people more than they can handle.

Maren: He's overestimating my abilities to hang on here.

Me: Where do you think I come in?

I stared at the screen, no bouncing dots, no nothing until the screen went dark. I sighed, thinking I'd probably said the wrong thing, and dropped the phone to my chest, staring at the ceiling in the dark when it buzzed against my chest.

Maren: I don't know what to say to that. I still don't really understand why you would do so much for me. I'm a total stranger. I guess it's just been an extremely long day. The holiday, missing my dad... they're coming for the hospice stuff the day after tomorrow and it's like I don't want them to take it. Like if they take it away, it's really real, you know? That he's not coming back...

Maren: I'm sorry. I'm babbling and it's probably really unattractive, me being all needy and washed out all the time.

I chuckled, amused that she was worried about being attractive. I mean shit, I should be considered a thirty-six-year-old, dirty old man by her seventeen-year-old standards. I squeezed my eyes shut and gave my head a little shake.

She was pretty. She had a bangin' body. She was over the age of consent and emancipated, but that didn't make any of what I was thinkin' anywhere close to right and the legalities were murky. I needed my fucking head examined, and right about now, I needed a cold shower too. Wasn't any way I was on board with becoming some kind of a pedo. Fuck that.

Me: U aren't being needy. Far from it. U been handling this like a champ so far and I can tell u, there ain't no wrong or right when it comes to this shit. Denial ain't just a river in Egypt, Maren. Welcome to it. It'll pass, and u'll go back to it. Then u gonna go through all sorts of other shit too. It's okay, it's normal, and ur not crazy. That's the most important thing. Ur, not crazy for any of these feelings. Ur hurting. Ur hurting bad. So is ur brother. I told u I am here to listen. U gotta cut you some slack, girl.

Again, there was a long pause before the dots started their shimmy across the bottom corner of the screen.

Maren: I don't think I can thank you enough.

Me: U cryin?

Maren: Yeah

Me: Good, u just let it out.

Maren: Why are you so patient and understanding? :-P

Me: Seems like not enough people have been for u.

Maren: The school administration and our social worker, they try. Most of my teachers have been pretty good.

Me: Most but not all?

Maren: Mrs. Kubrick, my English Lit teacher, is either a harpy or one of the furies, she wasn't going to give me an extension on my midterm until Mr. Thorpe, the principal, made her.

Me: LOL Well ur ahead of me on that score, I barely made it out of HS.

Maren: You did, though.

Me: I did.

Maren: So what did you end up becoming when you grew up? I mean, what does LMP stand for?

Me: Licensed Massage Practitioner.

Maren: Oh!

I couldn't help but smile, grinning to myself in the dark.

Me: Not what u expected?

Maren: I'm sorry, I must sound horribly judgmental.

Me: I'm used to it from citizens like u.

Maren: Ouch, not sure what you mean by that but yeah, I apologize. It was wrong of me to judge you like that when all you've been is nice to me.

Me: Sorry, sarcasm and joking don't come thru text the best. I'm in an MC – Citizen is what we call anyone not in the club with us. Ur a citizen, Sage is a citizen, anyone not in a patch is a citizen.

Maren: The way you make it sound, it sounds as if 'citizen' is either a dirty word or somehow less in your eyes.

Me: Maybe it does carry thru text just fine. :-P Seriously tho, it's hard to explain. I'll take you out to dinner sometime and tell you all about it if u want. Well, what I can say without giving up any club business.

Another long pause. I pictured her lying there, phone raised above her face, considering carefully what I'd just said. She had a habit of chewing the inside of her cheek when she was thinking, causing an adorable one-sided dimple when she did it. Finally, she texted back.

Maren: I think I'd like that, actually.

Me: Good, it's a date then. I texted it without thinking, and sighed thinking it was going to be a pain in the ass weaseling out of this one, my brain asking me, *now why the fuck did you do that, numb nuts? She's young enough to be your kid. A date? Really? She isn't even eighteen!*

Maren: Aren't I a little young for you? :-P

Me: Just a turn of phrase, Angel. Just a turn of phrase.

Maren: LOL I know, I just had to yank your chain a little.

Me: Ha ha. Very funny. Lemme ask you something.

Maren: Sure

Me: Did you smile?

Maren: Yes

Me: Are you smiling now?

Maren: Yes

Me: Do you feel better?

Maren: Yes, much. Thank you.

Me: Well alright then.

6

M aren…

Thank you, Jesus! I thought to myself. It was two days after Christmas and I was trying to spend my winter break getting the house in order and my English lit paper finished before Sage and I had to go back to school. I was scheduled to work later, trying to get as much of that in as possible too; but the snow had piled so high in front of the garage, that there would be no going to work unless someone shoveled the driveway. I'd been begging Sage to help me for like the last hour and finally, I heard the scrape of the snow shovel against the concrete out front.

I was in the garage, shivering and trying to fold the clothes out of the dryer double time so I could go back inside and get them put away, just so I could go on to the next tedious chore. It'd been like this for so long, I didn't really know any other way of life except how to be frazzled and tired all the time.

I dropped a pile of Sage's folded tee shirts into the laundry basket, followed them up with a bunch of his balled-up socks, and finished off the pile with his neatly folded jeans and boxer shorts. I hefted the basket, propped it against my hip, and went for the door leading into the house, gratefully. That first blast of warm air as I opened it up was a welcome one, let me tell you.

I took the basket in both hands and the stairs two at a time, nudging Sage's bedroom door open with my hip. I froze in the doorway and blinked at my brother sitting cross-legged, still in his PJ's at the end of his bed, game controller in his hands.

"Sage, what are you doing?" I demanded.

"What's it look like?"

"I asked you to shovel the driveway!"

"I'll do it later," he said but I was less concerned with that.

I set the basket of clothes down and told him, "Never mind that. Get off the game and put these away." He rolled his eyes so hard I was pretty sure he saw his own gray matter, but he paused the game and slid off the end of his bed, standing. He grabbed the basket off the floor and put it on his bed and started going through it.

"Thank you!" I called over my shoulder, my feet already carrying me back to the stairs, the front door the next target in my sights. I wanted to know who was out there. I pulled my coat off the line of hooks by the door and shrugged it on. I opened the front door, stepped onto the front porch and squinted in the direction of the drive, blinded by the sun reflecting off the snow, my eyes automatically watering as they struggled to adjust.

I blinked at the two bikers, snow shovels in hand, a pickup parked at the curb as they cleared out in front of my garage. They looked up and Nox gave a wave.

"Figured you could use a hand."

"You have no idea," I said back and rolled my eyes pretty hard. "I've been asking Sage to get out here all morning, but you should have said something or come to the door!"

"Nah, wanted to make sure you could get out, so you could get to work on time."

I smiled in spite of myself and wondered if my dad were up there, playing some kind of a funny on me, sending me angels dressed in black leather. The other biker stomped his feet on the drive.

"Is it okay if I salt this?" he asked. "Temperatures are supposed to drop, and if you come home after dark, it's gonna be an ice rink."

"Uh, no, no problem at all! Please, in fact."

"Cool, I'm Rush," he came forward and stuck out his hand, "I'm this retard's twin brother."

I shook his gloved hand and smiled. "Maren, and my retarded brother is upstairs."

The front door opened, and Sage cried, "I am not! You're retarded!" before he slammed the door and I heard him lock it.

I sighed and said, "Jokes on him, my keys are in my pocket."

Rush and Nox laughed, and Nox shook his head, eyes unreadable under his wraparound sunglasses.

"You want, I can have a talk with him later," he said.

I sighed again, and it was a heavy one this time. "It's okay, I wasn't exactly leading by example there, you know?"

"Don't be so hard on yourself, sweetheart," Rush said. "It ain't easy raising a kid at your age, let alone a pre-teen."

"Thanks," I murmured. "Um, can I get you guys something hot? Coffee, tea, some soup maybe?" I asked, remembering my manners.

"That'd be great," Nox said with a smile. "Whatever ya got, you know? Whatever's easiest," he said gently.

"What he said," Rush replied, going back to shoveling.

"Okay," I murmured, blushing lightly. I couldn't help it, Nox had a good smile.

I let myself back into the house and called up the stairs, "Sage! I'm making lunch, what do you want?"

"Food!" he called down over the heavy artillery of his video game.

"Fine but turn that down!" I yelled up.

He turned it up louder and I hung my head. "Pick your battles, Maren," I reminded myself under my breath and was shrugging out of my coat when the front door popped open. Nox winked at me, his sunglasses on the top of his head.

"Hey, Sage!" he called up the stairs.

"What?" my brother demanded rudely.

"Shut that off, man! I can hear it all the way outside. Better yet, why don't you come down here and help us out?" Nox called.

The violence upstairs suspended as if by magic, as I pulled my coat off the rest of the way and hung it back up.

"Awright!" Sage called down and I raised my eyebrows at Nox. He grinned at me, and with another wink, ducked back outside. I went into the kitchen to cook and heard Sage thunder down the stairs a minute later, the front door opening and slamming closed.

I jumped and closed my eyes, willing my heart back into my chest. No matter how many times I told him not to do that, he always did, and no matter how much I knew it was going to happen, how much I totally expected it to happen, it always startled me. I was just as bad with horror movies too. I had to cover my ears as much as my eyes to keep from startling at them, too. It was why I pretty much hated them and avoided watching them at all costs.

I went through my cupboards and fridge looking through everything and decided when it came to a meal that would both warm and fill four people I was pretty much limited to grilled cheese and tomato soup again, which was fine. The last time we'd had it had been the day before Christmas Eve; long enough ago now that Sage shouldn't complain.

I opened up three cans of soup and mixed them with the last of our milk, putting them on the stove to heat. Next, I brought out the last of our bread, cheddar cheese, and some butter and got to work whipping up the sandwiches while the soup gently started to steam. I made instant hot cocoa for them and tea for me; even going as far as to set the dining room table for the four of us. I went to the front door and opened it up.

"Come on guys, come and eat!" I called and the three of them marched across the frozen ground, knocking their boots on the porch's stairs, and wiping their feet on the mat in front of the door. It still boggled my mind that these bikers were such... such gentlemen. I sighed inwardly with a touch of regret that I could judge a book by its cover so thoroughly. My father had raised me better than that; me and Sage both.

"What 'cha got cookin' good lookin'?" Rush asked and Nox knocked him in the ribs with his elbow. I blushed to the roots of my hair.

"I'm afraid I need to go grocery shopping once I'm off my shift, so it's grilled cheese and tomato soup."

"Sounds good!" Nox said and I gestured for them to come on back to the kitchen and the little dining table in it.

We sat down, and I squeezed my tea bag, setting it on the edge of my plate.

"Hot cocoa and everything, alright!" Rush said and he and Nox were smiling. Sage remained quiet, almost sullen.

"You okay, Sage?" I asked quietly.

"Yeah," he said and I frowned.

"He's cool," Nox said. "Aren't you, Sage?"

"Yes, sir."

I blinked, surprised and Nox laughed. "Ain't gotta be so formal to me."

Sage dipped his sandwich into his soup and took a bite, so he didn't have to say anything. I did likewise and when I'd finished chewing and swallowing asked him, "Did you pack a bag with some stuff to do?"

"Yeah."

"Ariel is going to be here to pick you up in about an hour, so at least you'll get to spend some time with Ian tonight, right?" I said, trying to sound upbeat.

"Yeah, we're supposed to play Madden," he said glumly.

"What's wrong, Sage?" I asked, my concern growing.

"You know I don't mean to be a dick, right?" he asked, and his eyes welled up. Nox got up and moved so I could take his seat. I pulled my brother against me and he said, "I just really wish Mom were here!" he wailed, and I felt the last brittle bits of my heart sift into dust.

"Sage, you know that can't happen," I murmured and hugged him tight. "We're going to be okay, I promise. I'm doing everything I can —" He shoved me away hard.

"You aren't an adult, Maren! You're just a kid! Like me! We aren't going to be okay! Nothing's ever going to be okay again!"

"Hey!" Nox barked, as I sat back and tried not to let my own tears break free. I had been trying so very hard for Sage, to be everything he needed and then some, but still, every one of my fears had just come out of his mouth at me, sharp and accusatory.

"You and your sister are going to be fine, you've got people in your corner and like I said outside, you need to cut her some slack, buddy. Can't you see how hard she's trying?"

"Nox is right, man. She's busting her butt to keep you here, in the house you grew up in. So, what're you fighting her so hard for?"

"I don't know!" Sage bellowed. "I don't care, either!" He dodged around Nox and ran for the stairs, Nox went to go after and I grabbed his hand.

"Let him go," I said, hollowly. "Let him simmer down, he's just angry and confused, and this is a lot for him."

Nox sank into the seat I'd vacated and wrapped his long, strong fingers around mine. He jerked his chin at Rush, who picked up his plate and said, "It's a nice day out, I'm going to eat on the porch."

"No, it's okay. You don't have to," I said, and he just smiled at me and went out anyway.

I closed my eyes and tried to breathe through all the emotions welling up in me at once. Instead of calming down, though, I felt like I was losing ground containing them with every breath I took, rather than gaining any of the control I fought so hard to keep.

I looked at Nox who was sitting there, quietly, solid and sympathetic, without saying a single word and all I could whisper was, "He was my dad, too…" before my shoulders shook with the sobs I just couldn't suppress anymore.

"I know, baby," he soothed and pulled me into a tight hug, kneading the base of my skull with his fingertips, probing along my neck as if taking some kind of measure. He let me cry, and it was cathartic. One of those good, strong cries that left you feeling cleansed and regrouped and ready to take on more. I sat back and he gave me a paper towel off the roll in the standing dispenser in the middle of the table that we used for napkins.

I wiped off my face and blew my nose and he smiled a little wanly and asked, "Better?"

I nodded. "Better."

Rush came back through the front door and walked briskly back to where we were at. "I really hope y'all are good because it's cold as hell out there and I can't do it anymore."

I laughed lightly. "I'm sorry," I said.

"Don't be. This is the kind of shit you aren't supposed to go through until you're something like fifty."

I nodded silently and traded a look with Nox who smiled encouragingly. We'd texted throughout the holiday briefly, late Christmas night, and yesterday morning. I hadn't gotten to talk to him much yesterday throughout the day as he'd said he was at work. Just a few 'how are you doing' texts between clients for him and he'd put in a long day of appointments, crashing for the night early. I didn't know how he could do it with his hands, wondering *didn't they get tired?*

A knock fell at the front door interrupting my thoughts as we finished up our meal and I called out, "Sage! Get ready, I think that's Ariel!" Nox trailed me up the hallway as I slipped past Rush, I opened the door to two men in blue work uniforms standing on my porch, the one who'd knocked held a clipboard and I felt my face fall.

"Maren Tracy?" he asked, quiet and respectfully.

"Yes, please come in." I stepped back to let the men from the hospice equipment place into the house and stepped back lightly into Nox's chest. His hands fell on my shoulders and I jumped slightly, his thumbs digging in between my shoulder blades, releasing the knot of tension I had mounting there.

Sage came halfway down the stairs and Rush put up a hand to stop him. "Not for you, after all, little buddy. Let these guys do their thing, okay?"

Sage rolled his eyes and turned around. "Whatever," he muttered and jogged back up the staircase. I closed my eyes and let him go.

"I'm sorry, Rush."

"Don't be," Nox said, soothingly by my ear. "You doing okay?"

I nodded and watched them take the IV stand out first, and the medical tray table my dad took meals on—his last meals—my eyes watering up. I hugged myself and stood aside and let them take the bed and the other miscellaneous things out of the living room.

"I'm sorry for your loss, ma'am," the worker said and shook my hand. I signed that they had picked up the equipment with shaking fingers and sniffed.

"Is that why you came today?" I asked Nox, quietly.

"We figured you could use a hand moving the furniture back into place," he said and I burst into a fresh round of sobs. He swept a hand over his short, dark hair and turned me around, pulling me into another hug. Rubbing my back until the well ran itself dry again.

"Maren?" I looked up the stairs and felt my heart drop; Sage was three steps up and looking scared and uncertain. I sniffed and wiped my eyes on my sleeve and tried to get my shit together.

"It's okay, Sage. I'm sorry. What do you need?"

It was too late, though, he'd seen weakness and he dropped like a stone to the steps and burst into tears himself. I went and sat down next to him and we both sniffed and cried it out and I kept telling him, over and over, "I don't want you to be scared, Sage. It's okay, I'm doing everything I can, and everything is going to be okay, I promise."

"I thought you didn't care!" he wailed and I felt stricken.

"Of course I care, how could you think I didn't care?" I hugged my brother tightly.

"Then why didn't you cry? When dad died and they came and took him away, why weren't you upset?"

"I *was* upset, I *am* upset, Sage, I just didn't want you to see it. I'm trying to be strong for the both of us."

"You're a liar!" he screamed and shoved me off of him and bounded up the stairs. "You wanted him dead!" he shouted, disappearing into his room and slamming the door behind him. I sat there in stunned silence, the knife twisting deep in my heart and I was almost afraid that my relationship with my brother was forever changed in that instant. Rush broke the heavy silence hanging over the three of us remaining.

"Well, shit. That probably didn't go according to plan."

"Shut up, Rush," Nox grated at his brother. He sat down next to me while I tried to regain my composure.

"I'm okay," I lied, standing up abruptly. If Nox touched me, I couldn't guarantee I wouldn't fall completely apart again, and I couldn't risk it. Not with Ariel coming any minute.

"Um, let's just get the furniture moved back, please?" I asked, and I hated how my voice held that tremulous edge to it like I was a crazy person on the brink.

"Just breathe, Angel," Nox murmured, but when he stood, he made no move to touch me, just shrugged out of his jacket and hung it on the banister. I blinked, I hadn't realized he was so heavily tattooed. His one arm done from what looked like his shoulder, all the way to his wrist. The design ending in a neat line at his wrist, like he wore a skin-tight shirt sleeve on one arm.

"Where's the sofa go?" he asked gently and I shook my head. "It goes here, but let me run the vacuum over it first," I said, sniffing back new tears and got into the hall closet so I could pull out the vacuum.

I ran it over the area rug in the living room and set it aside just as Ariel knocked on the door.

"Just a minute!" I called softly, but Rush was already there, pulling the door open.

"Oh! Hi… um, who are you?" Ariel asked, both taken by surprise and nervous.

"Rush," he answered succinctly and Nox went over to him and smacked him on the shoulder.

"Gonna have to forgive my retarded twin; that's Logan, I'm Landon, and we were just helping Maren out, shoveling the driveway and now putting back the living room furniture for her." Nox turned to Rush and said, "Make yourself useful and let Sage know his ride's here."

He scowled at Rush and Rush looked back raising an eyebrow. It was subtle what they were doing, but the silence stretched on for almost a full minute, and in that time, it was as if they held an entire conversation that neither Ariel nor I were privy to.

"Sure thing," Rush said, and took the stairs two at a time, stopping outside Sage's door and knocking.

"You okay, Sweetie?" Ariel asked and I nodded.

"Sage is really upset, I'm trying but it's um…"

"Exhausting?" Ariel asked. "Overwhelming?" she supplied and I smiled nervously and nodded.

"Yeah," I agreed. Nox gently took my elbow in his hand.

"That's why we're here to help. Steady."

I nodded some more and Ariel eyed Nox cautiously. I could see her taking in his tattoos and his and his brother's jackets over the railing. Rush's had joined Nox's while I'd vacuumed the rug and I could tell Ariel was uneasy about their being here.

"It's fine, Ariel. I promise, these are the men I was telling you about, the ones that made sure Sage and I had Christmas."

"Oh," she said and didn't sound quite convinced.

"Sure did, we put together a charity ride. I was impressed with how much the club and its supporters put together on such short notice, but we did it." Nox smiled the smile that always managed to disarm me, and it apparently had the same effect on Ariel. She smiled back and some of her nervousness eased.

"Thank you so much for what you did for these kids," she said, and Sage came down the stairs, his backpack on and a gym bag over his shoulder. Rush came down just behind him, a hand on my brother's shoulder.

"Be good for Ariel, please," I asked him and managed to keep my voice even.

"I will," he said and pushed right past me out onto the porch, making his way to Ariel's car and his best friend, Ian, without so much as a goodbye.

"Is it bad?" she asked and winced at my expression.

"When he's not telling me that I wanted our dad to die, it's not even close to pleasant, why do you ask?" I said, voice dripping with sarcasm.

Ariel looked stricken. "Oh Maren, I'm so sorry!"

I grimaced. "It's alright, if he misbehaves, just call me and I'll come get him."

"I think it will be just fine, maybe he just needs to get out of the house," Ariel suggested.

"Yeah, I hope that's just it. Speaking of which, I need to finish this up and get myself to work. Thank you so much for taking him tonight."

"Sure, no problem, Sage has always been a pleasure."

"Like I said, if he's anything less than, please just call me and I'll come get him."

"Alright, I promise." She hugged me tight and said to Nox and Rush, "It was nice to meet you both. Thank you for what you've done for this family and God bless you."

49

"Thank you, ma'am," Rush said plastering on what I could tell was a fake as hell smile. I waved as she pulled out of the driveway with my brother and when I shut the door on the cold and the wind, I sagged with relief.

"Go get ready for work," Nox ordered gently. "We'll finish up in here, okay?"

I nodded. "Thanks." I didn't look back as I escaped up into my room. I supposed now I should start sleeping in here again as opposed to the couch. I scrubbed my face with my hands and with a sigh, pushed all of those thoughts aside and got ready for work. I needed to hurry now, or I was going to be late.

7

N ox...

"You really going to let her drive to work like that?" Rush asked.

"Nope."

"Didn't think so."

"Give us a ride over there, let's drop her off, and I'll pick her up in my cage later," I said and sighed, staring up at where she'd gone.

"Dude, this family is a mess. You sure about this?" my brother asked and I looked at him.

"Strangely, yes. Probably more sure about this than I've ever been before in my life. Don't ask me why, either," I said, cutting him off with the last. He closed his mouth and put up his hands.

"You sure it doesn't have anything to do with Archer and his new family?" he asked and I lifted one shoulder in a shrug.

"I couldn't tell you, Rush. All I can tell you is what I've been telling you. Something tells me I need to be here for these two."

"Never figured you for a Captain Save-a-..." He frowned and shut his mouth.

"Yeah, now you're starting to see it, huh?" I asked, grinning.

"Shut up," he said with a scowl.

He couldn't call her a 'ho' because she was both too young and too innocent, but that had been what he was going to say to me, that he couldn't see me being a Captain Save-a-ho. I wasn't, really. I mean, out of all four of us — me, Rush, Grind, and Arch — I'd never been afraid of tapping some spare pussy when it was around. Hell, I still hit Cherry back at the club on occasion, but surprisingly, not since I'd met Maren. Granted it'd only been a couple of weeks, but she made me want to clean up my act some, even though I had no intention of going there with a seventeen-year-old girl.

She came down the stairs dressed in the good ole Wally World standard uniform, face free of makeup, hair in a high ponytail, and even as somber as she was, she was beautiful.

"C'mon, Angel, we're gonna drive you to work. You're not fit to be behind the wheel like this."

She looked at me and a slight frown slipped across her features, "I'm okay, really. You've already gone way out of your way today – I couldn't possibly ask you to do anything else."

"You ain't askin' and we ain't taking no for an answer," Rush told her flatly and her eyes grew wide.

"Jesus Christ, Rush!" I hung my head and pulled on the back of my neck with one hand.

"What?"

"Could you have channeled Archer any harder right then?"

Rush rolled his eyes and I caught a small smile on Maren's lips.

"We'll drive you to work," I repeated gently. "And I promise I'll be there when you get off to drive you home."

She thought about it, chewing the inside of her cheek in that adorable way of hers before finally nodding.

"Okay," she murmured softly and came down the steps the rest of the way. She lifted her scarf off from the hook it was on and wound it around her throat, next she pulled on her coat and zipped it all the way up. A fluffy, purple thing filled with goose down but a little worse for wear. Probably last year's or the year before's coat.

Rush and I did the same with our jackets and cuts and made to follow her out. She paused in the archway leading into the living room and took in our furniture move job.

"Is it not right?" I asked and she shook her head.

"No, it's right," she intoned hollowly and slipped out the front door. Rush followed her, and I made sure the doors were locked before slipping out myself.

She rode in silence at my side, her leg pressed the length of mine where I sat bitch in my brother's truck. I didn't think she'd be comfortable smashed between us, so I'd climbed in next to my twin without a word. He kept glancing at me, giving me the side eye that said clearly, *Are you sure you know what the fuck you're doin'?*

I gave him a furtive look back that clearly said back, *Fuck no, but I'm doing it anyway.* Rush rolled his eyes skyward and gave his head a little shake, all the while Maren stared sightlessly out the passenger side window deep in thought. Her expression just plain gutted in the reflection against the window glass. It was as if she'd been hollowed completely out and the girl just wasn't there anymore; like her physical presence remained but emotionally and intellectually she was as checked out as she could get... although I supposed she didn't need to really be with it to be a cashier for groceries and shit.

We let her off in front of her store and she turned, a little apprehensive, and I smiled, "What time are you off, Angel?"

"Ten-thirty," she murmured.

"I'll be here at ten," I told her and the tenseness in her posture eased a little.

"Okay, thank you." She closed the door to the truck and went inside. I slid over on the seat, opened up the door and closed it for real, she hadn't closed it hard enough to latch. Rush let out an explosive breath.

"That girl is wrung the fuck out," he said, driving us along toward the exit.

"Who you tellin'?" I asked. "She's as emotionally exhausted as anyone could get."

"You can't save everybody, you know."

"Not trying to save everyone, jackass."

"Nope, just her and her little shit of a brother for right now."

"Can you blame me?"

"Yes." I looked at him and scowled, but he kept talking anyway, "Okay, no. I'd have a hard time not doing something about it, too, but watch yourself Nox. I don't care if she's emancipated, at or above the age of consent or whatever – she's still jailbait."

It was my turn to stare out at the passing scenery, even though it was dark already. I sighed and said to my reflection, "It isn't like that."

"And how the fuck would you know? You know how many guys have said that before? How many of 'em ended up on the registry because the girl –"

"Rush, stop. I'm a big fuckin' boy. You should know that. I can take care of myself."

My twin looked at me like he highly doubted that for a fraction of a second longer than what kept me cool, being that he was the one driving. I snapped at him, "Watch the fucking road," before I turned and stared out at the gloom and scenery whipping past the window.

I stared down at my cut across my knees and wondered if what I was doing was the right thing too. I mean, I'd known more than a few guys caught up by younger women and fucked over hard for it. I really just wanted to help her, but there wasn't any denying she was attractive. Part of that attraction was definitely how much she was handling and how much grace she was handling it with. I'd met some thirty-year-old women who couldn't handle half of what Maren was going through right now.

I mean, she just lost her dad and pretty much become a parent overnight. While I would catch her staring, wide-eyed and vacant, it was far from empty. You could just see the wheels turning as she worked through how she was going to handle this, or how she was going to deal with that.

It hadn't gone unnoticed by me how much she hoarded the money we'd given her. Instead of blowing it on more Christmas, or hell, even groceries for that matter, she held it aside like it was her lifeline, and to be honest, that was what it was meant for – in case something around her house broke to where I couldn't fix it or even one of the guys on a volunteer basis.

She was mature, way beyond her years for sure, but was she really? *Doesn't matter,* I told myself. *Attractive, sure, but that doesn't mean you are or should be looking for any kind of relationship other than friendship.*

"I'll be careful," I told my brother finally and Rush sighed.

"I know you will. Other than Arch, you're the most careful out of all of us."

"Arch can't hold that title anymore," I said grinning, and Rush laughed.

"Yeah, I guess not... still can't believe that bastard got married."

"It was a good call, though," I said.

"Real good," Rush agreed.

We rode back to the club talking about a little of this and a little of that, and when we got there, split off at the bar, as in Rush stayed for a drink and I headed back out to my room.

I'd saved a gang of money living here rather than finding a place to rent. I'd given half of it to Maren, and just kept on saving; paying my club dues, chipping away at some debt from back in Arizona. My cage was almost paid off; I hated the fuckin' thing, but I needed it to transport my massage tables and chair. It wasn't all bad. The club was like home. My twin was here, and it was better than back in Arizona. A fresh start that we'd all needed... Still missed Grind, but that was what it was.

You never know when your time is up. Maren's dad had been lucky in that regard, that he'd had a lingering illness was both the best and the worst luck. Best because he'd been able to hang on long enough to give his kids the strongest start that he could provide 'em... the worst because I couldn't imagine wasting away like that. I'd probably end it myself if I didn't have anyone like Maren or Sage. Maybe even Rush would help me out. Neither of us wanted to go out that way. We'd talked about it plenty when we were kids.

I watched some TV and kept an eye on the time, dragging myself to my feet at around nine-thirty. I pulled on my coat, kept my cut in my hands, and went on out to my cage. The club was quiet. It was just Rush, Dragon, Cell, Blue, and me living here right now. Everyone else had a woman, or family, or a place they called their own.

Disney had moved in with Aaron since even before Rev and Mandy had gotten married. Dray and Ev were on their own in their place. Who the fuck knew where Data went or what he did when he wasn't here. Then Zeb had a shitty little apartment above a bar that he bounced for, but the brother seemed happy and more power to him.

I got into my cage, a nice looking 2012 Hyundai Tucson. Nice looking, probably because I never really drove the fuckin' thing. So much so did I not drive it, it'd been sitting in the lot here more than a minute, to the point I half expected it not to start, but it did and it still had three-quarters of a tank left in it from the last time I'd driven it.

It'd been a bitch flying back to Arizona, packing it up, and making the long ass fuckin' drive back here trapped in its confines. Hell, Rush had had the same trouble – towing his pickup along with Archer in a fuckin' U-Haul full of his fuckin' furniture he'd created. He'd sold a bunch of it off before we'd left but still a good bit ended up coming out here with us.

I pulled into the lot of the Douglas St. Wally World right at nine fifty-eight and parked, killing the engine. I sat for about twenty minutes and watched for her. I knew it'd take a bit for her to wrap up, but I didn't want her to walk across the lot in the dark; plus, she didn't know what my cage looked like.

She came out the front entrance bundled in her tired purple parka, hands buried deep in her pockets and scanned the lot. I backed out of my space, went around, and pulled up in front of her. I picked up my cut from the passenger seat and hit the automatic locks so she could get in. She opened up the door, the cold air and her delicate scent swirling into the cage's interior. She smelled good. I'd never noticed before.

"Hi," she murmured.

"Hi."

I let her pull on her seatbelt and buckle it before laying the cut in her lap. She looked down at it, surprised, and let her fingers wander over the patches.

"Can you hang onto that while I drive?"

"Sure."

I put the cage in gear and headed for the exit when her soft voice filtered through the dark, close space, "Why do you take it off?"

"It's in our by-laws. You don't wear your cut in a cage, it's a disrespect on the patch; the club colors are meant to be free and in the wind."

"Oh, that explains a few things."

"What?"

"Why you keep calling your car a cage for one." She smiled and then made a face. "I can't imagine you like it much."

"What driving a cage? I don't."

"No, riding when the weather is cold and icy like this... it's dangerous."

I laughed a bit. "I'd rather be on two wheels than four no matter what the weather, but some things are worth making the exception for," I said glancing her way. She blushed and it was pretty on her.

"Thank you," she murmured and bowed her head. She looked tired, and I was glad Rush and I had made the right call. Even if she had driven herself to her job, she was damn sure in no shape to drive herself back. She sat quietly, her eyes closed and head slightly bowed, too exhausted to hold it up.

"Need to pick up your brother?"

"No, Ariel called me at work and asked if he could stay over with Ian. They've missed each other, and she said I looked like I could use a night to myself to catch up on sleep." Maren looked over at me with a little pleading in her eyes. "I don't look that bad, do I?" she asked.

She did, her skin pale to the point it was almost translucent, her eyes smudged with dark circles beneath them. Her shoulders slumped and she looked about ready to keel over any second; so I did the only thing a man was supposed to do in a situation like this when a woman had asked him about her appearance, I lied.

"Naw, honey, you don't look nothin' but a little bit tired is all. A good night's sleep and you'll be right as rain."

Her lips twisted with a wry and bitter amusement, and she nodded slightly. "It's okay Nox. You don't have to lie to me."

I chuckled. "You look beat, like if you weren't sitting there just now, you'd fall down. You need a good night's sleep, but you don't and could never, look 'bad'. You're a beautiful girl, Maren; both inside and out."

She looked thoughtful after that, for a time, making no extra comment. Instead, she got that real thoughtful look on her face again and leaned her head back on the rest, watching me as I drove. I tried not to let it distract me, and instead, kept my eye on the icy streets as I piloted my cage through them.

Finally, I pulled into her driveway, the house dark, not even a porch light on. I shut off the car and sighed, and when I turned to her, I found her eyes shut, head still tilted in my direction, but her expression, where it'd been pinched before, was now smooth and slack with sleep. I watched her for a minute or two, listening to the engine tick, the cold pressing in, creeping through the vents and into the car.

I touched her cheek with my thumb, cradling her face in my hand, and sighed, bummed I would have to break the magic and wake her up. As much as I wanted to carry her to her door, I needed her keys and the footing wasn't safe enough even after salting the drive.

"Maren, Angel, wake up, we're here," I said softly.

A small wrinkle between her brows and her head jerked, she pulled back and sucked in a deep, tremulous breath. I dropped my hand before she could open her eyes and see I touched her. She blinked several times and huffed a sigh.

"I'm sorry," she murmured and fished in her coat pocket, her keys ringing.

"Don't be, come on, I'll help you." I popped my door and went around to her side and opened her door for her. She held up my cut to me and I paused, looking at it for a moment in her delicate hands. I took it from her and swung it on deftly, holding out my hands for her to take.

She placed hers in mine and leveraged herself out of the seat, and I was struck by it. It was the action of an old person, or the heavily burdened, the way she got out of my cage and it made me want to lift it from her shoulders so badly. I wrapped an arm around her shoulders and let her lean on me. She tried once, twice, and before she could try a third, I took her keys gently from her fingers and unlocked her door for her.

She took off her coat and scarf and hung them up, then went immediately to the couch, dropping onto it with a heavy sigh, kicking off her shoes. I sat down on one end, lifting the pillow off of it and setting it in my lap. Maren just flopped over without a second thought, her head hit the pillow and she went limp like she was just done, and I couldn't blame her. I propped my heels on her coffee table, feeling pretty guiltless about it because a magazine was conveniently where I'd put 'em, cushioning my boot heels from the wood.

"Long day, huh?"

"Mm," and that was *it*. Her breathing evened and deepened, and she was *out*.

I sighed, and settled back, closing my eyes and just kind of enjoyed the closeness. A secret, guilty little pleasure, smoothing my fingers through her hair brushing it back off her face. I knew I couldn't sleep here. I wanted to though, I wanted to rest here, with her, and share her load, just for one night, but I knew I couldn't, so I did the next best thing.

I kept it appropriate. I let her fall into a deep, deep slumber, then I eased out from under her, found her room and turned down her bed, and I went and did what I'd wanted to in the first place — I went down, lifted her in my arms and carried her up to bed.

I didn't do anything I really wanted to do, like undress her so she would be more comfortable. Instead, I settled for pulling off her socks so she wouldn't get too warm, and pulled the blankets up over her, folding them beneath her chin.

I allowed myself the one guilty pleasure I could and kissed her forehead before I went down and let myself out, locking the place up tight behind me before exiting. It was the hardest thing I'd done in a while, leaving her alone like that. It just didn't feel right.

8

Maren...

The last time I'd seen Nox, he'd picked me up from work. I'd been so tired, I'd forgotten to buy the groceries, but then again, I'd been too tired to care. I remember him waking me up to go in the house and then I remember waking up the next morning, tucked into my bed when I could have sworn I'd fallen into an exhausted sleep on the couch. I'd immediately felt both incredibly rude and incredibly guilty, guessing I'd fallen asleep and he'd brought me up and tucked me in.

I'd raced downstairs to see if he was there, but of course, he'd gone. I'd found my phone in the pocket of my coat and there had been no messages. I had texted him, apologizing profusely but I hadn't heard anything back, at least not right away.

He'd texted back later that evening apologizing, saying that he'd been at work, and I had felt so incredibly stupid and so incredibly relieved at the same time it wasn't even funny. I had cried after the first three hours had gone by without a response. After two more, I had almost given up hope of ever hearing from him again.

Stupid, I know, but true. I didn't have any real friends anymore... he was my first one in a long time and I was surprised at how starved I had been for some positive human interaction.

Now it was the thirty-first and my brother was with Ian and a group of boys over at Ian's house. Ariel had put together a New Year's Eve party for them. It left me home soaking up the quiet which eventually let my mind wander, which naturally led to me wondering what Nox was up to tonight.

I was in front of the fire in the living room, a cup of tea at my elbow, and a book in my hands staring at my phone, wondering if I should text when the screen lit up, saving me from having to be the one.

God, I was pathetic.

Nox: So what are U doing for NYE?

Me: Sage is at a party, so I'm home alone catching up on some reading.

Those dots bounced forever, so I was expecting a long reply, but then they would stop, and then they would start and what finally came through surprised me.

Nox: That's bullshit. U can't bring in the NY alone.

I considered what to send back, capturing the inside of my cheek with my teeth and sighing. Nothing that came to mind didn't sound horribly desperate or lame...

Me: I just don't have any plans I guess.

Nox: U do now, be there in 20min, get dressed.

Me: How, I mean, where are we going?

Nox: Leave that to me, dress casual, be comfortable.

Me: Okay.

Little did he know, I was still dressed from my errands from the day in a comfy pair of fitted jeans and an oversized sweater; all I needed was my boots back on and I was good to go. I closed my tablet cover and set it aside with a sigh and banked the fire. I sat back down and pulled on my knee-high stylish riding boots and made sure my thick, long, cable-knit socks showed above them at the knee. I pulled my matching cable-knit sweater down over my ass to where it hit me mid-thigh and lamely went and checked my appearance in the bathroom mirror.

I ran a brush through my hair and pulled half of it up with a pewter clip I had in the shape of an owl, wings outspread. I stared at myself in the mirror for a few moments, put on a little lip balm, washed my hands, and went out into the living room to wait nervously. It was only eight o'clock and I had no idea what Nox had in mind.

When he knocked on the door, I jumped. I had expected him but hadn't heard him pull into the driveway. I went to the door and answered, and he smiled at me and I think my heart very nearly stopped in my chest.

"Hi," I murmured and I think I was blushing. His grin grew wider and that pretty much told me that yes, yes I was blushing like an idiot, which of course made me blush even harder. I stepped aside so he could come into the house and he did, just inside the door, but only long enough to pull down my coat and hold it open for me.

He, like me, was dressed comfortably in his motorcycle boots and a pair of butter soft jeans. He wore a plain, black, hooded sweatshirt beneath his leather biker jacket and club vest and it looked good on him. He was rakish and, I don't know... he just appeared so capable and it was gorgeous. He was a man who looked good, no matter what he wore.

"Have you eaten?" he asked, the timbre of his voice soothing to me after so many days without hearing it.

"Not yet," I murmured. I didn't want to tell him that I wasn't hungry, or that I hadn't really seen the point in just cooking for one. I was afraid to let anyone know the depths of my sadness lately.

"Okay, we'll do that first."

I shrugged into my coat and before I could flip my hair out of my collar, Nox's hands were doing it for me. It sent shivers down my spine that had nothing to do with the cold and almost suffused me with a warm glow. I told my raging hormones to take it down a notch. There was no way a grown ass man had any interest in a dumb teenage girl. Nox had made it clear over the last few days, we were just friends and it needed to stay that way; I agreed. I didn't want anyone to think ill of him, or for him to get into any kind of trouble. I didn't want that for him at all.

"You okay, Angel?" he asked me as I wound my scarf around my neck.

"I'm sorry, yes I'm fine. It's just another holiday, you know?"

"Another first without your pops?"

"Yeah."

He gave me a slightly sadder smile and held out his hand. I took it and he pulled me into a hug. I closed my eyes and breathed him in, his clean cologne wrapping me in an almost sense of safety. He gave me a squeeze before letting me go and murmured, "Let's see if we can't make some memories that'll get you through some of these tough times, okay?"

I smiled and gave a nod, "Sounds like a plan, do you think the fire will be okay like that? I had one going," I said, gesturing toward the fireplace. He went over, had a look, and gave a nod.

"You did a good job, it'll burn itself out and shouldn't be any trouble glassed in like that."

We locked up and left the house; only this time he made sure to switch on the porch light and told me to keep a lamp burning in the living room.

"For safety," he said.

I smiled and acquiesced even though I worried about what it might do to the electric bill. I smiled when he opened and held the car door for me.

"I didn't know anyone did this outside of books," I said.

Nox raised an eyebrow. "What kind of lunkheads do you go out with?"

"None, actually... I haven't had time to date in a very long time." I got into the car which was still residually warm from his drive over here. He jogged around back and shrugged out of his leather vest, he got into the driver's seat and laid it absentmindedly into my lap before reaching for his seatbelt.

"Surely you've gone on some dates already though?"

"A few, even managed to lose my virginity." I made a face at that and he raised both eyebrows in surprise as he started the car up.

"Not fun times, I take it?"

"Rushed and awkward, the second and third time with him wasn't much better; then my dad got sick and I got busy and he... I don't know, it's like he just didn't understand or didn't get it. I legitimately didn't have the time for him anymore, so we just kind of drifted apart..." except we hadn't. The breakup had been ugly, and sadly, at least for me, remained ugly. It was like I had hurt Lucas' pride or something, but it didn't matter, he had hooked up with Robin Brown, one of the cheerleaders, and they'd been steadily making my life hell ever since. *High School, ain't it grand?*

For some reason, I didn't want Nox to know about that part... the bullying and the humiliation. I was already pathetic enough as it was, why add to it?

"Yeah, well, he was a dumbass then. You're a great girl, Maren."

I blushed. "Thank you."

We'd texted so much on the days we couldn't see each other that I was comfortable talking with him about just about anything. Nox was different from anyone else I'd ever met. An adult, sure, but technically I was too now… but more than that, he wasn't my father, nor was he a social worker or school official. I didn't have to mind myself carefully around him. I didn't have to be afraid I would say or do anything he would consider wrong and go running to the powers that be over it. I didn't have to worry that he would say or do something; go to someone and get Sage taken away from me.

It was like I had all these people on my side or in my corner, but I still had to be afraid of them. All except for Nox. He was extremely forthright and transparent. If he said he was going to do something, he did it. Likewise, if he made a promise, he kept it. I could rely on him even when I didn't think I needed to. I could tell him things, and he listened and not only that, provided insight and perspective that I sorely needed coming from the standpoint of having never done any of this before.

"I promised to take you out to dinner a while ago, how does Italian sound?" he asked.

I blinked. "I love it; it sounds good."

"Cool, I have no idea where we're going, I've never been, but it's got good reviews and it's nearby. Give me just a second."

He fiddled with his phone and got the GPS working, Siri's voice flitting out into the car demanding he starts his route to an address that sounded familiar by going east, or right out of my driveway.

"Okay, here we go," he said and did his checks before pulling onto the street. I let my fingertips trace the patches and buttons on the front of his vest across my lap and watched him drive. I'd lived here all my life, so there was nothing new to me outside the window, but the high sculpted cheekbones and strong features of the man driving were not only still new, but much better scenery than outside the window.

"How was work?" I asked softly.

"Busy and long… a lot of gift certificates today. I'm glad I draw a paycheck, folks with gift certificates never, if ever, think to tip. Not that I get a lot of those anyway."

"I still don't know what I want to be when I grow up," I said, laughing a little lightly.

"Yeah? What did you think about before… you know?"

"A lot of things, really. When I was little, I wanted to be a vet, but then I wanted to be an archaeologist, a lawyer, but mostly I'm hoping I can be a writer someday."

"A writer, huh?"

"Yeah, I like to write and tell stories. I don't have any money for college now, my dad and I paid the house off with my college fund and left Sage's protected… I'll figure something out but yeah… I thought about culinary school, too."

He very nearly slammed on the brakes at my revelation and shook his head like he was coming up out of water when we came to the next stop light.

"You and your dad did *what?*" he demanded.

"It was either that or lose the roof over our heads. I want Sage to have every chance possible, so it was my college fund to the rescue. Don't worry, I'm smart and there're a few academic scholarships in my near future, as well as several grants I plan to apply for. I didn't have any real dreams in the first place, there's just so much to choose from. I'll figure something out."

He remained grimly silent and I shifted in my seat, worried I may have finally overshared in a way that would put our new friendship in some real danger. Finally, he sighed out harshly and asked me, "Is there any length you won't go for your brother, Angel?"

"No."

"You're too good to be real, you know that?"

I smiled to myself and blushed faintly; perking up when we made a turn onto a familiar street. "Are we going to Filiberto's?"

"Yeah, that's the name of the place."

"My dad used to bring us there all the time! I love it there, it's my very favorite place... but you're sure it's not too expensive?"

"Nope, not too expensive, not for you," he said, and pulled up to the curb out front, shutting off his car. He looked over at me, raised his eyebrows and smoothed his hands along the tops of his thighs over his light denim jeans. "Hang tight, I'll get your door."

"Okay," I said laughing lightly.

He came around to my side and opened up my door. I passed him his leather vest and he took it, swinging it on, before reaching down and taking my hand.

"Careful, it's slick."

"Thank you." I stood straight and he closed the door behind me and chirped his alarm. We walked up the sidewalk, two doors down, to the brick building with the green door. He opened it for me and ushered us inside.

"Welcome to Filiberto's, do you have a reservation?" the hostess asked and Nox smiled.

"Yes, for two, should be under Landon Fisher."

She looked and smiled at us professionally, despite the glint of unease in her eyes as her gaze roved Nox's vest.

"Right this way," she said and we followed her to the upstairs, toward the back to a little two-person table.

"Thanks," Nox murmured and pulled out my chair for me. I slid my jacket and scarf onto the back of the chair and he did likewise with his coat and vest on the back of his. He sat down, pushing back the long sleeves of his gray Henley over his forearms. I smiled and let my eyes roam over his tattoos.

"Why crows?" I asked looking over the sleeve on his left arm.

Nox smiled a little ruefully, "Harbingers of death, extremely smart, memories like iron traps... they're resourceful, everything I need and want to be."

"Seems to me you've got a lot of those qualities."

"Yeah?"

"Yeah, just look what you did for Sage and me... what you do for us."

"I try."

We were interrupted by the waitress coming to take our drink order, and then we spent a bit of time looking over the menu to order our food. For the first time in weeks, I was famished, and I think it had more to do with the good, relaxed mood I was in.

There were no demands on me when I was around Nox. It was like I could breathe and be me with no expectations of remaining grown up beyond my years; at the same time, Nox wasn't like the parents, school officials, and social workers. They all treated me like a kid they expected to fail — with pity, and a certain level of mistrust. While they said with their mouths they trusted me, with their eyes they said just as loudly that they expected me to fail.

Not Nox, he believed in me. It was in his eyes and in his voice, and it made all the difference. It felt like if he could believe, then I *should* believe.

"You okay?" he asked softly, and I looked up from where the menu swam in my vision.

"I um..." I cleared my throat. "I guess I didn't realize how..." I set down the menu and looked out over the restaurant while my eyes cleared. Nox covered my hand with his where it rested on the table.

"It's okay," he murmured. "It'll all be there when you get back to it. For now, deep breaths and try to enjoy your evening. You can't worry about things you can't do anything about all the time, Angel. That's how you worry yourself sick. So when you're with me, just let me handle it some, okay?"

I blinked, and nodded dumbly, and some of the stress just melted away. Nox smiled, gave my hand a squeeze and asked what was good. I flicked my gaze back to the familiar menu. We ordered, ate, and shared in some companionable, light conversation. It was a good start for me to be able to enjoy myself and really, just what I needed.

9

N ox...
She was beautiful in the dim light from above and the soft golden glow cast by the little candles on every table. She smiled and her whole face transformed to the point she looked like one of the angels in the frescoes on the walls and ceiling in here. I guess I'd hit that right, calling her Angel all the time. I don't know why I'd started doing it. It just came naturally, so I went with it.

We ate a good meal and I think it was the most I'd seen her put away since we'd first met. Over the last couple of weeks, I'd seen her cheekbones grow sharper, the delicate bones of her wrists stand out more against her skin. She'd been losing weight, likely more from the worries and concerns that consumed her than from lack of appetite.

It was good to see her smile, it was good to see her laugh, and it was damn good knowing I somehow made that difference. The waitress brought the check at the end of our meal and I smiled, peeling off some bills to pay and leaving a better than decent tip. The woman smiled broadly and put a hand on my shoulder.

"You know it's always so nice to see these daddy-daughter dates, no matter how old they get," she said, and I watched the smile disappear off of Maren's face.

Son of a bitch.

I plastered on a stiff, fake as hell smile and gave a slight nod. It was hard to keep my trap shut as I watched the knife twist in Maren's chest and the sparkle leave her eyes. Her face burned with her fight to hold back the threatening tears and I couldn't do anything about it. I mean sure, I could have ripped the woman to shreds, but she didn't know... either about Maren's dad dying or the fact she sure as hell wasn't my daughter. I guess, technically, I *was* old enough to be Maren's daddy. Shit, I'd have had to have had her when I was something like... I did the math, *Christ... nineteen.* I was nineteen when Maren was born, totally doable. I could totally be her dad... *why didn't that squick me out like it should? Why didn't I feel like a pedophile now?*

Because the woman sitting across from me at that dinner table was just that... a woman. Young, sure, but old enough to make her own decisions and to hold her own. Hell, I'd been watching her hold her own for a minute now.

"What are you thinking?" she asked as the waitress walked away.

"Not sure I should say, Angel."

She pursed her lips and nodded, her dark eyes flitting to the side, off my face, to the little guttering candle at the edge of our table.

"You're not a little girl, you're not *my* little girl, that's for sure. We're friends before anything else, but I sometimes wonder things I shouldn't." I swallowed hard and didn't say anything else. I just watched those luminous dark eyes return to my face, searching it with one of the gravest expressions I'd ever seen someone wear.

She studied me in silence for a full minute.

"Me too," she said softly, and I felt my spine turn liquid with relief. I hadn't scared her, and she hadn't scared me, but *now what?* It definitely felt like some sort of line had been drawn in the sand and crossed; like we'd turned a corner of some kind, but into what?

"Thank you for dinner," she murmured, and the spell was temporarily broken. I nodded and could pretend nothing had happened or that nothing was amiss, if she could.

"I figured we could go to the club, watch the ball drop on the big screen, what do you think?"

"Am I old enough?" she asked and I had to laugh.

"Not a nightclub, Angel. *The* club, as in the MC."

"Oh! You're sure they won't mind?"

"You're my guest, why would they mind?"

I stood and helped her into her coat and figured I wasn't going to get an answer when she finally said softly, "I'm just a kid."

I smiled but tried not to laugh, figuring that would just make things worse. "What did I just tell you, Angel?" I asked, voice low and somewhat chiding.

"That you don't see me as a kid, I know, but your friends – they might."

"I love my brothers and sisters at the club, but fuck 'em if they do."

Her eyes widened, and I captured her hand, tugging her along toward the stairs and the eventual exit. We hit the street and a wall of cold and I heard Maren gasp. I turned and tucked her under my arm as we made our way up the block to my cage, the lights flashing as I hit the button on my key.

"I hate the cold, why can't it be summer again?" she said as I opened her door for her.

"You think you're cold, I come from a land that has no winter!" I laid my cut across her lap and shut the door on her before she could say anything, mostly because I wanted to get the damn cage started and some heat going.

"I didn't think of that, I thought it snowed in parts of Arizona though."

"It does up around Flagstaff sometimes, but I was down in a small border town."

We chatted some while I drove us to the club and around back to spare her from going through the bar. When we pulled up on the track, there were a bunch of the guys standing around the fire pit, a bright blaze going in it, beers in hand. I got out of the cage and Maren slipped out on her own before I could grab her door for her.

"Hey, Jailbait!" my retarded, half lit, twin crowed and I think I saw Maren flinch slightly.

"Hi Rush," she called out softly.

"What you two doing here?" Dragon asked and sucked on his cigarette, the coal glowing in the dark. He stood behind the fire, and the flames licking up, casting shadow and throwing shade made his coal dark eyes darker somehow. Hell, it made the man look like the devil him-fucking-self.

"Nowhere else to go really, thought it'd be nice to bring in the New Year around my brothers." I clasped hands with Reaver and we drew in for one of our classic manly hugs.

"Well get on up close to the fire, girl! Before you freeze to death," Archer muttered.

Maren stepped up in between Archer and Trig and held her hands out to the heat. Trig stepped aside for me to take my place beside her. Archer sucked on a joint and passed it in front of Maren to me, but she took it and a drag. Dragon laughed and Maren passed it to me raising her eyebrows. I smiled and took a hit.

"Huh," Archer said, "I didn't figure a nice girl like you for a toker."

"My dad had it, for his cancer," she said. Her voice strained from holding her breath, she let it out in a plume of fragrant smoke and water vapor from her breath as it hit the cold air. "He'd have me light it up for him and let me take a hit every once in a while." She looked up at Archer, huddling in on herself, her hands pushed deep into her pockets. "Sorry if I wasn't supposed to."

Arch was typical Arch; he just gave a one-shouldered shrug and said, "I ain't your daddy."

Maren blushed hard and Rush took pity on her; before I could open my mouth, he said, "Translation — He don't give a fuck, you're adulting just fine; you do you."

"Ah," Maren said back as if Rush had just explained everything, and maybe he had.

Reaver turned to go inside and I called out, "Hey, bro! Grab me a beer?" The scary as fuck brother waved over his shoulder and disappeared into the club's back door.

"Where's little brother?" Rush asked.

"Staying the night at his best friend's."

"Ahh, was wondering what brought you out here."

"Actually, I expected to spend tonight alone, it was Nox who had other ideas."

I fucking loved how she smiled in my direction when she said it. It warmed me up better than the bonfire they had going. Trig chuckled beside me.

"That so?" he asked and Maren blushed.

"As in getting her out of the house, asshole. No one should be alone on New Year's Eve."

Reave banged out the back door and called back behind him, "Yeah, yeah! Got one more for your girl pile out here – I'm stayin' out here where it's safe for the time being!"

Peals of feminine laughter floated out from the club and he returned to the fire with three cold ones. He handed me one and Trig the other. The dead soldiers were piling up on the ground. Good fodder for the shooting range later.

"Who's out there with you that's a girl?" Everett called from the back door, hands on her hips. "Not fair that you're keeping her from all the fun!"

"I've got Maren with me!" I called back to her.

"Maren?" she sounded perplexed for a moment and then called, "Oh! *Maren!* Well, come on in here out of the cold, girlfriend! Let the boys be retarded, doesn't mean you have to suffer."

"I fuckin' heard that!" Dray called from beside his father.

"Don't fuckin' care if you did; not like I was keeping it some big damn secret."

"Oh, I am so gonna fuck that mouth of yours later," Dray said shaking his head and Everett laughed.

"Looking forward to it, baby! As always."

"That is one *dirty* fuckin' girl you've got there," Rush said with approval.

Maren remained silent, simply taking it all in. Her dark eyes aglow with firelight and the mellow high she'd attained from her hit of weed. If it was one thing this area had, it was some seriously good shit. One hit was usually all it took to mellow you out.

"Why don't you go on in, sweetheart? We'll all be in before the ball drops," Dragon suggested, but I knew when it wasn't a suggestion, and this was one of those. I nudged her lightly and she nodded.

"Thank you," she murmured and took the dismissal.

"Be right there," I assured her, and she trailed along in the dark, Everett opening up the door for her and greeting her warmly.

"I interrupt something out here?" I asked when she was gone.

"Not especially, just having a little pow wow about the upstate New York chapter."

"What about 'em?" I asked.

"Eh, they imploded a minute ago, but a few of the loyal brothers that were serving time are getting out and want to rekindle their chapter up there."

"There any question on if they're on board with the new, gentler regime?" Trigger asked.

"Can't be sure, but two does not a chapter make," Dragon said with a sigh.

"Thinking of bringing 'em down here?" I asked.

"Might just." Dragon didn't sound sure. More talk went around the fire about it, beer was drunk and I took a few more hits off the joints being passed around. Finally, Hayden and Ashton poked their heads out the back door.

"Countdown is starting!" Hayden called and we struck out in that direction.

I found Maren in the back corner of the media room, folded up on one of the stools from the bar. She was smiling and watching everyone and almost seemed a touch relieved when she saw me. I went over to her and she smiled, slipping off the stool and standing. I leaned my butt against it and the counting started, everyone shouting in unison.

"Eight!"

I smiled at the enthusiastic smile on Maren's lips as she counted with everyone else. The jubilation and excitement thrumming through the room a contagious thing.

"Six!"

"Five!"

"Four!"

I joined in on the count.

"Three!"

"Two!"

"One!"

"Happy New Year!"

The ball on the television flared bright, the room brightening as a result, the only light coming from the big screen. *Auld Lange Syne* as sung by the crowd in Times Square booming through the speakers. Maren turned and hugged me jovially and we drew apart and, in her enthusiasm, her lips landed on mine.

I'd seen it a thousand times in the movies and on TV. The guy and the girl, they kiss, and time – hell everything – just freezes around them. I'd never had it happen to me, though; not until right then. An electric tingle suffused my lips and it was like it jolted my heart, the damn thing skipping a beat entirely while that electric pleasure flowed through my veins and the hair stood up on the back of my neck. It was a split second our lips touched but it might as well have been the shortest eternity.

Maren drew back slightly, surprise painting her features as much as it probably painted mine. Her dark eyes wide and her equally dark hair tumbling around her face, I couldn't resist. I couldn't stop myself, and if I were going to hell for it, then so be it. I bent my head deliberately and kissed her again. I kissed her for real, tasting her this time, and I had zero fucking regrets.

10

Maren...

I held my breath, I hadn't meant to, I was just excited. I'd kissed him and I'd pulled back from it, longing squeezing my heart in its fist. He'd quickly glanced over my face, a deep, lusting longing in his eyes and had bowed his head, his arms tightening around my body and drawing me close.

He kissed me back.

He kissed me back, and it was everything every girl has imagined at one time or another. His mouth warm against mine, his tongue gently asking permission, touching lightly against my bottom lip. I gave him access and I swear to God, I melted. He deepened the contact, his tongue stroking expertly against mine, and I would have given him anything, anything at all that he wanted from me, had he only asked for it.

He didn't, however. If anything, the thing I admired about Nox, was his level of control. No matter what, no matter the situation, he always seemed in control and ready to handle it. This was no different. While I wanted to climb his body and have him take me anywhere but this room full of people to finish what I'd started; he had the patience to follow the wiser course of action. He broke the kiss, both of us breathless, chests heaving in shallow gasps.

He rested his forehead against mine and licked his sensual lips, his eyes opening to pin my gaze with his.

"I have to stop, Angel. We both have to stop."

"I know," I gasped, and I couldn't keep the mournful tone from my voice.

"Trust me, baby. I don't want to. I want to take you to my room and finish what we just started, but it's not a good idea."

"I know, it's not safe, for you or for me. They might take Sage and I can't let that happen."

"They might decide I need to serve some jail time, and I can't let that happen either."

I closed my eyes again and just tried to hold on to the intimate feeling like we were in our own private bubble.

"Take me to your place," I murmured. "I just want to be alone with you, to talk; to listen to something other than the worries and the heartache for a time."

His hold on me tightened just a little and he drew back to look at me before nodding, finally.

"I can leave the door open, come on this way." He took me by the hand and led me out of the cavernous family room into the club and back out the door we'd entered it from. Once outside, I followed him across the grass to the asphalt track, around past the big garage and shop building to another outbuilding. He opened the door on one end of it and ushered me inside.

It was warm, and a long sterile hall with doors lining it to either side. Nox took my hand again and pointed at the first one. "That's the bathroom if you need it, the door on the other end of the hall on the opposite side is one too."

"Okay," I murmured.

He led me about four doors down the hall and to the left opening the door. "This is my place," he muttered, flipping on the light.

The room was fairly good sized and held a bed and a couple of dressers. A television was perched on the top of one of them, along with a small cable box, Blu-ray player, and a few remotes. Everything was neat and orderly, the air scented faintly with something herbal. The bed was big and heavy, made from the same light wood as the dresser and armoire. The furniture pieces rustic, speaking of the country or life on a ranch. It seemed out of place from the rest of Nox, of course, nothing about him had fit the stereotypes of what you would expect from all the tattoos and black leather.

He took my coat from me and hung it on a hook on the back of the door, hanging his jacket and vest beside it. He swung the door wide, and while I would have liked a little more privacy, I understood. It stung that he didn't trust me, but what could be done about it? This was why we couldn't have nice things... people, both men, and girls, behaving badly, ruining it for the rest of us.

"You okay?" he asked me, smoothing his hands up and down my shoulders. I nodded, and wrapped my arms around his waist, hugging myself close, in the shelter of his much taller body. He wrapped his arms around me and held me, and I could have stayed there forever.

"I was just thinking about how this is why we can't have nice things, meaning people just wreck everything, you know?"

"I don't think I follow," he murmured.

"Like now, I want more than anything for you to trust me, and for you to close that door so we can just be, but I know you can't..."

"I trust you, Maren."

"You can't, at least not really," I said.

"Why do you think that?"

"Stop me if I'm wrong," I said. "What's to say you close that door, and we lay down, and I fall asleep and we just cuddle? Nothing inappropriate happens, you don't touch anything you're not supposed to, we don't even kiss. What's to say, a week, a month or even a year from now I don't get upset with you and as vindictive recourse, I go out and cry rape or something equally awful? You know I would never do that, I know I would never do that, but so many other girls that have gone before have done just that… which makes it unsafe for you or for me to close the door and have some privacy."

"By and far it's the same for you, isn't it?" he asked, smoothing his hands up and down my back over my thin cardigan. "What's to say I'm not some dirty old fucker? What's to say I don't pin you down and do things? Make you cry? Hurt you?"

"Because that's not who you are."

"Maybe not," he said, with a hint of a satisfied smile tinging his voice. "The rest of the world might have a different opinion about it, though."

"I wish we could just forget about what other people think."

"Me too, Angel. If it's the one thing I've definitely learned, it's that people don't know how, or just can't mind their own fucking business."

I sighed heavily and nodded wearily against his shoulder. "So what now?"

"I figure I leave the door open, we lie down, and talk about whatever you want. You fall asleep, I let you sleep, and I take you back in the morning."

"And then?"

"And then we Cinderella for a few months."

I laughed. "We what?"

He shrugged. "Dawn's our midnight; it comes, we go back to being pumpkins and pretend this was just a good dream – at least until you're eighteen and no one has a say about the shit that we do, or do not do."

I let him lead me to the bed and sat down at his urging. He kneeled and unzipped my knee-high boots, sliding them off and setting them neatly at the foot of the bed.

"People will still talk, won't they?"

"Yeah, people will always talk, but Maren, we don't exactly have to listen."

I smiled a bit wanly. "We don't now, do we?"

"Unfortunately, when it comes to the law, I do," he said and lifted my ankles, swinging them in toward the mattress. He laid my legs on his bed and I just naturally lay back to watch him. He came around to the other side, pulled off his boots and did the same as he did with mine, lined them up neatly at the foot of the bed on his side before he lay on his side to look at me. Our hands just sort of naturally met in the middle, on the mattress between us.

"I don't understand," I said. "What does the law have to say about it if I say everything is fine?"

"Not how the law always works, Angel. Even though you're perfectly capable of making your own decisions, even though you're legally emancipated, all it takes is one social justice warrior with a badge to say that you are still a minor and that I'm somehow victimizing you and bam! I'm walking around with a life sentence of having to be on some sexual predator registry. I'd lose my license, wouldn't be able to practice massage anymore. My livelihood, my ability to live where I wanted, anytime I tried to get hired on anywhere else, all of it would be in jeopardy even if we were still together or not."

"That's not fair," I murmured.

"Neither is life, Angel." He shrugged the shoulder he wasn't lying on and it was such a nonchalant motion over such a serious topic, the fact that he had just given up and knows this to be true – it broke my heart.

"Not everything has sinister connotations," I whispered and he gave me a crooked smile.

"No, not everything, but enough of the real-world situations do and so people just get to calling a spade a spade. I'm almost twenty years older than you. I like you, and for a whole hell of a lot more than your age or your body. You're a smart woman, Maren, and strong, even if you don't feel like it. You're interesting and not like other women I've met. I want to get to know you and I have to say, the best things in life are worth waiting for and I don't think you're an exception to that particular rule."

His last sentence made my breath catch in my throat, my eyes very nearly mist, and I felt galvanized of a sort. If he could wait and be patient, then so could I. After all he had done for me, and for Sage, I think I could wait forever if I had to.

Nox reached out and grazed his thumb gently in the corner of my eye, thumbing away the pool of moisture there. He leaned forward carefully and pressed a kiss to my forehead, sighing.

"It's okay," he murmured, lips against my skin. "We can do this. Hell, you can do anything, just look at all you've done so far."

I closed my eyes and basked in the comfort of his presence. It felt good to have someone acknowledge it out loud, you know? To recognize that it wasn't easy, being seventeen, being the only one available to help your only functional parent through their last days. Dealing with the paperwork, the social workers, the hospice workers, and the finances; managing your little brother and his feelings, his pain, on top of your own to the best of your ability. That it was hard maintaining a full-time job, on top of a full-time high school class schedule, all the legalities with inheritance and emancipation, becoming a legal guardian for a brother who had little to no interest in cooperating at all.

To have someone look at me and say that I could do anything I put my mind to, when I constantly felt like I was on a razor's edge of failure… that was something I needed. That was just the right thing at just the right time and I couldn't help it. I wept with relief that I wasn't crazy and that this really was as hard as it felt. I wept knowing that I finally wasn't doing it completely alone.

Nox let me shake and let me cry and smoothed my hair away from my face, making soothing sounds, keeping me warm and giving me a sense of safety – that it was finally safe for me to simply feel all of these things. I don't remember falling asleep, but I did, and it was probably the best sleep I had ever had; at least since my father told my brother and me of his diagnosis. When I woke up, light streamed in the high window and the door still stood wide, but Nox's side of the bed was empty, a blanket lay over the top of me and I sat up, shoving it off.

I slipped on my boots and brought down my coat and scarf from the back of the door where it remained; Nox's jacket and cut missing from the hook next to it. I used the bathroom at the end of the hall and slipped out the door we'd come in from. Frost, so thick it looked like snow, coated the grass and my breath fogged the open air. I winced as the sound of a table saw assaulted my ears and I marched across the grass to the open bay door to investigate its origins. That's where I found Nox's brother Rush in what I presumed to be his woodshop.

"Hey, Jailbait!" he called out and I felt myself blush.

"Hi," I called back as the saw whirred down.

"Lookin' for Nox?" he grunted and inspected the cut he'd just made. Something was different, it was like Rush was more reserved than he had been before last night and I felt myself sigh inwardly.

"Yeah, have you seen him?" I asked.

"Think he was making y'all some breakfast inside the main building. Just go through the back door and past the media room. The kitchen is behind the bar," he answered, his expression going back and forth as if he were struggling with things.

"Ah, thank you."

Rush nodded and looked me over, I waited for him to say what was on his mind knowing it was likely something I wasn't going to like.

"Just do me a favor, Maren," he said finally, and I nodded for him to go on. "Just don't fuck over my brother. He's a good guy, and for some reason, of all the chicks that are out there, he got stuck on you. Personally, in some ways, I think it's a good choice, you're one solid chick, but you're too young. Plain and simple, which makes it the wrong choice. I worry, you know?"

I nodded, and forced a smile. "I worry too, so I guess that's a good sign, yeah?"

Rush nodded. "Yeah, maybe it is."

He started up the saw and was all concentration behind his clear safety glasses as he made his next cut, and I felt as dismissed as anyone could be. I escaped the grating high-pitched noise by trudging through the white-coated grass towards the back door of the club, past Nox's car which was iced over pretty good. So, he hadn't left at all, which eased my anxiety.

I wiped my boots on the mat outside the back door and slipped inside the warmth of the main building. I slipped through the archways and found the bar easily enough, but paused before going in. Even though I was emancipated, and considered an adult in every regard, I was still legally a minor when it came to both alcohol and cigarettes. I couldn't buy them, and I couldn't just waltz into a bar.

"Come on in here, he's in the kitchen in the back. Somehow, I doubt any law enforcement is gonna jump out and bite ya," an older man said. He was bald and had a trucker's mustache. He was sitting at a table across from Dragon who looked half asleep, smoke curling out of his nose. I returned my gaze to the older man and he looked at me with watery blue eyes over half-moon spectacles. He clutched a thick romance novel, of all things, between his hands and I blushed.

"I'm looking for Nox," I murmured and the old man smiled.

"I gathered that, honey, the way you was suckin' face last night. An' like I said, he's in the kitchen, through there. Go on now, it's booze, not anything that's gonna get you."

"Thank you," I murmured and yet still felt uneasy stepping into the room and past the two men at the table. Dragon chuckled and shook his head.

"Were we ever that young, Doc?"

"Yeah, we were just fearless when we were..."

I left the men to their conversation, reminiscing over this and that and slipped behind the bar and into the kitchen beyond. Nox smiled over his shoulder at me as he stood at the range, waiting on what looked like sausage patties.

"You'll take a hit off of a joint which is illegal all the time, but you're afraid to even walk into a room full of alcohol which you only gotta wait four more years for?" he asked, and his tone was gently teasing.

I shrugged, blushing harder and said, "I never said I was consistent, just serious."

He laughed outright and turned back to the range, flipping the patties gently with a metal spatula.

"Was making breakfast sandwiches, what time you gotta pick Sage up?"

"Noon, unless Ariel calls sooner. I don't think she'll be watching him overnight for a while," I said making a face. Nox's face fell and he cocked his head.

"Why not? What's going on?"

"Sage being Sage, I guess. She wasn't specific, just said that it would be a while before she could do an overnight. When I offered to let Ian come over for an overnight at our house, she said no, that it was okay and I get it, I guess." I mean, I was only seventeen, and I was apparently doing a real bang-up job as a single parent type with Sage. Nox nodded slowly and simply stood, raking his eyes over me, like he was trying to decide if I was telling him the whole truth.

"It'll be okay," he murmured and I nodded.

"It will all get figured out," I agreed softly.

He opened his mouth to speak and it was cut off by the shrill trilling of my ringtone. I dug my phone out of the pocket of my coat.

"Speak of the devil," I muttered, flashing him Ariel's name on the screen. He nodded and went back to cooking. I answered the phone before it could ring a third time.

"Hello?"

"Maren, hi, um… can I ask, where are you?"

"I'm having breakfast with a friend, why, what's up?"

"I'm at your house with Sage. Um, I need to drop him off a little early."

I closed my eyes. "What's happened?" I asked.

"It will probably be better if we talked in person."

"Yes, you know what, I'm sorry you're absolutely correct," I said in my best parenting voice, whatever that was. "I'll be home in just a few minutes. Twenty at the most."

"Okay, thank you. I really, honestly expected you to be home."

"Yes, I'm sorry, I figured I was only a phone call away…"

"Right, well, see you in about twenty minutes."

"Twenty minutes," I agreed.

By the time I hung up, Nox was handing me a breakfast sandwich wrapped in a paper towel.

"Guess breakfast is 'to-go' this morning," he said with a charming half-smile. It made me smile in return.

"We'd better hurry."

"You bet, come on."

I followed him back out to his car, worry gnawing at me. I wondered what had been done, had Sage broken something? Had he hurt Ian or Ian's little sister? *What on earth was going on?*

When Nox and I pulled up to the curb outside of my house, the breakfast sandwich had decided to sit in my stomach like lead. I got out of the car before he could even shut it off and met Ariel half way down the driveway. She had been sitting in her car, while my little brother had been sitting huddled on the porch swing near the front door.

"Keys," Nox called and I pulled mine out, tossing them to him. He went for Sage while I went for Ariel.

"Ariel, why is my little brother sitting out in the cold while you sit in your car?" I asked, not rudely, not angrily, I simply asked.

"Maren, it was his choice," she said putting up her hands, "after I told him that he and Ian needed to take a break for a little while."

I felt my back go up and I gritted my teeth. "Don't you think that maybe we should have talked about that before you said something to him?" I asked.

Ariel looked uncertain. "Well, you're so young—"

"And I'm still his guardian, would you mind filling me in on what exactly is going on?"

"I just think that Sage is going through a lot right now and that he's maybe becoming a bad influence on Ian as a result."

I rubbed my forehead and looked at Ariel plainly. "Can you tell me why you reached that conclusion?" I asked.

"I overheard Sage telling Ian last night that Ian didn't have to listen to me, or his father, just like Sage doesn't have to listen to you…"

"And your control over Ian is *so* fragile that you thought Sage's opinion would make that much of a difference?" I asked, and I couldn't help being bitter and even snarky about it.

"Maren, it's not like that—"

"Then what is it like, Ariel? Were you even going to give me the chance to fix it? To talk to Sage?"

She was silent for a time and finally said, "You know all about kids and peer pressure these days. I just think it's a good idea that Sage takes a time-out; that you and he sort some things out."

"I don't disagree, but wow. Just wow. I'm going to go inside and do just that, but I think you need to leave."

"Maren!"

"Thank you for everything that you've done so far, Ariel. I really do appreciate it. I mean that," I called over my shoulder and I went into my house without another backward glance.

I found Nox standing in the living room, arms crossed over his chest, staring down at my little brother who was huddled on the couch, sniffling. I dropped onto the cushion beside him and tried not to cry myself. I felt like I was screwing just everything up for him, but had to admit, Sage needed to take some responsibility too.

"Do you want to talk about it?" I asked gently.

"No."

"Well," Nox drawled, "that's too bad this time, buddy. You need to listen to your sister."

"Why?" Sage demanded. "She's only six years older than me! She gets to do whatever she wants, why can't I?"

I couldn't help the harsh, choked, bitter laugh that escaped me. "Is that what you think? Because if I were doing what I wanted, I would probably be a lot happier," I said, staring at Nox, who caught my meaning and inclined his head with a sad little smile. Neither one of us were having much fun having reverted to pumpkin status.

Sage brought up his head and glared at me savagely and I stared right back, calmly, waiting for it. "It's like you're pretending to be all grown up and you're all of a sudden the boss of me! You're not! I don't have to listen to you, you're just my stupid sister!" he shouted, and Nox hung his head and let out a jagged laugh.

"No, you're right, you're right. You don't have to listen to her, you don't have to listen to me either, but what you have to do is live with the consequences of not listening. You feel me, little man?"

Sage glared at both me and Nox, but finally looked a little uncertain. I asked him, "Do you know what happens if you won't listen to me? If you get into trouble? They'll think I can't take care of you. They'll take you away from me and put you into a foster home."

"So?" Sage demanded, but I could tell he was losing steam.

Nox cut in, "I can tell you all about foster homes, Sage. It's not a vacation. You go to live with strangers. If you're lucky, they aren't too bad. Then there are the kind who don't care if you eat and beat you for the smallest thing. Most of the time you get the kind that just treats you like you're a paycheck. Feed you and make sure you don't die on your way to school, but other than that?" Nox shook his head. "You can forget help with your homework, you can forget getting any of your favorite foods, or going out to play, or playing video games or a lot of the things you get here with Maren. You won't get to see her, you won't get to use the phone to call her, and you probably won't get to do anything like learning how to drive when you turn sixteen, unless you steal a car.

"You can pretty much be guaranteed to get caught, and spend some time in Juvie…" He paused and took a deep breath, reordering his thoughts before going on, "It's a spiral you see, down, down and down. If you're not lucky, like me, you get put into a home with foster parents like Norma Rae and Duncan. Where a couple of boys barely older than you are the ones who raise you. Your foster parents spend the money that's supposed to feed and clothe you on booze and cigarettes, your foster father beats you with his belt for stealing a French fry off his stack even though you're so hungry, you'd eat just about anything—"

"*Nox!*" I said sharply, horrified and hoping this wasn't how he'd grown up, but deep down, looking at the pain etched into every line of his face, looking at the well of deep pain in his eyes… somehow, I knew it was.

"That doesn't happen!" Sage said defiantly, but he looked scared. I wanted to agree, to tell him he was right and that nothing like that ever happened, but wasn't it the exact thing I was terrified was *going* to happen to him?

I felt awful, I felt trapped; I felt like no matter what I had tried to do to get him gently through this, it wasn't working. I felt like the last thing I wanted to do was to terrify him into behaving, believing wholeheartedly, that fear wasn't how you should motivate or steer a child through life. However, I was at a crossroads here with my little brother. My way had, quite literally, lost him his best friend. I wasn't sure how that would end up working out or if it would at all.

"Truth is best," Nox murmured and I covered my face with my hands, scrubbing as if I could scrub all of this away.

"Nox isn't lying, it does happen, and I don't want that for you. I want you to stay here, with me, I don't want to lose the only family I have left. It's just you and me now."

"No, it's not! And you know it!" Sage exploded and pushed off the couch. He went for the stairs and slammed up them; I closed my eyes and sighed.

"I'm not going to ask," Nox said gently, "but I'm around when you're ready to talk."

I nodded, grateful for that, because as soon as I told him about my mother, I was pretty certain he would walk away, and I was growing to depend on him — on his emotional support. I stood up and he pulled me into his arms, resting his chin on top of my head.

"Thank you," I murmured.

"For?"

"One last minute of closeness before the clock strikes pumpkin hour."

Nox chuckled lightly and kissed the top of my head. "You're welcome, Angel."

I closed my eyes and breathed in his crisp, clean scent of man and leather before I had to let him go.

11

N ox...

"Dude, what the fuck are you doing? You're gonna end up in jail and listed on some sex offender's registry as a total pedo," Rush said, dropping onto the couch in the media room next to me. I scowled at my twin.

"Fuck you. I am not," I said, scoffing. Rush scowled right back.

"Man, you had your tongue halfway down her throat in here last night, then the both of you disappeared."

"Yeah, they were in his room with the door wide open, quit yer fuckin' bitchin'. You ain't his mom," Duracell said from one of the recliners.

"No, I'm his fucking twin, asshat. Fuck you, mind your own business." I had to laugh when Duracell flipped him the bird, saluted my brother with his beer and took a drink of it. Blue laughed silently from the other recliner at the opposite end of the couch from Cell. Those two were fuckin' weird. None of us could tell if they had something going like Disney and Aaron, and whenever anyone brought it up, Cell typically flew off the handle about how he wasn't some faggot. Confusing as fuck if you asked me, because short of holding hands and kissing, the two were inseparable and even slept in each other's room sometimes.

Rush was talking, droning on in one of his fucking lectures like he was somehow magically older or wiser; I cut him off with, "Motherfucker, you're older than me by a few minutes. What the fuck do you know about it, anyway? I'm not going to do shit to put myself in any crosshairs. She's a grown woman despite her age, and she knows what could happen. Chill the fuck out and mind your own business on this one."

Rush pushed to his feet, his expression stormy. "Fuck you, then. I'll be in my shop." He left out the media room and I followed him with my gaze, meeting Duracell's half-charmed smile.

"Admit it," he said. "You hit that nubile teen pussy already."

"Can't admit to something that didn't happen, bro."

"You could," he said, settling back, "but you'd be a liar. I would have fuckin' hit it by now."

"Yeah, but you have no limits, plus, we already have our sights set on someone," Blue said softly, and I startled, looking in his direction.

"Shit man, that's the most I've heard outta you in months. Who is she?"

"No one," Duracell grunted, "Blue doesn't know what the fuck he's talking about."

Blue rolled his eyes so hard he probably saw his own brain, and I chuckled. "Does that mean you two are some kind of a thing?

"Man, fuck that. Why everybody have to be accusing me of being gay and shit?"

Again, Blue rolled his eyes and I laughed outright. The rest of the evening passed pretty peacefully. I kept a hand wrapped around my phone, waiting for it to go off, though. Finally, around nine o'clock, it did.

Maren: He still won't talk to me. Won't come out of his room, either.

Me: Let him sulk if he wants to. He doesn't have to like it, he just has to put up with it, and do what u say for the next, what, seven years?

Maren: Ugh, don't remind me... he's not even a teenager yet. Eleven going on thirty.

Me: LOL how are u doing tho?

Maren: Okay, I guess. I miss you. It's okay that I say that right? I mean, I don't sound stupidly desperate, do I?

Me: No Angel, and I miss u 2.

Maren: God, sometimes I feel like such an immature little girl next to you.

Me: Growing old is mandatory. Growing up is optional.

Maren: LOL! That explains so much.

Me: U have school 2morrow, right?

Maren: *Sigh* Yes. Don't remind me.

Me: Tough luck, baby. I just did. U should get some sleep.

Maren: I will.

Me: Now... not l8r.

Maren: Fine, I'm going to bed now.

Me: Sweet dreams.

Maren: If you're in them, then yes.

Me: ☺

The girl sure did know how to give me a boner. *Jesus.*

12

Maren...

"Sage, come on! Stop playing around and get down here! You've already missed the bus and if I have to come up there one more time, I'm dragging you to school behind the car!" I shouted up the stairs and stopped only when my brother appeared at the top of them, dragging on his coat.

"I don't want to take the bus anymore," he said, sulking and I sighed and tried to count to ten before I said something unfortunate.

"We'll talk about it tonight, over dinner," I said.

"Yeah, right," he said pushing past me and I just snapped.

"That's it. Get in the car, now! I'm sick of this attitude problem of yours, Sage. Now move it. I'm not going to put my education on hold and be late because you refuse to act your age rather than your shoe size. This is getting past ridiculous. Honestly, what do you think Dad would say?"

Sage stopped cold and glared at me, but didn't say a word; finally, he popped off at me with, "You're a real bitch, you know that?"

"Not impressed. I get called worse on a daily basis at school, or did you forget that? Get. In. The. Car." I turned him by his shoulders and gave him a shove in the direction of the garage and he went. We got in the car, tears stinging the backs of my eyes even though I wouldn't let them out. Just like the assholes at school, I wouldn't give Sage the satisfaction.

I backed us out of the garage and out of the driveway, making sure the garage door shut firmly behind us, the headlights beaming on its painted surface, before backing completely onto the street. I drove Sage to school, pulling up to the waiting line of cars. I'd barely made it off the street into the school's driveway when Sage unbuckled his seat-belt and opened the passenger door.

"Do you have your key?" I demanded.

"Yeah, I'll take the bus, whatever." He slammed the car door so hard it rocked the vehicle on its frame and I sighed, already tired before my day could even really begin. I drove myself to school in the early dawn gloom. Shutting off in my assigned space and practically sprinting for the front door, my backpack bouncing hard enough against my back to almost knock the wind out of me, I barely made it before the bell.

Anxiety hummed through my veins and I thought of Nox. There was still so much we didn't know about each other. Still so much I hid from him, afraid if he knew, that it would be too much... one of those things was my very ex-boyfriend, Lucas Triggs.

"Maren! Heard you finally finished off your dad, the house is all yours now, huh?" he called from down the hallway to a course of masculine laughter. I knew it was going to be bad, but I managed to resist folding like cheap origami. Instead, I slipped into my class just as the bell rang its last and rushed over to my seat, taking it and digging in my book bag for my text.

I sat, cheeks stinging as I felt their eyes bore into me, their whispers and commentary filtering to me in snatches.

"Did she really kill her dad?"

"No, he's been sick for a long time… then again, maybe she did, so she wouldn't have to take care of him anymore."

"I heard she's trying to get her brother into foster care, so she doesn't have to take care of him anymore either."

"Probably," someone agreed.

"Isn't her mom –"

"Alright! That's enough!" Mr. Miller, the history teacher called out, drowning out the comments. "Open up to page two hundred and eighty-four, the French Revolution is upon us. Who can tell me…"

I listened halfheartedly and tried to breathe around the crushing pain and anxiety weighting the center of my chest.

You knew it was going to be bad, I told myself, but still, nothing really prepares you, you know? Just when you think you've thought of just about everything they could come at you with, they come up with the one thing you didn't think of. Or in this case, the one thing I figured they would have the decency not to pick on.

I swallowed hard and took a swig out of my water bottle to drown the threatening tears, concentrating on what the teacher was trying to teach and already bored to tears for having researched it all before on my own with my dad. I liked learning new things. I liked excelling at my studies, it was one of the few things that were uniquely mine that these bullying bastards couldn't take from me.

"Maren, I know you know the answer to this, why don't you enlighten the class seeing as no one else could be bothered to read the material," Mr. Miller said, and his gaze was squarely on me. I licked my lips and took a deep breath.

"I'm sorry, I'm afraid I was a little lost inside my own head there for a second. Can you repeat the question?" I smoothed my lips together as the class erupted in light laughter at my expense.

Mr. Miller frowned. "Are you sure it isn't too soon for you to come back, Maren?" he asked me, and I nodded quickly.

"Yes, if you'll just repeat the question, please."

"Even the super nerd isn't listening to you today, maybe it's time you retire!" someone called from the back and Mr. Miller looked up.

"Or maybe it's time you served a little detention, Mr. Swanson; see me after class."

A chorus of 'Ooooooos went around, low and sweeping, and more laughter ensued. I closed my eyes and counted to six before Mr. Miller repeated his question, "What was the ultimate cause of the French Revolution, Ms. Tracy?" he asked me.

"Ah, that would be a financial strain on the people from old debt and their continued witnessing of the upper-royal classes' wasteful expenditure and excess."

"Do you know the famous quote that attributed to the French people's outrage?" he asked.

"Yes, when the people complained they were starving, that they couldn't even afford a loaf of bread, the queen, Marie Antoinette, is quoted as saying 'then let them eat cake!' though it has never been proven that she actually said those exact words."

"Very good. Thank you, Maren."

"Yeah, Maren. What would he ever do without you?" one of the girls mocked in a voice where you could just hear her rolling her eyes. Chelsea Day was a cheerleader and my very ex-boyfriend's current girlfriend. She was welcome to him.

"Likely, I would feel as if I were a complete failure as an instructor, such as I do in your case, Ms. Day," Mr. Miller quipped to a round of laughter.

"What's that supposed to mean?" she demanded.

"Google it," he said with a smile and I felt myself sink lower in my chair. Likely her embarrassment would translate, somehow, into being my fault. It always did. I still couldn't follow her logic on that one, but she did a superb job of making me pay for her mistakes.

The day just dragged, the insults and comments about murdering my sick father kept coming and by the time the last bell rang, I was mentally and emotionally exhausted but the day, the day wasn't done with me yet. I got into my car, turned the key, and *click*.

"No!" I moaned and put my forehead against the steering wheel. "Why?" I cried to no one in particular.

I got out of the car and closed the door, pulling my phone from my pocket. I, sadly, only had one person I could call and he, thankfully, picked up on the second ring.

"Hey, Angel, good timing, I have about two more minutes before my next client shows." I felt my shoulders slump. "How was school?" he asked.

"It would be better if I hadn't left my lights on — my car is dead," I told him sheepishly.

"Ooo!" I heard him suck in a breath between his teeth. "I can't come, I have a client, uh – hold that thought. I'll call you or text you right back. It'll be okay."

I jumped and yelped, a glass bottle shattering at my feet. Lucas, leaning out the passenger side of his best friend's car as they zoomed by, shouted, "I'm going to make you suck my dick, you murdering whore!" The boys laughed and peeled out and I pressed a hand to my chest, waiting for my heart to calm down.

There were several heartbeats of silence on the other end of the line and Nox asked calmly, "Maren, who was that?"

"No one," I said. "It was nothing."

"Right, I'm going to go and call in a favor, you get in your car and lock your doors. I'll call you right back."

"Okay."

"And Maren?"

"Yes?"

"We'll talk about why you just lied to me a little while later, alright?"

I shut my car door and locked it. "Yes, alright," I said quietly, guiltily.

"Be right back," he promised and ended the call. I watched the minutes tick by, all three of them, and my phone lit up with Nox calling again. I answered immediately.

"Hello?"

"My brother is leaving the garage now, he'll be there in a few to give you a jump. Okay?"

"Okay, thank you. I'm so sorry for being an inconvenience, Nox –"

"Hey, no, none of that, baby. Okay? Everything is going to be fine, it's what I signed up for, remember?"

"Okay," I murmured.

"I've got to go, I'll see you tonight."

"Right, um, I'm supposed to have a talk with Sage, maybe tonight isn't the best. As it is, I need to call him."

"We'll talk about it when I get off work."

"Okay."

"Hi Jennifer, I'll be right with you, two seconds I promise," I heard him say, his voice a little distant as he pulled the phone away from his mouth.

"I'll talk to you later, you'd better go," I said before he could say anything.

"Later, I promise."

He ended the call and I huddled in my dad's old car, one of the many things I inherited, and tried to keep warm. It was the reason I'd stepped out. It was cold outside, but the sun was shining and when I stood in it, it was at least marginally warmer. I waited for Rush to get here and when I heard the rumble of a motorcycle, I looked up.

He pulled up next to my car, but it wasn't Rush on the bike. I got out and Archer pulled the thick scarf off from around his face and the sunglasses off from over his eyes. He took the time to take off his helmet, eyeing me suspiciously.

"I forgot to turn off my headlights this morning," I said sheepishly. "I was running late."

"Should have left earlier," Archer grunted, swinging a leg over his bike and standing. He went to the back of his bike and one of the saddle-bags, unbuckling it.

"It was my brother, he missed the bus and was dragging his feet," I explained.

"Should have got 'im by the ear, showed him who's boss."

"Um, I'd rather he not be put into foster care," I said laughing uncomfortably.

Archer grunted. "I can agree with you there. Pop the hood for me, Jailbait."

I blushed at the awful nickname and did as he asked. He pulled a jumper box out of his saddlebag and went to the front of my car, lifting the hood and hooking it to my battery with the giant clips.

"Turn it over," he ordered and I did, the car was sluggish but kicked over.

I got out, "Thank you so –"

"Maren, are you alright?" I turned to Mr. Hunter, our school's vice principal making his way toward me.

"She's fine," Archer declared, dropping the hood with a clang. He picked up the jumper box and put the clips back into their housing.

"If it's all the same, I would like to hear as much from my student."

"I'm fine, Mr. Hunter. Archer is a friend," I said.

"How do you know each other exactly?"

"She doesn't know me, she knows my little brother."

"Ah," Mr. Hunter looked relieved, and I let him assume, which clearly, he did, that Archer's little brother was my age. I felt myself blushing hotly, but I could probably get away with him assuming it was just the cold.

"Thank you for coming on such short notice," I told Archer and he gave a sharp nod.

"No problem, I'd do anything for my brothers, but you know that already, I'm guessing."

"I do," I said and smiled.

"How long is it to your place?" Archer asked, Mr. Hunter standing by and watching the exchange. Archer put the jumper box back into his saddlebag and closed it up, buckling it tight.

"About five minutes or so."

"Ideally you should drive it for thirty to make sure the battery is fully charged." He straightened and pulled on his wallet chain, bringing the rectangle of battered leather out of his back pocket. He opened up his wallet and pulled out a twenty. "Take the kid to his favorite fast food place for dinner tonight; that ought to do it."

"Oh, that's too much, I can't—"

"Don't worry about it," he said, folding my fingers around the crumpled bill. "My wife would have my balls if I let your car die on you again and I'll wring the twenty outta Nox."

"Then I will be sure to pay him back," I said laughing softly.

"Do whatever you're gonna do, just make sure that thing runs for a good half hour before you shut it off for me."

"I'll do that."

I took the money and he got back on his bike. "Satisfied I'm not a chimo now?" he asked my vice principal.

Mr. Hunter frowned, and Archer laughed. "See you around, Jailbait."

I colored at the nickname and nodded faintly. "See you later," I said, and he pulled up the scarf around his face and rode off. Mr. Hunter rounded on me, concern written all over his face.

"Maren, that was a Sacred Heart," he said and I nodded.

"I know what you're going to say," I started, but he cut me off, saying it already.

"Do you know what kind of a reputation they have around here?" he asked.

I shook my head. "No, and I don't care to hear it. They've always been nice to me. I met one of them the day my dad died and the next thing I knew, they were at my house the day before Christmas Eve with toys and gifts, and money to make sure my brother and I had a good holiday and then some. They're good people."

"Maren, I don't think you understand—" I raised my hand to stop him.

"Mr. Hunter, I can appreciate that you're looking out for me, but they've only shown themselves to be good people to me. Abraham Lincoln once said, 'character is like a tree and reputation its shadow. While the shadow is what we think of it; the tree is the real thing.' I called one of them because I didn't have anyone else to call when my car just died. He was here in less than five minutes. Don't let the shadow of their rough appearance fool you. I'm glad I didn't. I don't know where Sage and I would be without them."

Mr. Hunter sighed and ran a hand through his light thinning hair, searching my face with his blue eyes so full of concern. Finally, he nodded. "There you go, the student teaching the master… again, might I add."

"Not the first time, eh?" I asked smiling.

"Not by far, Ms. Tracy. You should get home to your brother."

"I really should. Thanks, Mr. Hunter, for looking out for me."

"Of course."

I did what Archer told me. I picked up Sage, running into the house just long enough to call him down from his ivory tower so we could go get tacos from his favorite fast food Mexican place.

"Seriously?" he asked and I nodded. He came down without a complaint and got into his coat, and then the car.

We drove in silence for a minute, Sage staring out the window and finally he said, "Sorry I was mean this morning."

Surprised I said, "It's okay."

"I thought you were going to forget."

"Forget about what?" I asked and he looked at me.

"Taco Tuesday."

I blinked, *was it Tuesday?* I smiled and said, "How the heck did you think I would forget about Taco Tuesday? I know I'm busy, and the holidays were crazy, and that they aren't homemade, but I figured you'd forgive me for the fast food version."

Sage nodded. "I really don't want to take the bus anymore."

"Listen, about that; I will try to take you to school every morning, but you're going to have to take the bus home on the nights I have work. Okay?"

Sage nodded after a time and said, "Deal."

"And Sage?" I said after some more silence.

"Yeah?"

"If I forget things, like Taco Tuesday, all you gotta do is say something. This whole being an adult thing has a lot to it. I can't always remember everything. Some stuff gets lost in the shuffle."

"Okay," he said with a nod and it looked like he was about to cry.

"I love you," I said, and Sage went back to staring out the window.

"I love you, too."

Meanwhile, inside my head, I thanked my dad, Nox, and Archer for the confluence of events that led to saving Taco Tuesday for my brother. That led to having this small heart-to-heart and a truce or two declared on some things. I mean what was it, if not some divine intervention? How weird, right?

13

N^{ox…}

"What can you tell me?" I asked when I picked up the phone.
Archer never was one for formalities and always appreciated the short
version. He didn't like long stories, and so I tried to keep everything
simple. It was just how we were. So, my picking up the phone and
asking straight out what I wanted to know wasn't exactly frowned
upon or considered rude. It just was what it was.

"There was glass. Looked like a bottle of some kind, whatever that shit
kids like to drink with the fuckin' lizards on the label. Anyway, she
was safe, in her car. Hooked up the jump starter and she fired right up.
You owe me twenty bucks by the way."

"What the fuck for?"

"She needed to drive the thing for a half hour or so to make sure the
battery was charged. I gave her a twenty and told her to take her kid
brother out for some fast food for a change."

"Oh, good call. I'll get you back next time I see you."

"Fuckin' yeah, you will."

"Cheap bastard," I accused.

"Dumb cunt. Anyway, her principal or some shit came out to make sure I wasn't some kind of pedo. I think he was keepin' an eye on her from inside. He didn't look any kind of thrilled about one of us showing up for the save. Better watch your ass. Maren may be a good kid, but she ain't what you gotta worry about. One of these well-meaning bastard's will be the ones to have you up on charges and Arizona was downright liberal compared to these bible thumping assholes out here."

I rolled my eyes, "I get you, Bro. Later."

"Bye."

I hung up with Arch and sighed. My hands ached some, and I still had some clean up to do. I'd do it, and then I'd call Maren, see what I could get out of her. I'd heard that little cock-weasel on the line clear as day, threatening my girl. Something wasn't right. That wasn't nobody and it sure as hell wasn't nothing.

I stripped down my table and threw the sheets in the in-house washer, tossing in a couple pillow packs of soap. I'd turn it on first thing in the morning. Then, between massages, I'd throw the shit from the washer into the dryer. By the time my second massage of the day was up, they'd be dry and ready to use.

I made up the table tonight, that way it was one less thing I had to do come first thing in the morning. I drank down a bottle of water from the mini-fridge, crushed down the bottle, capped it, and tossed its little carcass into the recycling underneath one of my cabinets where I kept it alongside a gallon jug of massage oil. I washed my hands at the sink in my area and dried them off before picking up my phone to call my girl.

She picked up on the fourth ring. "Hello?"

"Hey, Angel. Heard your car started right up."

She blew out an explosive breath and said, "Yes, thank you. I'm sorry I had to call you. I promise to pay better attention to what I'm doing in the future."

"It's no problem. Archer treat you okay?"

"He's... intense," she said, and I laughed.

"Yeah, yeah he is. Always been that way, too. So what are you doing?"

"Um, took Sage out for Taco Tuesday and now we're at the table doing our homework."

"Aw, shit! I missed Taco Tuesday?"

She laughed. "Yeah, yeah you did."

"How's homework going? Almost done?

"Yeah, it's almost bedtime for us. What about you? Late night at the office?"

"Yeah, Tuesday nights aren't usually, but I've been trying to fit one or two extra massages in to clear up the gift certificates from over the holidays. Been putting in some tens rather than my usual eights."

"Going home to get some sleep yourself then?"

"After we talk about what I heard earlier, yeah. Can I come by?"

Silence on the other end of the line, and finally she murmured, "Tonight isn't the best night."

"Okay," I said slowly, disappointed, and sure, now more than ever, that something wasn't right. "You guys got much longer on your homework?"

"Not too much longer. Like I said, we both need to get to bed soon."

"Tell you what, I'm gonna head back to my place, fix some dinner and by the time I do that, and grab a shower, you should be in bed. Call me or text me when you are and we'll finish this conversation that way... and Maren?"

"Yeah?"

"You're not in trouble, Angel. I just really didn't like what I heard, and I need to know what's up. I can't fix it if I don't know what's wrong."

"Nox, it's okay, really... there's nothing for you to fix."

"If it makes you sad, it needs to be fixed." She sighed heavily, and it was a frustrated sound. I said, "Call me or text me when you go to bed."

"I will," she promised, and I nodded before I realized she couldn't see it.

"Talk to you then."

We hung up, and I pulled on my riding gear over my scrubs, glad for the ride home, despite how fucking cold it was going to be. When I got to it, I skipped pulling up out front and rode around back, heeling down the kickstand in front of the outbuilding that housed my room. I went in and took a hot shower, pulling on some comfortable sweats. I skipped food, I just wasn't hungry or feeling it right then.

Instead, I flopped down on my bed and waited for my phone to ring or chime. It finally did around nine-thirty. It was a text, not a call.

Maren: He's my ex-boyfriend, Lucas. When my dad started getting sick to the point I needed to take care of him more, I broke it off with Luke. He didn't take it well. Started some rumors about me; that I gave him the clap – which I never did. I will even go to the doctor and prove it if you need me to. Anyway, things have gotten progressively worse, the more that time goes on. There's nothing the faculty can or will do about it except to tell me to ignore it, so I do my best. Today was a tough day. The newest rumor is that I murdered my dad, sped things along for him so I could inherit everything and that getting rid of Sage is next on my

list of priorities. I'm doing everything I can to protect my brother and keep him with me and everyone is saying I'd do anything to get rid of him. That I killed my dad. As if that wasn't bad enough, I don't know, I guess it's just exhausting listening to their shit. Just when I thought that they couldn't get more evil... there you go.

I squeezed my eyes shut and opened them a few times as I worked my way through the wall of text on my phone, my blood growing hotter by the second until it very nearly boiled.

Me: He ever hurt u with more than just words?

Those three bouncing dots sure took their sweet fucking time as I waited for her to respond. *Shit, hasn't this girl been through enough?* I wondered. I mean fuck, how low can you go? Treating a girl who was losing her dad like shit because you got temporarily shut down? Fuck, as far as reasons for a break up go, that is a pretty fucking understandable one.

Maren: He was the boy I lost my virginity to before I found out he was such a selfish ass. He's 'accidentally' bumped into me in the halls, knocking me off balance into lockers and things, but other than that... no. He hasn't put his hands on me. As for the hurt me with more than just words? He's the boy I lost my virginity to. My first love and all of that. So I guess, yeah. Who am I kidding? It all hurts. It all hurts a lot. I hate going to school, which sucks because I love learning. I lost the one place that made things bearable before my dad died, then I lost my dad and it's everything I have left in me to hold onto what I have left that's dear. My brother, my home... I thought that was going to be it for me, you know? And then you showed up, and I'm scared if you knew just how monumentally screwed up things are in my world that you'll leave. Too much drama, you know?

I sighed sharply. "Fuck!" I uttered out loud and decided I needed to get one thing straight with her, right this minute.

Me: Here's the deal, Maren. I'm sure that u noticed but I'm a grown ass, fuckin man. U got more shit going on than most grown fuckin women twice ur age. That being said, I ain't going nowhere – because I'm a *grown ass fucking man* and grown men handle their shit, and when they find a woman of quality? They don't make shit worse for her – they make it better which is just what I'm gonna do. Am I crystal fuckin' clear?

Those dots remained maddeningly absent for a really long time. I watched the little message below what I just sent read 'read' for a long time and I pictured her, laying in her bed, that dark hair of hers splashed across the pillow, her smooth skin lit with the blue glow of her screen as she read and reread the message I just sent and I couldn't help it. I popped a serious fucking boner at the thought. Finally, those damn dots started their shimmy and their shake across the bottom corner of my screen, but only after I'd had to wake up my phone twice.

Maren: I don't know what to say except I think I love you for so many things right now. For listening to me. For coming to the rescue as much as you have and even for things that I didn't even think I needed rescuing from until you were there to do it. Lucas is an ass. He's a little boy and annoying, but I can handle it. It's only for a few more months until I graduate, anyway. It will be okay.

I let out a breath I hadn't realized I was holding.

Me: Maren, Angel, u just don't get how this works, baby. I'm here to take care of u, and part of that means I'm here to protect u from asshats like this.

Maren: That's sweet, Nox. Really, but there isn't anything anyone can do. There just isn't.

I smiled, and I knew it wasn't one hundred percent nice. I sat up and typed back quickly, thumbs flying across the screen.

Me: U forget something, Angel. There isn't anything anyone can

do that follows citizen rules. I'm not your average citizen. Just give me the kid's name and I'll handle it.

Maren: You won't hurt him, will you?

Me: Club's rule is 'no women, no children' he's a minor, so no – I won't hurt him.

Maren: Then how would you get him to stop?

Me: U leave that to me.

I waited for a long time and finally grew a little impatient.

Me: U want it to stop, don't u?

Maren: Lucas Triggs

Me: Thank you.

Maren: Be careful, his dad is a piece of work. When I dated Lucas, I kind of wondered how he could be so sweet when his dad, well, wasn't. Now I know better.

Me: Don't u worry about me, Angel. I'll try and get things taken care of by the end of next week.

Maren: You're too good to me. You know that?

Me: I ain't even got started yet.

～

I ASKED Maren how her day was and practically grilled her on asshat's behavior every day for the rest of the week. Between my work schedule and her work schedule, I wouldn't be seeing her until Sunday night, which was a major bummer. With Sage's best friend's mom being the twat of the century, Maren was worried about what she'd do with Sage on Sunday during the day when she put in another ten-hour shift, so I volunteered to spend some time with him.

I went over and made it about an hour after she'd left for the Douglas Street Wally World. Sage opened up the door and glared at me.

"She's lying to you," he said by way of greeting and I felt myself scowl.

"Spill," I told him, and he sighed, stepping aside to let me into the house for our great superhero movie spree.

"I hear her talk to you, she says it's not bad, and that everything is fine, but I hear her cry herself to sleep at night. I don't care if you hurt him. I want you to hurt him, or at least scare the piss out of him."

"Now, Sage," I said, dropping a hand on the kid's shoulder, "you know that violence doesn't always solve problems, right? That Maren has it right, just because he's mean to her, doesn't necessarily mean that he needs to be hurt for it."

Sage jerked his shoulder out from under my hand and sighed, he went over to the couch and flopped down on it dramatically.

"Yeah, I get that, but it's not just him being mean to her, he's got all of them doing it. I'm tired of her crying all the time and being all stressed out. It's bullshit."

"Language," I said sternly, and he arched an eyebrow at me and it was so like his sister I had a real tough time not laughing.

"You swear all the time."

"I'm over the age of eighteen."

"Yeah, *way over,*" he said rolling his eyes.

I couldn't help it. I did laugh at that. I went around and dropped onto the other end of the couch and faced Maren's kid brother. He was a skinny kid, lanky; a real beanpole. He was going to be tall, and probably a basketball player if he had any interest in the sport, which judging by the fact he'd asked if we could put the hoop up in front of the garage? I was betting there was at least something there. He had dark hair, just like his sister, and chocolate brown eyes. He was just about old enough to start hitting the weights and I thought about that for a minute. He'd be an unlikely workout partner, but it might keep him out of trouble.

"What do you mean when you say he's got all of 'em doing it?" I asked.

Sage rolled his eyes. "He's like the star quarterback or something. Mr. Popular all the way, he's got like the entire school making fun of her and doing things to her. It's stupid."

I considered him, trying to judge if he was being melodramatic or what, but after searching his oh-so-serious face, I decided even if he was exaggerating it wasn't by much.

"Why you narcing on your sister?" I asked him finally, and he jerked his head back.

"I'm not. I thought you wanted to know what was up, so you could do something about it."

I shook my head. "I'm gonna do something about it regardless, but don't you think if she'd wanted me to know what's up, she would have told me?"

Sage huffed out a really big sigh. "My sister thinks she's gotta do all of everything all of the time. She's turned into a real control freak. She can't though, can she?"

"Can't what?"

"Do all of the things all of the time, I mean, no one can do it all alone, can they?"

I shook my head. "I used to think that, but then I met your sister. She does a pretty good job of it, don't you think?"

"If she does such a good job of it why's she crying all the time?" he asked.

I shrugged, he had me there, of course, there was also… "Girls are like that," I said wisely. "They get overwhelmed and sh-stuff, and they melt down and cry it out and before you know it they're back at it again, stronger and harder than before. Girls are kind of amazing that way. Dudes give up, girls just have a cry and go at whatever's in front of them again and again and again until they beat it. I ain't seen nothing like it anywhere else."

Sage gave me a look like he wasn't impressed. "Are you saying girls are better than boys?" he asked.

"No, I'm saying girls are different from boys on how they handle things, but the way your sister deals with shi-stuff, yeah, I think she's better than most guys I know at handling things."

"Yeah, she kind of is," Sage agreed. "I'll totally deny it if you tell her I told you so, though."

"My lips are sealed, man."

"You know, you're not so bad," he said, and I laughed.

"You're not so bad yourself, you just got a lot going on like your sister."

"Not as much. I'm more of a pain in her," I gave him a look and he gave me one right back, "ass than I should be."

"You got an outlaw's spirit, kid. I can respect that."

He frowned. "Thanks, I think."

"You're welcome," I said to assure him I'd meant it as a compliment.

"What are we watching first?" he asked.

"Your choice."

"Batman."

"Ahh, a DC kind of kid?"

"Not really, Batman is really the only one worth anything out of all of them. Marvel just does comics better."

"Finally, some common ground," I muttered and pulled the CD holder out of my coat sleeve. I had it loaded with dvds and Blu-rays of every superhero movie I could scrounge when this thing had been set up. I'd borrowed heavily out of the club's library and left post-it notes in every one of the cases on the shelves stating who had the disc if anyone came looking for it.

"We going early '90s Batman movies first or getting right to the good stuff and the Christopher Nolan directed stuff?"

"*Dark Knight* all the way," Sage said.

"My man!"

We were almost all the way through the third film when Maren came in the front door. Sage and I were chillin' on the couch in the midst of the wreckage of our popcorn fight and when Maren saw it, she wilted a little more around the edges which looked frayed as it was. I pushed myself to my feet and pulled her over murmuring, "Don't worry about the mess, I'll clean it up."

I pulled her down onto the center cushion and against me, and before five minutes had elapsed on screen, she was breathing deeply and evenly against me; fast asleep.

"Told you," Sage said simply, and I nodded. I think it was a mark of how worried he was about his sister that he was behaving so well for her lately. I was pretty sure, that when Maren was feeling stronger and the outside threat was neutralized, he'd go back to being one serious pain in the ass, but I think the state she was in scared him. He wasn't entirely alone in that regard. I made it a point, right then and there, to take care of this little problem before she had to go back to school tomorrow.

We went through the last of *The Dark Knight* trilogy and were into the second *Iron Man* movie when Maren finally stirred. She pushed off of me and swept some of the loose tendrils of hair off her face, scrubbing it with her hands and pressing her fingertips into her eyes.

"What time is it?" she asked, and Sage answered her.

"Almost time to go to bed."

"Oh, jeez, I'm so sorry, Nox!" She bit her bottom lip and it was everything not to say fuck it and pull her mouth against mine, so I could suck on it for her.

"It's not a problem. If you're tired, you're tired," I told her with a shrug. I wished I could tell her how good it'd felt to just hold her, warm and close against me, but Sage was here, and we were all in this holding pattern of truce that I didn't exactly want to ruin.

"Why don't you guys go on and get ready for bed, while I clean up our mess down here," I suggested. Maren nodded tiredly, and Sage looked over to his sister. I could tell he wanted to protest, but instead, he impressed me with a compromise.

"If you promise to come back some night this week and watch *The Avengers* with me, I won't argue right now."

Maren stilled and looked at her brother like it was an invasion of the body snatchers or some shit. "I'll totally do it if only to spare your sister some grief," I said. Sage held out his fist and I bumped it with my own.

"Thanks, guys. Although, why do I feel like this is some axis of evil coming together and that later I'm going to regret not being more suspicious?"

Sage pushed to his feet and stretched. "Bro code prevents us from speaking on it, right Nox?"

"Absolutely," I said solemnly.

"Later," Sage called over his shoulder and went for the stairs.

"Later, little man."

"I'm not little!" he called down and Maren sagged with relief.

"There he is," she said quietly, and I chuckled.

"He's worried about you," I said and she looked up at me from beneath her long, dark, lashes. Fuck that was hot.

"Oh yeah?"

"Narced you out cold, the second he opened the door." I rolled my lips together and eyed her carefully. She suddenly looked nervous and I sighed.

"Maren, this douche is the ringleader of a bunch of kids who are hurting you. That's not cool and I'm going to deal with it. Now, what is going on?"

She hung her head and put a stray lock of hair behind her ear and the movement was both alluring and fucking heartbreaking with the expression she had on her face. She licked her lips and shifted in her seat and sighed heavily.

"Mostly, it's just things like what you heard on the phone," she murmured. "A loud, sudden noise followed by a threat, usually of some form of rape. It's disturbing and disconcerting, and I've tried to talk to the faculty about it, but they say they can't do anything unless they see the behavior first hand, which, of course, he doesn't do it in front of them."

"You're afraid," I said and there wasn't any question about it.

"Yes," she said, unequivocally. "I'm afraid that he'll show up here, or that he will catch me alone somewhere at school and make good on his threats."

"Nope, not going to happen," I said, and pulled her tight against my chest. I tucked her head beneath my chin and wound my fingers in her silky hair, placing my lips on the top of her head. She melted into the embrace willingly and it wasn't but a second or two later she was crying softly into my fuckin' Henley.

Oh, I was *so* talking to Duracell when I got back to the club; maybe even Reaver. Minor or not, I think it was time for this kid to get a lesson or two in fear, so he knew what it was like.

"I've got you, Angel. Nothin's gonna happen to you, baby." I made soothing noises and held Maren close and thought just about what I was gonna do, because — Fuck. This. Shit.

14

M aren...

"Did you brush your teeth?" I asked my brother and he rolled his eyes at me.

"Did *you?*" he demanded, and I huffed a small laugh.

"On my way, now. You didn't answer my question, though."

"I'm not five and you're not Dad. What, do you want me to come breathe on you?"

"No, just say 'yes', and I'm sorry for treating you like you're five." I put my hands on my chest, a most sincere gesture. "You're right, you're eleven and old enough that if you want to skip brushing your teeth and have your teeth rot out of your head? Well, that's one decision you're now forever allowed to make on your own."

Sage made a grossed-out face. "Well when you put it *that way*," he said.

"Well, it's true, just trying to keep you out of the dentist's chair because we all know how much you *love* that."

"Which is why I brushed my teeth already! God, Maren." He got up and came to his door. "Good night!" he cried and slammed it in my face.

"God grant me the patience…" I muttered and sighed.

I turned around and went into the bathroom to brush my teeth and put my hair into a braid over my shoulder, listening to the vacuum run downstairs as Nox cleaned up his and my brother's disaster area. Truthfully, I didn't mind the mess. Especially when Sage seemed almost happy when I'd come home. Honestly, I was grateful that Nox was cleaning it up. I just didn't have the energy; I was so deeply mentally, and emotionally exhausted.

I shut off the tap after spitting a final time and rinsed my brush to total silence in the house. When I stood up, I jumped and clapped my hands over my mouth to keep from screaming. Nox frowned at me from over my shoulder in the bathroom mirror.

"Jesus, Angel," he whispered. "He's got you jumping at everything."

"I'm sorry," I muttered quietly, lowering my hands from my mouth and smoothing over my nightgown. Nox raised an eyebrow, noticing it for the first time. It was black satin and ankle length, clinging to what curves I had, with lace panels just beneath my breasts, along the ribs. Not exactly something I advertise, but I liked to wear nice things to bed. I just usually had a robe on over them. My scruffy, fluffy bathrobe hung on the back of the door, just inside my reach. I tended to have water drip down my arm when I brushed and when it caught the edge of my sleeve, I *hated* that. It was like tiny wet kisses against my wrist from Satan with how much I detested it.

"I like this," Nox said softly, and his eyes, for as pale as they were, went dark with a hunger that had nothing to do with food.

I swallowed hard and whispered, "Pumpkins, remember?"

"I do," he murmured back, but that didn't stop him from capturing my hand with his and drawing me closer. He lifted my hand to his mouth and turned it, placing his lips softly to the inside of my wrist.

"Everything is cleaned up, downstairs."

"Thank you," I murmured, throat tight with the urge I had to just pull myself the rest of the way into his arms and put my lips up against his. The struggle was absolutely real, and I could tell it was for both of us. What I couldn't tell was if that made things easier or if that made things just that much harder.

"Come on, let an old man tuck you in," he said, teasing.

"You're not old," I murmured and took the last step into his personal space. His hands smoothed over the satin over my hips and he closed his eyes as if committing the feel of me beneath it to memory.

"This isn't easy," he said.

"No, it's not," I agreed, my voice strained, and his mouth was on mine. We kissed, and the fact that it was a mutually stolen one, despite our pact to remain chaste until my eighteenth birthday, made it both sweet and forbidden. My heart picked up its pace until it felt as though I'd been running, even though I stood perfectly still.

Nox pulled back first, though it was reluctantly, and stared into my eyes from inches away. I closed mine, unprepared for the sheer magnitude and intensity of that look, and he backed off a step. The air suddenly seemed breathable again, the sexual tension backing off, alleviating suddenly with the empty space between us.

"I'm sorry," I uttered and slipped past him into the hall.

"I'm not," he whispered. "Still have to watch myself, though."

"You aren't the only one."

He slipped into my bedroom before me and pulled back the blankets on my bed for me. I went to the jewelry box that'd been gifted to me for

Christmas and opened it. I bit my lip gently and pulled out the spare house keys. I turned to Nox and held it out to him.

"What's this?" he asked.

"Someone should have them, in case something happens... You're the only one I trust enough to give one to. Plus, if you're up here with me, and plan on tucking me in, you need to have the ability to lock up. Right?"

He laughed softly and plucked the keys from my fingers. I sat on the edge of the bed and he bent, lifting my feet onto it the rest of the way as if it were a long-practiced motion, and perhaps it was. He pulled the blankets to my chin and kissed my forehead before going and turning out the light. I felt cherished; warm and safe for the first time all week. It surprised me when he came back over, rounding the bed and sitting on top of the covers. He laid down behind me and pulled me back against him, the thick comforter and blankets separating us.

"What are you doing?"

"Holding you until you fall asleep."

"Oh..."

"Would you rather I not?" he asked softly, a hint of amusement in his voice.

"No... I mean yes! It's nice, keep doing it please."

He chuckled softly and laid a kiss behind my ear. "Sleep, Angel. There's no bad here. Not while I'm on watch."

I closed my eyes and it was true, there was nothing that could hurt me when Nox was around. I believed wholeheartedly that he would do anything to protect me. Both me and Sage. I melted back into his warmth and embrace, and I slept; sad, that once again, he would be gone when I woke. I liked this, probably way more than I should. I mean if anyone found out, there would be no way they would believe that nothing had ever happened sexually between us. I didn't want him to get into trouble. I didn't want them to take my brother for poor judgment on my part, but I was simply too tired to resist the siren's call of the safety of Nox's arms.

15

N^{ox...}
Maren's alarm went off, waking us both.

Shit!

Maren's alarm went off, waking us both!

I was still on top of the covers, Maren snug beneath them and still snug in the cradle of my body, her phone screeching that it was time to wake up. She reached a hand out from beneath the quilt on her bed and pulled it off the nightstand, silencing it.

"Morning, Angel," I murmured, and she froze.

"Holy shit, you're still here!" she whispered harshly.

"I think I fell asleep," I muttered.

"This is not good! What about Sage?"

"Shit, uh, he up yet?" The toilet flushing across the hall said that yep, the kid was up.

I rolled off the bed, and onto the floor and stayed there, frozen to the hardwood and area rug beneath Maren's bed.

"Morning, Sage!" she called out.

"Whatever," was his grumpy sleepy reply. His door shut, and I sat up, pushing quietly to my feet. I brushed my lips against Maren's who was trying like hell not to laugh, and I slipped downstairs grabbing my jacket and cut off the hook by the front door and slipped outside. I pushed my bike down the frozen pavement for like half a block before getting on it.

My phone buzzed in my pocket and I pulled it out to look.

Maren: OMG that was close!

Me: Sorry, Angel. Didn't mean to fall asleep. Try 2 have a good day at school. U work tonight?

Maren: Yes, I do.

Me: Ok, B careful.

Maren: You too. Call me later?

Me: U know it.

Maren: XOXO

Me: ☺

I fired up the bike which was cranky about the cold; the brisk as fuck ride better than any cup of coffee at waking my ass up. It being Monday, I had the day off. It was my Sunday, and I had some shit to do. I felt guilty as fuck that Maren was going to have to go through the wringer at least one more time, but I really needed to talk to Cell and Reaver. They were the best men for the job when it came to putting the fear of God, the Devil, and anything and everything in between, into a man.

As luck would have it, Cell and Blue were throwing their shit into the back of their pickup when I pulled up into the club's lot. I pulled up right behind their massive cage and pulled the bandana off my face, calling out, "Hey Cell! You got some time for me later tonight, brother?"

Cell raised one of his ginger eyebrows at me and said, "Yeah, man. Be back around seven, that cool?"

"Yeah, gonna try and get Reave's help with it, too."

"Now I really wanna know what's up," he said and Blue nodded deftly from across the bed of the truck, curiosity written all over his expressive face.

"See you at seven," I said and got out of their way. I needed to get into a hot shower and phone up Reave.

"Okay, where's the fuckin' fire at?" Reaver asked dropping into a seat at my table out in the barroom. Duracell dropped into the one across from Reaver's and I leaned forward.

"Maren's got a bullying problem that's way out of pocket, some ex-boything of hers is fuckin' terrorizing her on top of all the other shit she's going through. Threatening her with all kinds of rape. I heard it myself when her car died last week."

Cell and Reaver exchanged a look. "Kid's a minor, what do you want us to do about it?" Reaver asked, but I could tell his interest was piqued.

"Who fucking cares, the kid wants to act all big and tough? Let's show him what it's like to roll with the big dogs," Cell said coolly, leaning way back in his seat, tipping the front legs off the floor.

Reaver shook his head. "Club doctrine, man. No women, no children."

"I thought about that," I said. "I figured I'd go over there and have a talk with the kid's dad. I mean, he's gotta learn it from somewhere, am I right?"

"So, what do you want us there for?" Cell asked confused.

"According to Maren, Daddy's a piece of work and is where his bouncing baby boy gets it from," I said.

"Uh huh, well, sounds like a date to me. It's been a little tame around here lately," Reaver said with a gusty sigh.

"You got this kid's address?" Cell asked. I pulled a piece of paper out of the inside pocket of my cut.

"Courtesy of Data. That dude really can find anything."

"Cool, then let's roll." Cell stood up and I stood with him and Reaver.

"Good deal, thanks for the help," I said.

I should have known better than to call in the fucking big guns right off the bat. I really should have. We rode out to the address on the slip of paper and it was a fairly nice house. I went to the door, Reave and Cell both flanking me to either side and standing just a little behind me. We had our glasses on, to cut the wind, and still had our scarfs and bandanas covering our faces for warmth as we stood bouncing on the stone front stoop of the house waiting for someone to come and answer the bell. It was fucking cold out here.

The door opened to the kid standing there, a burly guy, probably the star fucking football player. Shit. If he put hands on Maren, she wouldn't have a chance. The words were out of my mouth before I could even ask for the kid's dad.

"You Lucas?"

"Yeah, who wants to know?" he demanded.

"Your daddy home?" Reaver asked from behind me.

"Who the fuck wants to know?" the kid demanded, and I exchanged a look with my brothers.

"Friends of Maren Tracy," I said.

"Luke, who is it?"

"Some assholes, say they're friends with that bitch Maren," Luke called back.

"Oh, hell no, you did not just say that," Cell uttered.

The father appeared in the doorway. "What do you want?" he demanded sternly.

"We want your son to stop bullying Maren," I said.

"I've heard all the bitching and complaints I'm gonna over that stupid girl. She's over sensitive and can't take a joke. You ask me, she's just jealous Luke doesn't want her back. She never had it so good." I blinked and exchanged looks with my brothers.

"Excuse me?" I said, not believing I just heard this asshole right.

"You heard me."

"Sir," I said, the honorific leaving an oily taste in my mouth, "were you aware your son's been threatening that girl with rape?" I demanded.

"So?" the father demanded.

"Fuck this shit," Duracell uttered and reached past me, dragging the man out of his entry way by the front of his shirt.

"Dad!" the kid cried and darted out right behind him. I stepped aside, and the dude wasn't so fucking tough now that Duracell had a gun jammed against the guy's forehead and was pushing him down to his knees.

"Nope! C'mere. You're going to get a harsh life lesson on why it doesn't pay to be a dick to people," I heard Reaver say and he had a knife to the boy's throat and was pushing him to his knees as well.

This was getting out of hand.

"Now just what the fuck have you been teaching your kid?" Duracell demanded.

"What every man should know. *How to be a man,*" the father said defiantly.

"And how's that?" I asked. "By telling women that he's going to make them suck his dick? Threatening to hold her down and face fuck her?" I was losing what little pity I had for this douche canoe, real fast.

"That little bitch has it coming! Breaking up with my boy, and for what?"

"Is he fucking serious?" Reaver asked.

"Nah, nah, nah, nah, nah!" Duracell crowed. "You know, God ruined a perfectly good asshole when he put teeth in your mouth." Cell pressed the barrel of his gun harder into the man's forehead to the point it made him rock back on his knees. I watched, mouth a little dry, but I had to trust that my club brother knew what he was doing. Duracell lifted his shoulders in a shrug and said, "Meh, I'm going to fuck it anyways," before he reached for his zipper to let it down. It was only then I realized that his cock, was indeed, straining at the denim of his jeans to get out.

What the fuck?

"Whoa, bro, what are you doing?" Reaver asked, taken just as far aback as I was. Duracell ignored Reaver's question and spoke to Lucas' daddy.

"Life lesson number one-thirteen," Duracell said. "If you're gonna threaten something, you need to know just what it is you're threatening to do. If you're gonna teach little Lucas here that it's okay to mouth-rape someone, I think you should know just how it feels." He cocked back the hammer of his gun and ordered sternly, "Open your mouth."

Fuck, he was serious. He was totally fucking serious.

"Man, I don't know about this…" I said and Cell gave a shrug.

"He's not a kid, that's the kid right there and a few more months he won't be a kid either. If not Maren, then who? Who you willin' to sentence to a life of consequences because this fuckwit taught his son that consent isn't required where a girl or woman is concerned? These boys need to fuckin' learn what they're advocating. I think it's the only clear-cut thing to do, don't you? Now open your mouth!"

The father glared up defiantly, and Cell let him have it, crashing the butt of his gun into the side of the dad's head. "Open your mouth, you son of a bitch or I'll blow a fucking hole in it and fuck that instead! You're so keen on your boy threatening this, like it's okay or some shit? Let him see what it's like first hand when someone he gives a fuck about is on the receiving end!"

Cell fucking did it, too. The son kneeled there crying and I just shut down all pity, thinking about Maren. Thinking about her exhaustion and her tears. Thinking about her jumping at every sound and shadow, about how this fool was making her life a million times worse during the absolute worse time of her life and how he was recruiting everyone else in the fuckin' school to do it too.

I watched Cell mouth rape this little cock weasel's daddy and I can't say I felt too much about it. I was more disturbed by my brother's intensity than I was about the fact that he'd just victimized a man on his own front steps in front of his seventeen-year-old son. I think the only thing saving our ass at this point was the fact that there were no visible security cameras, and the house was pretty fuckin' secluded, set a ways back from the road and on a big enough piece of property the neighbors weren't any kind of nearby.

God, we were all so fucked up in our own ways, I thought to myself and sighed inwardly. The fact I was more worried about our skins than what was fuckin' happening right in front of me was a testament to how jaded and warped my worldview was.

Cell zipped up and put his gun back in the waistband of his pants. Reaver's knife disappeared as if it'd never been and he shoved the kid at his dad who was throwing up in front of his garage. Both of them with tear-stained faces.

"Next time you look at a woman, son, it'd better be with some fuckin' respect," Duracell said. "Or I'ma come find you when you're eighteen and give you a taste. You hear?"

With those parting words, we took off, and I hoped to hell it'd taught these fucks a lesson and that Maren would be left alone. I wanted to see her, but I didn't. I wanted a shower, but there were some stains that wouldn't come off your soul no matter how much hot water you used. This was definitely one of those, but if it kept her safe, I'd do it all over again if need be.

16

M aren…
"What did you do?" I demanded when I opened the front
door. Nox blinked and stared down at me impassively.

"I didn't do anything, Angel."

"Don't lie to me, Nox! You did something, and by the looks of it, you
did something awful. Why, when I asked you not to?"

He sighed heavily and looked at me plaintively and said, "I protected
you, Maren. That's what a man does when someone fucks with his
woman. I protected you, and I did it the only way I knew how. Now
seriously, what brought this on?" he demanded. "That little cock bite
do something to you today?"

I opened the front door wider and stepped aside to let him into my
house. He came in and stopped, looking at me, expecting an answer
and I felt my shoulders drop.

"He just… *changed*, overnight. This morning, his girlfriend, Chelsea,
said something to me and he snapped at her. He looked *scared*, Nox,

like absolutely terrified, and he apologized to me immediately. I just knew that you'd done something."

"Did he tell you what?" he asked.

I shook my head. "He stays away from me now like I'm Satan or something. He just stares at me, subdued. It's really just… I don't know… *eerie*. It's sort of sad." I covered my face with my hands and scrubbed, so conflicted over it all. While on the one hand I was so *relieved* that he was just leaving me alone, the haunted, fearful, look in Lucas' eyes still found its way to the soft spot I had. Whatever had happened, I was certain I wouldn't wish on anyone. Not with the way Lucas looked at me now.

"Angel, he was hurting you. He was driving you crazy and was going to do some permanent damage to your psyche, and you feel bad for him?" Nox shook his head and sighed, gripping the back of his neck to ease the tension there.

That's when Sage chose to thunder down the stairs. "We watching a movie?" he asked excitedly.

"Not now, Sage. It's almost time for bed," I said and I just felt tired.

"Then why is he here?" Sage asked and Nox smiled at him.

"Sister and I are just clearing something up, buddy. We still on for Sunday?"

"Yeah," Sage said then looked at me. "You better not screw this up for us," he said. "I like him."

"Sage," Nox said sharply, "you need to start treating your sister with a little more respect, dude."

"Whatever," my brother muttered at his sullen pre-teen best, before he took the stairs two at a time to retreat to his bedroom. I fixed Nox with a silent stare. I really didn't know what to think, but the fear, the abject terror in Lucas' eyes had been very real when he'd said, '*You didn't have to send them.*' It'd been all he said on the matter but math had always been a fairly decent subject of mine and putting two and two together hadn't been difficult.

"Maren, they were hurting you. What would your dad have done?" Nox asked.

"My dad did do everything he could. He went to the principal, called the principal, all of that, even though he was so sick."

Nox sighed and reached up halfheartedly before dropping his hand back down. I was surprised to find how much I just ached for the proffered comforting touch and it broke off a piece of my heart that he thought I was so angry I wouldn't want him to touch me. I let my hand fall from the door knob and hugged myself. A sort of cold that had nothing to do with the frigid air swirling in from outside.

"And what did the principal do?" he asked evenly, taking a careful step inside over the threshold, swinging the door shut behind him. He eyed me carefully waiting for my answer.

I swallowed hard. "Nothing," I admitted, voice hollow. "Mr. Barber didn't do anything. He just told me that I needed to ignore it, get a thicker skin... that if I ignored it they'd eventually stop."

"And did they?" he asked gently.

"You know they didn't," I answered quietly, dejectedly.

Nox sighed before pulling me in against him, giving me the comfort I so desperately needed. He kissed the top of my head and said softly, "This is what the outlaw life is sometimes, Angel. I bet you and your dad did everything you could, at least by citizen's convention, but we ain't about that. We handle our own. We protect our own with a fierce devotion and loyalty. No one hurts our property and gets away with it, baby."

Outrageous!

I shoved off of him and put some space between us. "Is that what I am to you?" I demanded. "Property? Like a piece of cattle or something?

Or maybe it's more like a lost kitten." Anger bubbled up inside me and I could feel every throb of my heartbeat in my face which I knew was likely a garnet to match my Christmas gift.

"Okay, poor choice of words right off the bat, but do you think you can put it on ice long enough for an explanation or are you just going to blow a gasket right here right now?" he asked.

I paused and tried valiantly to shove my rage away long enough to hear him out and the only reason I managed to was because this felt like so many arguments or fights that had gone before. Ones that ended like me and Luke, with the forever kind of hurt and mad that neither party could come back from and that scared me. I didn't want that. I didn't want that at all. I was doing my very best at adulting and part of that was holding on to my emotions and *talking it out*, wasn't it?

Nox took my silence as the go-ahead to go on, saying, "You fit into my life so perfect it's easy to forget that you don't know all the jargon or lingo."

Like flipping a switch, my feminist outrage cooled to room temperature and I felt my shoulders drop. "Explain," I said curtly with none of the actual feeling that should have gone behind it.

"You want I should get back on the other side of the door so you can keep heating West County? Or you want I stay in here?" he asked with a devilish twinkle in his eye and he knew he'd already won me over. I wanted to make him go back outside just for yanking my chain but my electric bill was already disagreeing with its treatment. I stepped aside to let him further into the house.

"Sit," I ordered and his grin broadened.

"Anything you say, Angel."

He stepped lightly across my living room floor, his boot steps still sounding heavy against the hardwood. It was so quiet otherwise that I could hear the blood rushing in my ears as adrenaline and a little fear pushed it through my veins. Nox searched my face with those light-colored eyes of his and his face fell.

"Hey, are you okay?"

"Explain, please?" I said and latched the door behind me, turning the deadbolt until the lock gave a satisfying click.

"In a minute, first you need to tell me what's up."

"Nothing!" I lied and he frowned even harder.

"Okay," he said as if he didn't believe me, and the pulse-pounding well of emotion very nearly choked me.

He sat down in the chair by the fire and I moved to the couch, woodenly, mechanically, and sat down. Nox explained, "In the club life, there are sometimes no real words to express how we feel about something so in the early days, we adopted some mundane ones and sort of gave 'em new meaning. You get me?"

I think I nodded. "Property, let's start with that one."

Nox's eyes narrowed. "Angel, you having a panic attack or something?" he asked and I startled.

"I… I don't know what's wrong with me. Why are you asking me that?"

He got up and sat down next to me, the leather of his jacket and vest creaking, he left some space between us and I was surprised to find I was grateful for it.

"It's okay," he soothed. "Everything is okay."

"We'll see," I said. "Explain the alternate meaning of property, and we'll see."

He nodded and covered my hand with his. "In this life, there's property, like a cage, or a house, or a boat, right? Then there's *property*, like a man's bike or a man's woman but it's not like a house, okay? To us, a house burns down and fuck, that sucks, but whatever, you know? You just build or buy a new one. When it come to a man's *property* like his bike or his family, another man doesn't get to just fuck with that and walk away. That kind of property is something worth killing over. That kind of property, you, are worth dying for. Make sense?"

I stared at him, taken aback by his intensity, mouth slightly agape. He took one finger and tapped beneath my chin causing me to close my mouth, a sad, gentle smile playing on his lips that I suddenly wanted fiercely to kiss.

"Really?" I squeaked.

"Yeah, really," he laughed. "Now about this anxiety of yours, what's going on there?"

"I… I don't know," I stammered.

He gave me a patient look and said gently, "I told you mine, Angel. It's only fair you tell me yours."

I blushed crimson with embarrassment. It seemed like such a stupid thing to be afraid of now. Nox lightly brushed a thumb over the back of my hand, waiting me out patiently.

I swallowed hard to clear the lump in my throat before I could speak. "I thought this was going to be it."

"It?"

"Yeah, *it,* over, finished; the grand finale, last curtain, done like last night's dinner."

He laughed lightly at my litany and pulled me against him, tucking my head beneath his chin. "Angel, it's done only when you say it's done. You get me?"

"I feel so neurotic," I confessed, floundering and at a loss; hopelessness tugging at my edges, eroding my confidence like the sea to stones, the constant surge and retreat pulverizing them to sand.

"You have every right to be. No idea what happened to your mom, but your dad getting sick and dying? Leaving you all on your own with Sage? Pretty sure that's enough to give anybody some kind of abandonment issues, not to mention a little separation anxiety."

The lightbulb went off. He was right, first mom, then Luke — my first real relationship outside of the family. I mean, sure, I'd been the one to break up with him, but to have him turn on me like he did, and then to have my father die, I could see Nox's point. I let him hold me, the fire crackling in front of us and felt myself calm considerably.

"Need me to score you some weed for times like these?" he asked me suddenly. I startled.

"That bad?" I asked vaguely, lulled by the warmth and the steady beat of his heart beneath my ear.

"I don't like seeing you like this, all wound up, white as a sheet and looking like you're going to fly apart any second. You need to chill, Angel. You need to relax, sometimes. You can't do it all. I don't fuckin' care what everyone expects, it just ain't practical."

I closed my eyes and sighed. "Is that why you did whatever you did?"

"Yes." Unequivocal; a solid, one-word response.

I swallowed hard. "What did you do?"

Nox kissed the top of my head. "Two reasons why I'm not going to tell you that. One, it's club business and we don't share club business, not even with our girlfriends or ol' ladies. Two, it'd probably make you an accessory after the fact, and I'm not going to do that to you. That'd really be risking everything. There's this thing called plausible deniability and you have it. In fact, this little conversation right here didn't even happen. You get me?"

"Yes," I said dully.

"Ain't gotta like it, Angel, just have to do it; for your protection. Get me?"

I nodded and pulled from his embrace, even though I didn't want to.

"We okay?" he asked, carefully neutral.

"Yeah! I just need to check on Sage, make sure he's off his game and actually gone to bed."

"Okay."

"Be here when I come back down?"

"You want me to be?"

"Yes." From me, an unequivocal, one-word answer; full of all the certainty I could muster and put behind it.

"Okay, I'll be here," he said softly, and I knew that he would. It was nice to have someone solid, someone that I could depend on and believe in when he said something. Even if he could do frightening things.

"Hey, Maren," he called gently, as I was halfway up the stairs.

"Yes?"

It was as if he pulled the thoughts from my mind, saying, "I got no problem doing bad things for you, but never in a million years would I do bad things to you. You know that right?"

I smiled. "I do now."

Nox nodded. "Good."

I took a half step forward and paused. "Hey, Nox?"

"Yes?"

"What if I asked? Would you do bad things to me then?"

He laughed, and the mood lightened considerably. "I'd do anything for you, Angel."

"Good to know," I said and finished my temporary retreat up the stairs.

17

Nox...

I hadn't heard from Maren. It was odd, we texted and talked daily, sometimes sneaking texts between my clients and her classes, but today she'd been eerily silent. Only one or two word responses and not at all like herself. It bothered me, even though our heaviest talk to date, about the club, about the label of property, had been well over three weeks, maybe even a month ago now. Valentine's Day was coming up quick, then, after a couple more weeks, it would be her birthday. I couldn't wait for that day, let me tell you.

I'd been spending a lot of time with Sage on Sundays and had become a regular fixture at Taco Tuesday which had only been a few nights ago. Maren had been just fine, then. Now, it was radio silence and it was freaking me out. I kept watching the clock, the time dragging; my agitation at the situation growing as I worked on a groaning Mrs. Robinson type. You'd like to think I was giving her the best sex she'd ever had, rather than just a massage, but I guess for some people it could be as good. I didn't want to think about that too hard, I really didn't.

I finished up and did my usual routine; forcing myself to deal with the necessities of stripping the table of its linens, remaking it, and washing my hands before I went for my phone.

Me: Are u okay?

Maren: I'm fine.

My last text asking her if she was alright had been sent an hour and fifteen minutes ago. Her response, short, clipped and to the point, had come in fifteen minutes ago. I frowned. The more comfortable Maren became with me, the more animated, the more open, and the more expressive she had become. These one and two word short clipped answers weren't her style. My angel wasn't prone to the short version.

I checked my client schedule to see if there was any chance of me getting out of here early or on time. No fucking dice. Well shit. I typed out a fast text.

Me: Ur not fine. I'm coming over.

I kept checking obsessively and got nothing back by way of reply before my next client came in. Dammit. She would be out of school inside the next hour. Best I could hope for was kicking my ass into high gear between clients and that everyone would show up early so I could get them in earlier. I would not, under any circumstances, gyp them of their time on my table but if I got lucky, I could get out of here up to a half hour early. We'd have to see.

I checked my phone after all three clients, no answer from Maren. That straight up cemented my belief that something was clearly wrong, so I skipped remaking my table after my last client and took off. I could do it in the morning. When I got to Maren and Sage's, Sage was the one to answer the door.

"Everything okay, man?" I asked. Sage looked past me at my bike ticking and cooling in their driveway. He rolled his eyes and stepped back further, opening the door wide.

"Yeah, let me guess, she's not answering her phone."

"Uh yeah, how'd you guess?"

Sage laughed. "She always gets super emo this time of the month."

Stupid me, I blurted out, "I don't follow."

Sage said, "She's on her period, she's in her room." He was laughing now, tears gathering at the corners of his eyes.

"Hey, knock it off," I said pushing past him. I went up the stairs, easing my way down the hall until I could glance in Maren's doorway. She wasn't in that sexy as hell nightgown of hers. No, she was in some raggedy-ass sweats, curled on her side, arms around her stomach. She looked asleep, so I backed off and nearly collided with Sage who looked amused.

"I'll be back in a bit, gonna give it my best shot to fix this. Answer the door when I get back," I told him.

He rolled his eyes at me again and I bent down nose to nose with him. "Disrespect me again," I said; voice low, controlled, and even.

He swallowed visibly and said, voice shaking, "Sorry, Nox."

I straightened up and nodded once. "Glad we understand each other." I ruffled his hair and left him at his bedroom door, jogging down the stairs on a mission.

18

M aren…

I hated how much my cramps took it out of me. I couldn't bear to be around people when they hit. I didn't even feel human. All I could do was curl on my side and wait for it to pass which, thankfully, only took the better part of the first day, with tolerable pain the second. I took two Tylenol the moment I got home and crawled into my favorite sweats. I lay curled on my side on my bed wishing for death or for the damn pain to just stop when a light touch fell on my head, smoothing aside my hair. I jerked, startled, and looked up into Nox's gently smiling face.

"Oh God, did you try to call?" I asked.

"No, Angel, your texts have been off your baseline all day. I texted to say I was coming over. Found you like this after Sage let me in. I left out and came back. Let's see what we can do to make you more comfortable, okay?"

"Honestly, I'm not really up for any company right now, Nox." I said and hugged my middle, the cramps in my stomach close to unbearable, twisting down so tightly I thought my spine should suffer permanent damage.

"Not going to let you suffer like this, Angel. Not when there's something I can do about it. Come on, up you go." He helped me into a sitting position and I sighed.

"All I can do is take my Tylenol, which I did, and wait for it to stop, which I am," I said glumly.

"First off, fuck Tylenol; take ibuprofen. Second, have you ever tried heat or massage?"

"Okay, and no I haven't... what does heat do?" I asked curiously.

"I take it your dad didn't know much about these kinds of problems?"

"No," I murmured.

"And your mom?"

I gritted my teeth, but not from pain and said, "Not around."

"Not here to push, just here to help," he said and he did help me to my feet. I let him take me downstairs and blinked at the crazy setup in my living room.

Nox stood by the table and held out a hand. "Hop up here. No need to take anything off, I can work around it for now. Someday, though, I'd like to do this for you for real."

I hopped up on the side of the table and sat there, Nox came around and touched the side of my face, his fingertips lightly resting on the pulse point in my neck, his thumb grazing my jaw. I shivered and closed my eyes for a second, relishing the touch despite how I hurt to the point of nausea. God, I hated being a woman sometimes, and the march of the red menace was definitely at the top of my list of times I hated being female.

"You trust me, don't you, Maren?" he asked low and the quality in his voice made me shiver again.

"Yes," I said breathily, and it didn't have anything to do with the pain.

He put an arm around my legs, cradling my head still with the hand that he'd touched me so gently with, letting it slide to the back of my head. I moved with him, easily, doing what he wanted, almost instinctively by touch alone as he laid me back, face up on the table.

He lifted my sweatshirt a bit and tugged down the corner of my yoga pants until he could dip his fingers below the waistline of both the pants and my panties beneath. My breath caught, and I closed my eyes and tried not to think about how this would look if anyone came in here, like Sage.

"I'm going to press, and I'm going to lift your leg against my shoulder, I need you to remember to breathe, you get me, baby?"

"I… I think so."

He lifted my leg with his free hand and braced it against his shoulder in a stretch I'd seen the cheerleaders do a thousand times with one another at my school. Then, he pressed a couple of inches down and to the side of my right hipbone, in the soft spot and holy God that hurt! I yipped and bit down on the sound, whimpering and holding my breath as he mercilessly worked the spot.

"Breathe, Angel," he ordered, and I sucked in a deep breath, tears stinging the corners of my eyes. "That's it, let it out." Nox breathed exaggeratedly, in a bid for me to follow by example and I did.

"That hurts!" I cried and he nodded.

"Only for a little bit, just breathe for me, baby," he said but he backed off to where the pain was tolerable. He flexed my leg back and forth and pressed in that same damn spot, ordering me to breathe as he worked the muscles loose on first the right side before starting on the left.

A knock fell at the front door, and Nox called out, "Come in!" I tried to sit up, but he put a hand to my chest and pressed me back down. He pressed in that spot hard enough to make me go, "Ouch!" just as my brother and my caseworker from the state walked through the door.

"Oh my God, Pam!" I cried and covered my face with my hands as it flamed away.

Nox, not to be deterred, said sternly, "Maren, I need you to breathe." I immediately sucked in a deep breath and wished I could melt into the floor.

"What are you doing here?" I asked, voice muffled as it was still hiding right along with me behind my hands.

"Sage called, said someone was hurting you. I can see the rumors of your impending death were greatly exaggerated, as I suspected they would be." Her voice was tinged with amusement and I lowered my hands.

"Hi, I'm Nox," Nox said and followed it up quickly with, "Probably looks bad, but I'm licensed and working here, do you mind? She's tensed up as it is and it's not making my job any easier."

Pam fought to suppress her smile and said, "By all means, I'll wait in the kitchen."

"Do me a favor and start some water for some hot tea?" he called.

"Huh," Pam muttered, looking Nox over before turning and walking into the kitchen. I tried to sit up again and Nox pressed me back down.

"Relax, Maren. I can't help you if you don't relax."

"Kind of hard, don't you think!?" I demanded, and he sighed, letting me up.

"We aren't done here," he murmured low, with a sexy growl next to my ear that made me bite my lower lip. I told my teenaged overwrought sex drive to chill and swung my legs over the edge of the table, blinking, my cramps much diminished but still there. I looked at Nox who smirked, bemused.

"Okay," I griped. "We aren't done but let me deal with one disaster at a time, this one takes priority."

"I don't disagree," he said and held out his hands. I put mine gently in them and he helped me hop off the table, trailing into the kitchen behind me.

"So, you're Nox," Pam said switching on the stove beneath our kettle. I slid into a seat at the kitchen table while Nox moved around my kitchen getting down tea and sugar, cups and saucers. It never failed to amaze me just how civilized he was, for being a rough and tumble biker.

"I'm Nox," he confirmed. I'd told Pam about him before, and she eyed him critically now.

"Somehow I pictured you a little…"

"Younger?" he supplied. Pam's response was for her mouth to flatten down into a thin line. Nox set down cups and saucers and asked, "What kind of tea would you like?"

"All due respect, I'm not here for the tea," she said and I closed my eyes. Her tone wasn't especially thrilled and I cleared my throat.

"I can explain," I murmured and Pam's keen brown eyes flicked to me.

She tucked some of her long, frizzy, dyed blonde hair behind her ear from where it was parted on the side and said, "I'm all ears."

Shit, she wasn't happy. I scrambled. "I wasn't feeling well." I flamed a special kind of crimson. "Cramps, and well, Nox was just trying to help…"

I was flailing for the right things to say, tripping over myself, when Nox's hands fell to my shoulders and his thumbs dug just right between them, easing out some of the tension gathered there.

"What did Sage tell you on the phone?" he asked succinctly. "Can't fix what's broken if we don't know why you're here."

Pam eyed him critically, and said, "Sage called and said that Maren's much older boyfriend had forced his way into the house and was hurting his sister and that I needed to come quick."

I let my face fall into my hands and Nox pressed just a little bit harder, a silent plea for me to chill. I looked at Pam's angular face and sighed. "That's not what happened at all," I said.

"First of all, I'm just a friend," Nox said. "Second, I was texting with Maren and she seemed... off all day, so I swung by to check on her and Sage. Sage was the one to let me in the front door and pardon my French, but he was acting like a disrespectful little shit. So, I checked him. Maren was napping up in her room and looked pretty wrecked, and Sage seemed to think it was awfully funny that Maren was in pain. Probably because he's an eleven-year-old kid and doesn't get that a woman's period is a natural part of life and they aren't funny, especially when it's taking it out of his sister like that."

His hands disappeared and one reappeared over my shoulder, reaching past me to hand Pam a laminated card. "Third, I'm a licensed massage practitioner and knew I could lend a professional hand for this particular set of circumstances, so I left back out and came back with my gear to do what I could to ease her discomfort. Seems to me, we might need to have a little talk with Sage."

Pam considered the card for a long minute before handing it back to Nox. "Before we call Sage down here, I'd like to know exactly what he did and precisely what you did, to quote-unquote," she raised her fingers and made quotation marks in the air, "check him."

"He rolled his eyes at me, so I did this." He stepped around my seat and leaned down putting his nose inches from Pam's. His face grew stern, his look blank and frightening and he said in an even, controlled tone, "Disrespect me again."

Pam's eyes widened, and he sat up. She asked him quietly, "And what did Sage do?"

"He told me he was sorry, I ruffled his hair and I left out."

"That was it?" Pam asked.

"That was it," Nox agreed.

"You didn't grab him or lay a hand on him?" she asked.

"Nope."

"I see."

I swallowed hard. "You see what?" I asked, mouth dry as the kettle began to whistle, filling the silence left behind; the air thicker with the gravity of the situation. My heart pounded and my mind raced, and all I kept thinking was *please don't take him away. Please don't take him away. Please don't take him away.*

Pam looked from me to Nox and sighed. "Maren, it's fine, really. Mr. Fisher didn't do anything wrong, except, perhaps, come on a little too strongly, but I somehow gather that this isn't the first time Sage has been disrespectful in his presence?"

"Not by a long shot," Nox declared from the kitchen island where he poured three cups of tea. He brought them over and set one in front of me and one in front of Pam before fetching his cup and pulling out a seat next to mine.

"I see," Pam said.

"Listen, I didn't do anything to Sage that I haven't done to my nephew, Noah, a time or two. There's no sense in yelling when that type of calm does so much better, am I right?"

Pam smirked and added sugar to her tea, meanwhile, I felt my eyes mist with tears at the sheer anxiety crushing me from the inside, like a black hole had taken up residence in the center of my chest and was sucking me down and inside out from the force.

"I'm really failing at this whole parenting thing, aren't I?" I asked, a few tears sneaking out and down my face. I sniffed and wiped at them, and Pam looked both empathetic and sad.

"You're doing a lot better than you think, Maren. There comes a point where it's up to Sage and no one else. I believe he is acting out simply because he didn't appreciate Mr. Fisher calling him out on his bad behavior. He's testing his limits and it is up to us as the adults to set the boundaries Sage must abide by. Mr. Fisher did that tonight and Sage didn't like it. He's resourceful, just like his sister."

"All due respect, I don't think Sage has a mind towards consequences," Nox said tiredly.

"Oh?" Pam said, and she sounded interested. She took up her tea in her hands and blew on it, staring over the rim at Nox.

"I've explained to him that he could wind up in foster care," I said helplessly.

"Yeah, but he doesn't know exactly what that means. I grew up in the system with the worst of the worst; I do." Pam looked at Nox who didn't look happy about making his revelation.

"Where at?" she asked. "If I may ask."

"Arizona."

"I see."

"Is there any way to show him?" I asked, and Pam smiled.

"I don't think it's come to scare tactics yet, I would keep it in reserve. Sage is smart, he called me instead of the police, if either you or he were in any real danger I know that he would have called 9-1-1, not his case worker." Pam looked thoughtful. "Could this be jealousy?" she asked.

Nox sighed. "Hadn't thought of that, honestly."

I looked back and forth between them as if I were at one of the world's most interesting tennis matches. "Jealousy?" I echoed.

"I've been spending a lot of big brother type time with Sage lately," Nox said.

"His coming over here for the sole purpose of checking on you could have upset Sage."

I put my face in my hands again and scrubbed, doctored my tea as my mind worked the problem and sipped the hot liquid carefully after blowing on it like Pam had done.

"I can see the point."

"Call him down here, let's have a chat, shall we?" Pam said, and I could tell she was feeling better about all of this. I wished I were.

I went to the foot of the stairs and called up, "Sage Hunter Tracy, get down here now!"

"Oh dear," Pam said and looked chagrined and I immediately felt the lowest of the low.

"What?" I asked.

"Let's not put him on the defensive right off the bat, Angel," Nox said gently and Pam side-eyed him but nodded in agreement with what he was saying.

God, could I get anything right?

The conversation with Sage did not go well. As was typical lately, it was a whole lot of the three adults, well... okay, two-and-a-half adults in the room, trying to explain the consequences of his actions and getting nothing but a whole lot of histrionics in return. The entire thing culminated in Sage running back upstairs after screaming at us that we didn't get him, and we didn't care about him, the silence heavy after he punctuated his outburst by slamming the door.

Pam sighed and looked at me with sympathy. I closed my eyes and just wanted to die. To melt into the floor and disappear. Nox sighed harshly and I opened my eyes to see him grip the back of his head with both hands, his long fingers laced together as he pulled on his head, bouncing it slightly to give his neck and back a good stretch. Guilt settled onto my shoulders, weighing them significantly.

"I'm so sorry I am screwing all of this up. I just don't know what to do. I'm doing my best but I'm well aware my best isn't enough." I looked at Pam helplessly and she smiled sadly. "I'm losing my brother, aren't I?" I asked and the tears started.

"No, honey. No, you're doing a remarkable job with what you've been given, actually. I don't think you're doing anything wrong, I just don't think you know how to reach Sage. I don't think any of us do."

"Not helpful," I uttered, and I hadn't meant for it to be said out loud, but she answered.

"I know, and I'm sorry."

I scrubbed a hand over my face and sighed, wilting into the back of my kitchen chair. Pam smiled apologetically and said, "You're doing everything you can, Maren. Welcome to what it is to be the parent of a smart, albeit somewhat unruly, child."

"Is he going to be taken, Pam? Are you going to take my brother away?"

She laughed a little. "No, sweetie. It would take something extreme for that to happen. You're actually doing fine, you may need to work on your technique a little, but that can't be learned overnight."

"If it's one thing I've learned from Archer and Mel? It's that parent-hood doesn't come with an instruction manual. It's just a part of life," Nox said. I turned my head to look at him, where he leaned up against one of the kitchen counters, his arms crossed over his chest. I let my eyes slide over the black crows and roses of his sleeve tattoo and tried not to let the monumental sense of failure swamp me.

Pam sighed. "I'd better get going. Mr. Fisher, it was nice to meet you," she said and held out her hand. Nox stepped forward and shook it.

"You too, ma'am."

"Hang in there, Maren."

"I will," I said somberly.

Nox saw Pam out and when he came back into the kitchen, it was to me wiping my tears. I confessed to him, "I feel like I'm screwing everything up."

"Come here, get up here," he ordered pulling me gently to my feet. He wrapped me in his arms and held me tight and I felt a little more solid, a little more grounded.

"You're hurting, you're tired, you're under a tremendous amount of stress and Sage is a typical eleven-year-old. He isn't making anything easy on you. He's doing what every pre-teen does, he's testing limits and seeing what he can and can't get away with. You've been doing a remarkable job so far of holding him accountable, of not letting him get away with anything. It's a tough line to walk, you're seventeen; you're his sister not his mother." I stiffened, and Nox sighed, he touched the side of my face, tilting my head back. His light-colored eyes searched mine and he sighed.

"Kiss me," I asked and he smiled.

"Thought you'd never ask," he murmured low and covered my mouth with his. My eyes slipped shut and the kiss was everything I needed. Patient, kind, and gentle. Full of promise that things would get better.

He pulled me tightly against his body and the kiss deepened to almost frantic. His hands slipped beneath my sweatshirt, smoothing against my skin and causing me to shiver. I ignored my cramps and held tightly to him and poured all of my worries, cares, and concerns onto the floor and let him fill me up with hope.

19

Nox...

She was warm and fit herself so well against me, it was every-thing in me to maintain even a little control. I crushed her to me and held her tightly and murmured into her hair, "I'm here, I'll help any way I can and I'm going to take care of some things. I promise you." She nodded, and I sighed, content for the time being.

I don't think she realized she did it, but she whimpered, and I remembered why I'd come in the first place. I pulled away from her so I could look at her and said, "Come on, Angel. Let me take care of you."

"Okay," she whispered and the fight was just clean out of her for now. She was tired, she was hurting, and emotionally, she was pretty raw. She needed some love, some support, and for sure a good night's sleep. I could help with all of that.

I led her past my massage table, which sat forlorn and sad in the living room, and up the stairs. A waste of my good intentions thanks to Sage's antics. He hadn't really said why he'd called their caseworker, but I knew it was because he was pissed at me for knocking his little ass down a peg. He couldn't hit me, he knew that was a bad idea, so the manipulative little shit tried the next best thing. Too bad for him that didn't work either. I wasn't going anywhere, and I wasn't giving up on him, either. I think it was time to 'fess up to myself that I was too far gone on his sister to do any of those things.

"Here, lie down," I murmured, pulling back her blankets. She got into bed obediently and I pulled them up to her chin. "I'll be right back," I promised, and I went downstairs to grab what I needed. I slipped back up to her room and handed her the round tablet I'd brought with me.

"What is it?" she asked.

"Muscle relaxer, take it. You aren't going to school tomorrow. You need a fucking day off from everything. I'll take Sage to his school and drop him off, then I'll swing by yours to get your assignments."

"Won't you be late to work?"

"Don't you worry about that, my first client isn't until nine, I've got plenty of time to get shit done. Take this and let me get the rest of this hooked up."

She took the pill from my palm and it disappeared between those soft lips before she pressed the water glass from her bedside table to them. Satisfied that she was going along with my mini-vacation plan, I plugged in the heating pad I'd brought with me and set it to its highest setting. I lifted the blankets and tucked it against her stomach.

"Anti-inflammatories from now on, like ibuprofen or a NSAID, you got it?" She nodded, and I went on, "Also, use this. Heat helps relax the muscles. If it gets really bad, I can massage you, but I'm also going to show you some stretches that will help."

"Okay," she said softly.

I bent down and kissed her again and fuck I was hard to the point of pain. *Six more weeks, five more days. Six more weeks, five more days,* I reminded myself, and fuck yes, I was counting. Still, I had no intention of fucking her on her birthday. Something about the idea of it felt classless and tacky.

I had something special planned for it, but sex with Maren would come in its own time, when the time was right and not a minute before.

"Stay with me?" she asked, and I wanted to. Shit did I want to, but we had eyes on us now thanks to Sage… and fuck it.

"Yeah."

I kicked off my boots and went around the end of the bed. I stayed on top of the quilts and laid up against Maren's back, pulling her lightly against me. She wriggled back until we were snug, and I was pretty sure my cock called me a son of a bitch.

"I love you," she murmured, drowsing heavily, the drug I'd given her turning her as limp as a wet noodle. I smiled to myself.

"Good shit, huh?"

"No, not for that," she said and sounded annoyed. "I love you."

I cuddled her closer and said, "I love you, too, Angel."

"Mean it?"

"Oh, I mean it."

"Good."

I laid with her until after she fell asleep, then I took her phone and my phone downstairs with me so when the alarms went off in the morning, they wouldn't wake her. I packed my table and the shit that went with it out to my cage, before heading back inside. I wanted to go back upstairs, lie down with her and hold her, protect her while she slept, but Sage was pretty much an unknown quantity on whether he would flip a bitch or rat us out. The kid had broken trust with me, and that wasn't shit that was easy to come by.

He'd be hard pressed to earn it back. It was one of those tough life lessons he was about to go through. I'd been his friend up to this point, but it was pretty clear friendship wasn't as needed as some structure and discipline. I could provide that too, for a while, and see which he preferred. I settled down on the couch, in the dark, and slept uneasily. It was going to be a long night and I didn't do well in unfamiliar places. It just wasn't my thing. It was a good thing I would do anything for Maren. It was a real good thing.

~

"WHERE'S MAREN?" Sage asked, poking his head outside his bedroom door.

"Asleep." *And not going to deal with whatever petty bullshit you cook up today,* I thought to myself. Out loud I said, "Get dressed. I'm taking you to school. You're taking the bus home and I mean straight home. Do I make myself clear?"

He blinked up at me owlishly and cocked his head to the side. *Just try it,* I thought. I waited for which way he'd go. Mean or sulking comment or sullen silence, any of which were likely to be punctuated by the bedroom door being slammed in my face. That wasn't about to go well for him either.

"The only reason you pretended to be friends with me is because you want to fuck my sister, huh?" he asked and went to slam the door. My hand stopped it, flat against the wood with a hard shove that bowled the kid on his ass in the middle of the hardwood of his bedroom floor. I stepped into the room and shut the door behind me. I didn't want to wake Maren, and Sage and I needed to have a little chat.

"It's time for you to grow the fuck up, Sage. Your sister had to, way before her time, to take care of your whiny, sorry ass. Now it's your turn to give back a little. She's trying way too hard for you to turn around and turn into a disrespectful little shit."

He stood up and took a swing at me and I caught it, hooking my arm at his elbow, sidestepping his follow through. His fist whizzed through the empty air and I had his arms hung up behind his back. He struggled, and I put some torsion into my hold until he yelped and backed off in his struggles. I pushed him away from me and he flopped onto his bed.

"That's the first and last time you take a swing at me. Get dressed and get your ass down to my cage. I'm taking you to school and if you even think about waking up your sister, you're going to regret it. Play-time is over, boy. Your lessons on what it is to be the man of the house begin now."

I punctuated my harsh words with the occasional stabs of my finger at him in the air. He was wide-eyed with disbelief and I couldn't say that I gave much of a fuck. Maren deserved so much better than anything he'd been dishing out and it was clear the kind and patient approach that was so uniquely his sister's, wasn't working. It was my turn, and I was giving him a bit of a taste of how I was raised to make a point.

I left him wide-eyed and staring at me and opened up the bedroom door telling him, "You've got five minutes. Move it or lose it."

I waited downstairs and I timed him; he had two minutes, thirty-seven seconds on the clock when he came thundering down the staircase. I raised a hand, palm out to stop him.

"You wake up your sister, I'm whooping your ass."

He froze. "You can't say that to me!" he said, indignantly.

"Who's going to stop me?" I demanded, and he blustered a second and fell silent.

"No, go on, think about it… I want you to really think about the posi-tion you've put yourself in, Sage." I crossed my arms over my chest, the leather of my jacket and cut creaking while I watched the cogs and wheels whir and click behind his brown eyes. He needed a haircut, the dark strands, just like his sister's, getting into his eyes.

"Why are you being so mean to me?" he asked and sounded fragile, vulnerable.

"Could ask you the same thing, kid."

More contemplative silence.

"I thought you really liked me, but it was just my sister the whole time."

"Did I ever say that?" He looked at me sharply. "Come on, let's go. If we move it, we have time for breakfast."

He slung his backpack higher on his shoulder and I took it off him, the navy-blue canvas had seen better days, and I made a mental note to either mend it or to get him a new one. He pulled on his coat, hat, and scarf, turning to take back his bag.

"You've got two choices, Sage," I said to him. "You can either work with us, do what you're told, and stop giving your sister a hard time. Do that, and we can go back to the older, nicer version of me; or," and I rested my hand on his shoulder, "you can keep doing what you're doing, going behind Maren's back, making shit up and making sneaky phone calls and end up in a place where you get worse than the new, angrier me."

"Worse?" he echoed swallowing hard.

"I just stopped you from hitting me. Where I come from, I would have had my ass whooped with a belt until I bled. Broken bones? They weren't out of the question either."

"They can't do that!" he said astonished. I put my hand on his shoulder.

"Lesson one, just because they can't don't mean they won't. They did, and they knew just what to say and how to say it to get right off the hook, which brings me to lesson two — you are never as smart as you think you are. There is always someone smarter."

Sage looked thoughtful and then looked up at me. "You aren't making this up?"

"Lesson three, a man has no honor if he's a fucking liar. I'm not making it up, I have the scars to prove it. Look at me when I tell you this." His eyes snapped back up to mine. "I love your sister the way she ought to be loved, and I love you like a little brother I never had. You have it in you to be a great kid, but the fighting at school, the not listening to adults, the attempts to get other kids to act out and misbehave… like I said, playtime is over, kid. Time to grow up some and face your demons. I'm right here if you ever want to talk about it – I am your friend. Always have been, always will be. There's nothing pretend about that. I just happen to love your sister, too."

He dropped his eyes to the floor and his shoulders hitched in a silent sob. It was sometimes hard to remember that Sage was just a kid, for all tough and proud he acted. I pulled him in and hugged him fiercely, smacking a kiss on the top of his head the way Grind used to do to me or Rush when we'd been pushed too far as kids by him or Arch. I was new to this whole parenting-like gig but was grateful for the sharp lessons in it.

"McDonald's?" I asked ignoring the elephant in the room for now, following the bro-code I'd grown up with which was let 'em cry it out a second, then move right along to the next thing; ignoring it, like it didn't happen.

"Yeah," he said glumly.

"Cool, and Sage?"

"Yeah?"

"Watch your mouth at school and in front of your sister."

"You swear all the time," he said as we moved to the door.

"Yeah, and so can you, after you're eighteen. First milestone, that one."

"Okay," he said with a little laugh.

We hit the drive-thru, got more food than we probably should have, and I took him to school dropping him off. He leaned in and I rolled down the window.

"Thanks, Nox."

"No problem, kid. I mean it about the bus, your sister is pretty much done like last night's dinner and needs a rest. Give it to her for today, yeah?"

Sage looked thoughtful. "Yeah, okay."

"You're a good kid when you want to be."

He gave me a cheeky grin. "Which isn't very often."

I rolled my eyes. "Born outlaw troublemaker. I know the type."

He grinned wider and reached through the open window of my cage. We bumped fists and he ran off and into the building. I watched him go in and when one of the other citizen parents honked their horns behind me, I gave them the good old one-fingered salute through my rear window.

Real mature and way to lead by example, I know, but I was out of fucks to give at the moment.

I headed to Maren's school next, pretty much dreading walking in, and trying to figure out how in the fuck to handle this shit diplomatically by citizen standards; especially after having gone the non-traditional route with Sage.

I pulled into a visitor's parking space and got out of my cage. I took my cut out of the backseat and ground my teeth as I locked it in the back-hatch area of my cage, tucking it carefully under some clean sheets to keep it out of view. It felt like too much disrespect to my colors for my liking, but I knew for a fact that they weren't going to buy me any favors in a public high school, at least not from the faculty. Tucking them under the sheets was for their safety, being as I didn't want a window smashed and the colors taken because then I really would have to go kill somebody. Not to mention face the consequences the club would have to dish out to me – which was likely a fate *worse* than death.

I went through the front door of the school to a lot of stares and kids putting their heads together, whispering. My age, plus the biker jacket, which happened to be the only one I owned, drawing a lot of attention. I caught sight of Lucas out of the corner of my eye and he sort of half blanched, staring at me intently and eying my jacket, as if trying to figure out if I were one of the boogeymen from that night. I gave him a second glance, before going into the main office, trying to judge if he recognized me, uneasy that I couldn't be sure he didn't.

"Can I help you?" the secretary asked from behind her rhinestone purple granny glasses on their tasteful bead chain. I smiled at her, she looked to be about D's age. So, late fifties maybe early sixties. Her white hair was in a fringe of bangs over her blue eyes and she was skinny, almost too skinny. She wrapped her purple cardigan tighter around her as I rested my hands on the desk, and I didn't think it was because she was cold.

"Yeah, that'd be great. I'm Landon Fisher. Maren Tracy isn't feeling well, and I stopped by to get her assignments for her so she could get 'em done from home." I laid the manila folder of her last night's home-work on the wrap-up around the secretary's desk and said, "These are her completed assignments she wanted to turn in."

The secretary blinked at me and picked up the phone, her eyes never leaving mine. She punched in a three-digit code on the keypad without missing a beat and said into the receiver; "Yes, I believe Maren Tracy's… boyfriend?" she asked me over the receiver and I felt my lips twist into a wry grin.

Well played old gal, well played, I thought to myself.

"Friend," I said unequivocally.

"Yes, Maren Tracy's friend is here to collect her assignments, it seems she won't be in school today." She paused. "Yes, of course."

"Vice Principal Hunter would like to see you. He's just through there." She pointed and I raised my eyebrows, picking up the folder of Maren's assignments that I'd taken from her backpack.

"Sent to the Vice Principal's office just for walking through the door, that's a record even for me," I said lightly and dryly, trying to inject a little humor into the situation. The secretary did not look amused. *Okay, then.* I gave a nod, and said, "Thank you, ma'am."

She reverted her eyes back to her screen, back straight, shoulders back, perfect posture. I tried not to laugh and went to the door she'd indicated, which opened up to a man in a suit, looking me up and down. He stood aside, and let me in, greeting me with a simple, "Mister...?"

"Call me Nox. Mr. Fisher would just make me feel like I'm in some kind of trouble," I said smiling.

"Should you be?" the Vice Principal shot back.

"Not for the reasons you're clearly thinkin'," I said coolly.

"Have a seat, Mr. Fisher," he said and again I told him to call me Nox. I took a seat in one of the two chairs opposite his desk, and he sank into the expensive looking leather office chair across the expanse of, what looked like, cherry wood. Rush would have been so proud at the identification.

We stared at one another for a long minute that may have even stretched into two, and I have to say, he had this Vice Principal shit down because I was beginning to sweat. I finally broke the silence with, "Are you going to take these and turn them in, and get me the assignments she has to do for today, or not?"

I tapped the manila file folder against the edge of his desk and gave it a toss onto the blotter in front of him. He picked it up and gave me a sardonic grin.

"It's against school policy to accept work, or to give work to anyone but a student or their immediate family, such as a parent or guardian."

I let my look flatten out. "Guess you best make an exception to the rule in Maren's case. She doesn't have any immediate family left, and in case you weren't paying attention to the goings on around here," I leaned forward and said conspiratorially, "I'm most definitely her guardian, even if it isn't by any official citizen standard."

His blue eyes grew keen and his gaze sharpened on me. He picked up his phone and punched in three numbers. When whoever picked up on the other end spoke, he answered into the receiver, "Yes, Jean, do me a favor and pick up these assignments I have here in my office, make a quick tour of Maren Tracy's classes and get the next assignments from her teachers." He paused and then said, "Now, please, I believe this gentleman has places to be."

He hung up the phone and we waited, staring each other down. The door opened, and he handed the folder to the secretary saying, "Thank you, Ms. Cox." I tried not to snort. *More like Ms. Cocks,* I thought to myself as she gave me a sour expression before shutting the door behind her.

"I've noticed that Maren has been... safer in these halls the last few weeks. That was you?"

"What was me?" I asked raising my eyebrows.

He shifted in his seat uncomfortably. "Fair enough. It's probably best I don't know."

"You have to be pretty smart to get the job as a Vice Principal, I take it."

He smiled but it held no humor. "Quite."

"Good to know," I said.

"What precisely is it that you do Mr- "

"Nox, and I'm a massage therapist."

Hunter looked surprised and I chuckled a little, I think he was warming up to me a little. I certainly was thawing out in his direction.

"You know I can't approve of a thirty-six-year-old man and a seventeen-year-old girl being together. I can't quite fathom how something like that even came to be."

Well alright, if he wanted to be blunt, I could be too.

"I think we both know Maren might be seventeen but she's way older than that; given everything that's happened. Trust me, I never once went for anything remotely resembling jailbait before but something about her is different. Plus, not that it likely makes any difference to you, I haven't laid a hand on her. I like my life, I like my practice, and I'm not about to flush either for anyone or anything. If it's going to go anywhere, it can wait until she's eighteen and legal. I'm just trying to lend a helping hand around the house and with that brother of hers."

"I see," he said and leaned back in his seat, fingers pressed in a steeple before him. He rested his ankle from his opposite foot on his knee and regarded me carefully.

"Ask her yourself if you don't believe me."

"I intend to," he admitted, and we sat in a stalemated silence. I gritted my teeth. The last thing I'd wanted to do by coming here was cause Maren any more grief.

"Why that look, Mr. Nox?"

I rolled my eyes. "It's just Nox, and in case you hadn't noticed, I'm trying to make Maren's life easier, not harder. So if you're going to get involved, or get the authorities up my ass – which good luck on that one, she's emancipated and considered an adult anyhow... just do me a favor and don't be giving her the third degree."

We deadlocked into another stare while he considered my words until we were finally interrupted by the secretary who looked like she could use some cock. She rapped lightly on the door and Hunter called out for her to come in. She slipped into the office with the same manila file folder I'd brought Maren's work in, only this time it was filled with crisp, flat paper — fresh sheets of new assignments.

"Ms. Tracy's assignments," she said handing it over to her boss, smartly.

"Thank you," he said and after another careful look in my direction handed the folder over. The secretary ducked out and closed the door behind her. I stood up, I needed to get going if I wanted to stop back over at Maren's before I had to head to work.

"Will there be anything else, Nox?" the Vice Principal asked standing with me, buttoning his suit jacket. I was hit with a flash of sudden inspiration.

"Yeah, when you catch me breaking into Maren's car on Valentine's Day," I opened the door, "do me a favor and don't call the cops."

I shut the door on his perplexed expression and gave a nod to the secretary on the way out. "Ms. Cox."

She looked startled as if she hadn't expected the nicety, and she probably hadn't which is exactly why I'd done it. I really was out to make my girl's life easier, not harder, but on some things, it looked like we were in this struggle together. Dammit.

20

M aren...

"Wake up, Angel."

I shifted slightly and winced, feeling as if I'd somehow rusted overnight. Nox brushed my hair away from my face and I cracked open my eyes.

"What time is it?" I asked, and even my voice sounded rusty with disuse. *Jesus, what had I taken?*

Nox chuckled lightly and said, "It's eight-thirty," and I bolted upright.

"Oh my God, I'm late!"

"Easy, Angel, you aren't late, you aren't going anywhere." I stared at him in disbelief as he lightly gripped my shoulders and eased me back into the pillows.

"I've already dropped Sage off at school, he's taking the bus home. Plus, I've already been to your school and turned your work in. While I was at it," he lightly plucked my manila homework folder off my nightstand, "I picked up your next round of homework. You can do it today while you take a rest and reset."

I stared at him, speechless. "Why would you do all that?" I asked when I could finally find my voice.

"Because you're at the end of your rope and need to regroup, so I bought you some time to do it." He stood up. "Now as much as I hate to say it, I've got to go. I'm going to be late if I don't."

He bent down to place his lips against my forehead, but I jerked my chin up at the last moment, so they landed on mine. Nox made a slightly surprised noise but it quickly gave way to a guttural moan of approval. I twined my fingers in his dark hair and kissed him soundly, and he returned the favor, breaking it at the last possible second.

"Angel, I've got to go," he murmured, and I let him go.

"Sorry," I said breathlessly, and he straightened.

"Don't be," he said seriously and left out my bedroom door.

I stared for a long time at the empty space where he'd been, my heart thundering against the inside of my ribs with the impression of his kiss, his body, pressed against mine.

A LITTLE UNDER two weeks or so later, I was back to struggling again, not with Lucas, but with his now ex-girlfriend, Chelsea Day. She and her little group of girlfriends were back to tormenting me again because Lucas had dumped her ass for not leaving me alone. He was still treating me like I had a case of the plague, punctuated here and there with a bizarre but pleasant behavior such as holding doors for me. Which given the way he'd treated me up until now, I was still fine with either of those things. Still, I just wanted to be left alone by all of them.

They still didn't know about Nox, which was fine by me; still, the remarks about being alone on Valentine's Day and no one caring was still cutting a little close for comfort. Especially because I had sent a 'Happy Valentine's Day' text to my much older boyfriend that morning and hadn't received anything back.

Speaking of much older boyfriends — my first day back to school had been somewhat of an adventure. Mr. Hunter had pulled me aside like first thing to have a little chat about Nox and whether I felt safe and if Nox had done anything inappropriate. I'd had to sigh and endure this talking to like I was Mr. Hunter's own daughter for a good forty-five minutes and it'd left me with some seriously mixed feelings.

I didn't know whether to be grateful, that anyone would look out for me in such a way or if I should feel annoyed at the fact that no one seemed to think I could handle myself anymore. I think I fell somewhat on the side of the latter and it was a turning point of sorts. I pulled myself up a little more by the bootstraps and went to my doctor. She prescribed me a low-grade mood stabilizer, not just an anti-depressant but also an anti-anxiety pill, for as long as I needed it.

It helped, surprisingly so, and I felt like I probably should have gone in for it a little sooner.

The bell rang, and I heaved a sigh of relief. I was seriously bored in my last class of the day, being leaps and bounds ahead of the curriculum. English had always been my strong suit and while we were supposed to be on chapter ten of the required reading, I had finished it my first night. So, I spent most of my time, while my English teacher droned on about it, working on my homework so I could get a head start on it. Except it'd been a light homework day, so I'd finished it in the first twenty minutes of the class.

I just wanted to go home, but nope, I had to work tonight. Too bad Valentine's Day wasn't considered a holiday. Time and a half, even at minimum wage, sounded really good right about now.

"Have fun spending the night alone!" Chelsea quipped as I shut my locker and I smiled sweetly at her.

"You too!"

She gave me a dirty look and I wrapped my fingers around my keys in my pocket until they dug into my flesh uncomfortably. I checked my phone for like the millionth time and sighed out harshly.

Still nothing.

I stopped just beyond my car and had to push through the kids surrounding it and taking pictures. Some were laughing and pointing, and I felt my heart sink. *What did Chelsea and her fucking friends do to it?* was my first thought, but when I got through the crowd, I just stopped. It wasn't that. It wasn't her at all.

This had to be Nox.

A larger-than-life teddy bear sat in the passenger seat, buckled in and ready to go. I could see his rounded head and ears just barely over the dozens and dozens of red roses that packed the back seat. I carefully stepped to the driver's side and unlocked the car that I was sure I had locked when I'd left it that morning.

Despite how cold the weather was, the smell of roses rolled out to greet me. I shook my head and plucked the envelope taped to my steering wheel off of it, written on the front was *I bet you thought I forgot...*

I opened it to a beautifully hand drawn card, and when I opened that, read the message penned inside:

I could never forget you on a day like today. It's been killing me maintaining silence all day. I wanted to surprise you and let you see just how loved you are. Call me.

Nox.

I put my bag in the trunk and shooed my classmates away, taking a particular bit of satisfaction in the fact that Chelsea was glaring at me with her single rose from whichever basketball player she was sucking off now.

I didn't wave or even acknowledge her, instead, I got into my car and started it up so it could warm up while I phoned Nox. He picked up on the first ring as if he was waiting for me and I think that melted my heart even more.

"Hey, Angel."

"Oh my God, I love you," I said breathlessly, the first happy tears sneaking free. I was getting a good look at the giant chenille teddy bear and it had a motorcycle vest or cut on it. A Sacred Hearts' one and it said Nox on the little name patch.

It was ridiculous and goofy, and just so *perfect*.

"You okay?" Nox asked laughing.

"You know I am! I'm surprised you didn't get arrested breaking into my car."

"Nah, I sort of pre-arranged it with your Vice Principal the last time I was there."

"Mr. Hunter was in on this?"

"Not exactly, I just told him not to call the cops and have me arrested if he saw me breaking into your car on Valentine's."

I laughed, and murmured, "I wish I could see you tonight."

"Night's not over yet, Angel."

"That's a bit dangerous isn't it?" I asked. My birthday was something like three and a half or four more weeks away.

"Probably, but I like to live dangerously."

"I miss you," I told him, and he was quiet for a half a second.

"I miss you, too. This is taking forever," he sighed harshly.

"You always want what you can't quite have, don't you?" I said.

"Yeah, something like that."

"Won't be long now," I promised, and I heard him smile, his breath hitching in a small laugh.

"Twenty-four more days."

"You're counting?" I asked surprised.

"You bet your sweet ass I am."

I felt myself grin and said, "I've got to go or I'm going to be late to work."

"Okay, Angel. Be careful."

"I will, and thank you, they're all so beautiful," I said twisting in my seat to look into the back.

"Not half as beautiful as you. I'll see you later."

"Okay."

I left the school feeling energized and renewed, and I hated that I could only stop at home long enough to bring in the flowers and teddy bear, taking three trips to get it all up to my room; only so I could change clothes and rush off to work.

Sage wasn't home yet, which wasn't completely unusual. Sometimes he liked to stay for the after-school program and sometimes he didn't; when he did, I would pick him up. Today just wasn't the day, though.

I tried calling him, but his phone went straight to voicemail.

"Dammit!" I muttered harshly and went back out to the garage. I got in the car and tried him again. Straight to voicemail.

I was going to kill him.

I drove to his school and found him in the after-school program area playing Ping-Pong with one of his teachers.

"Sage!" I called out and he turned, smiling which took some of the edge off my mad. His face fell a little and I tried to head off the souring of his mood right off the bat with, "I was worried about you, did you turn off your phone?"

"Oh, yeah!" he cried and pulled it out of his pocket.

"Come on, I'm already late. I'm just glad you're okay." I hugged him around the shoulders and he squirmed out of it but not angrily.

I exchanged pleasantries with his teacher and raced my brother home. He got out of the car at the curb and said, "I'm really sorry, Maren. Mrs. Trenkle made me turn off my phone and I forgot to turn it back on."

"It's okay, Sage. Just be a little more careful? I need your help on some of these things. It's the only way we're going to keep making this work."

He looked a little sad. "You shouldn't have to do all of this stuff by yourself," he said.

I laughed a little. "No one else to do it, bud."

"I know," he said, a weird look on his face.

"Close the door, I've got to go!" He grinned at me and slammed the car door. I waited the extra two minutes for him to run to the front door and unlock it, only taking my foot off the brake when he disappeared inside.

Despite my best efforts, I was over ten minutes late to work. I breezed into the back room and clocked in at the computer. My manager looked up and sighed.

"I'll need to talk to you at the end of your shift, Maren," she said tiredly.

"I know, Holly. I'm sorry, I had to go get Sage."

"Just come find me before you clock out."

"Okay."

I felt yet another write-up in my future as I took myself to my till and spent the next five and a half hours cashiering. By the end of my shift, all I wanted was to go home, fix a sandwich, and go to bed. I almost forgot to go find Holly, but Holly found me as I was finishing up just before clocking out.

"Maren, good, glad I found you… listen… I really hate to tell you this, but I'm going to have to let you go."

I blinked and said, "I'm sorry?"

"You've just been late too many times. Well past what corporate will tolerate."

"Holly, you know me! You know it's not always my fault, I need this job!" I wailed and tried valiantly not to cry, my eyes misting up on their own.

Can I please just catch a break!? I thought savagely to whatever powers that be might be listening. *Yeah right, if they were listening or cared they wouldn't keep doing this to you,* I thought with a heavy sigh.

Holly looked like this was killing her and I scrubbed my face with my hands. I let out another heavy sigh and sniffed and said, "It's okay, Holly, I know this isn't your choice."

"It's really not," she said miserably. "You're one of my best employees except for the tardiness lately, which I completely understand, but this is a big box chain, they don't care about anything but timetables and numbers. I'm really, and I mean, really, sorry."

"Happy Valentine's Day to me," I muttered under my breath and swung into my coat.

Holly winced. "Your last check will be mailed to you," she said.

"Thanks," I muttered and left quietly, without a fuss. I pulled my phone from my pocket and then the tears really did start. How was I going to tell Nox? Was he going to be disappointed? Would my dad if he were here? What was I going to do for a job? This was the first one I'd ever had, and now I was fired for being unreliable. How would I ever get another one?

The phone rang in my ear and I closed my eyes; trying to breathe slowly and keep the panic at bay.

21

N ox…

"Aw shit, baby. Really? I'm so sorry." I slipped further up the hall and turned my back on the curious looks from my club brothers and sisters. Maren sobbed piteously on the other end of the line, in full meltdown, I assumed in the parking lot where she worked – scratch that, where she used to work.

"I just can't seem to get ahead no matter what I do!" she wailed, and her breath stuttered and hitched. My heart damn near broke for her and I sighed. I didn't think there was a fucking thing I could do to make this one better.

"It's just a job, Angel, and I know it seems like the end of the world right now, but we'll figure it out. Okay? One day at a time. So tomorrow, when you get out of school, you and me will get online and start looking and putting in applications. Okay?"

A hand fell on my shoulder and I turned, Everett smiled at me and gently took the phone out of my hand.

"Maren, honey? It's Evy," she said evenly. "Hi, yeah I was shamelessly eavesdropping, and I want you to calm down, because if you want it, Mandy and I have a job for you at *Soul Fuel* any time you're available." She paused, and it was a long one while Maren spoke.

"Yeah, we own it. You didn't know?" Everett laughed a little and said, "It's fine, we get your situation and ten or even twenty minutes late isn't that big of a deal. As long as you're pretty good about not missing days entirely and can make up coming in late by staying later or coming in early the next day, we can totally work with that."

I looked past Everett to the rest of the club and the smiles and looks of patience on everyone's faces. Dray and Rev had mixed looks of love and pride on their faces for their women and I have to admit, it was a sentiment I shared by like a lot right now.

Maren and Sage were sort of semi-fixtures around here lately. Sage had even made a friend in Reaver's son, Connor, as they were only a couple of years apart. They would sometimes come over here for movies on the big screen and the occasional club Sunday dinner, and it hadn't taken too long for most of the club to see what I saw in Maren. Not everyone had come around, though.

Everett's voice drew me back to the conversation. "Can you come by tomorrow after school? We can have you fill out an application and the rest of the paperwork, maybe talk about it some more?"

I mouthed 'thank you' at Everett and she waved me off like it was nothing when actually, this was pretty fucking huge.

"Okay, four o'clock sounds good. Just remember, when one door closes another one opens, okay?" She listened some more and smiled. "Okay, I'm going to hand you back over to your man."

She handed me the phone and I pressed it back to my ear. "Well I didn't expect that," I said, "but there you have it."

Maren sniffed on the other end of the line, my heart went out to her; she was absolutely right, she just couldn't seem to catch a break lately, at least until just now with Evy. I felt my shoulders drop. Even though we agreed that we couldn't really viably pull off seeing each other between our work schedules tonight, she'd had it rough and all I really wanted to do was hold her.

"Want me to come over?" I asked.

"Yes," she said miserably, and it was all I needed.

"I'll bring ice cream," I said, and I heard the smile in her voice when she said, "You know me so well."

I laughed a little and told her I'd see her soon and hung up. It was getting harder, the closer we got to her birthday, to maintain control, and I swore up and down to keep it in my pants tonight. I stepped back into the common room of the club to a bunch of expectant looks.

"See you later, bro," my twin said and waved. He didn't even take his eyes off his poker hand.

I rolled my eyes and told him, "If it were your woman, you'd do the same thing."

"You ain't lyin'," he said, and half his mouth went up in a sardonic smile, but then he ruined it by adding, "'Cept she ain't a woman; she's a little girl. Don't end up in prison, asshole." I knew Rush was a little on the lonely side. He didn't do club sluts as a general rule, and even though the two we had left were lookers, Cherry was a fucking cunt, and Moira was all but spoken for. She wasn't really interested in anybody but Lucky and Lucky wasn't really interested in anyone but her.

Still, where Lucky and Moira were concerned? The dude was dense as fuck and wouldn't make 'em official which was total bullshit. I always thought Moira deserved better than that. It was a weird dynamic, those two. Of course, who was I to judge? Like Rush pointed out, I was the thirty-six-year-old perv with a seventeen-year-old girl. Even if she didn't feel seventeen in my head, or even when I was with her, it was still there. She was above the age of consent, sure, but I was smack in the middle of the fucking Bible belt. Consent would be inconsequential to a bunch of these motherfuckers out here. Just sayin'.

I'd be lying if I said it didn't bother me sometimes, or if I said it never occurred to me, Maren's age. Sometimes it didn't, but then, sometimes, like tonight, when she freaked out so heartily over the loss of her fuckin' minimum wage job at the fuckin' corporate ninth circle of hell, well… then I was reminded and reminded hard that she was still brand fuckin' new to this life shit. She should probably still be writing in her diary about her latest crush and not being a parent to her snot-nosed little brother or worrying about how she's going to pay the fuckin' electric bill. *Or hooking herself up to a dude old enough to be her father. Right, you damn prick?*

I shoved the voice of self-deprecation away and instead thought to myself how her situation was so damn tragic. All I wanted to do was fix it, but it wasn't my job to fix it for her all the time. That's how we landed in this mess with a bunch of millennial fuckin' whack-job kiddies in the first place. Mommy and Daddy doin' everything for them and not letting them do for themselves.

That wasn't my goal as Maren's boyfriend. My goal was to be there when she fell to help her back up, sure, but she had plenty of this shit to do on her own. I could encourage, I could love her, but I couldn't do it for her, as much as I wanted to. The girl had just plain been through enough and she couldn't do it all by herself. Assists were needed.

"Hey, Nox."

I turned around and lifted my chin. "What's up?"

Dragon, who I'd last seen in the club's barroom, didn't say anything right away, but finally, he came out with, "Be careful, it's icy."

"Yeah, sure, P, no problem."

That was weird, I thought to myself, as I shrugged into my jacket and cut, and picked up my helmet off the edge of my dresser. Dragon had come all the way back here to my room in the outbuilding, just to tell me to be careful? I mean he was a good dude and an even better president, but he'd never done that before.

I didn't know if it was more of a silent comment or judgment on myself and Maren, the age difference, or what. For the most part, I could ignore the looks of concern, but every once in a while, like with what just happened now, my brothers made it hard to ignore. I found my president smoking a cigarette under the eaves of the main club building, outside its back door. I set my helmet aside on one of the picnic tables and leaned a shoulder against one of the posts supporting the little slant of the roof to keep the weather off the back stoop.

"Got something you wanna say, D?" The conversation had taken a turn I didn't like, to be sure. I dropped the honorific of 'P' and went with 'D' instead. It was bordering on disrespect but wasn't quite over the line. I needed the outlet, though, and I think my president could sense that because he didn't call me on my bullshit.

Instead, he sighed, and blew smoke into the night. "She's a looker, Nox. Ain't no one denyin' that, but yer playin' with fire an' it's more 'n just a lil bit here, isn't it? Just be careful, right?"

"Just a few more weeks," I muttered.

"Ain't gonna change us worryin' about you none. Not 'til the statute of limitations runs out. You know how it goes."

"Not really sure I take your meaning, D. You tryin' to say I'm breaking club guidelines on the jailbait clause? 'Cause I ain't. I know our by-laws just as ready as the next dude and it's fuckin' bullshit the way everyone walks around here with accusations in their eyes of shit that ain't happening."

"No one is sayin' you're breakin' club doctrine –"

"Really? Because it sure as fuck sounds like that's exactly what's goin' on here. Not only from you but from my own fuckin' twin. I would never, I have never. Maren and me, we've kissed a couple of times, but that's it, D. Not that I really have to fuckin' explain myself to any of you on that." I shook my head. "Jesus Christ, I'm getting tired of the side-eyed looks around here."

"Can you blame us for being worried?" he asked simply and took another drag. I sighed out harshly and raked a hand back through my hair.

"I can't," I said. "Still would be nice to feel like y'all had a little more faith in me than what you do, though."

Dragon chuckled. "Is that what you think? That we ain't got any faith in you?" I stared my president down and he shook his head ruefully and said, "Nox, if we didn't, we wouldn't be keeping our mouths shut."

I arched an eyebrow and asked, "And this is what this is? Keeping your mouth shut?" Dragon gave me a flat look, bordering on unfriendly, but not quite there yet.

"You're really done in by this girl, eh?"

"She's mine," I stated flatly.

"Ever done that before? Declared someone your property?"

"Nope, always hoped someone would come along, but no one did, not until Maren. I'd lay down my life for her without a second thought."

"That's what we're worried about, Nox. Might not be her that asks it of you, you see what I'm sayin'? There are other ways to give up your life other than just dyin'. You know that, though, don't ya?"

"Yeah, I know. Blue almost did it, and Cell, for this club."

"Yeah, yeah they did. You're straight telling me she's worth risking it all?"

"D, if she weren't worth risking everything for, we wouldn't be having this conversation," I said tiredly. "Now if you don't mind, Maren is out there, she's scared, she's tired of being run through the mill, and she needs me right now. I know her, she wouldn't ask if she really didn't need me. She's made of some pretty tough stuff.

You should try and get to know her a little bit more past the fresh face."

Dragon looked thoughtful. "I reckon I should."

I let that be it between us and swept up my helmet. I got on my bike and made one quick stop on the way to my girl's; the woman who made me laugh, who made me feel lighter when the shit got heavy at work or around the club. I just about always found that I couldn't wait to see her and when we parted? I almost started missing her before she was even out of sight.

When she opened the door, I looked up and damn near had a heart attack. I hadn't expected her to be in that black satin number that made my cock jump on sight. Usually, she had on some leggings or something. I gave up holding up the damn paper bag with her favorite ice cream in it and settled for crossing the threshold and kicking the door shut behind me.

I dropped the bag and pulled her into me, Dragon's questions still scalding my mind, adding to the heat that was rising in my fuckin' jeans. I covered Maren's mouth with mine and folded her tightly in my arms where she went limp with relief. I held her to me, hands smoothing over all that satin, craving the feel of her warm, supple skin beneath – *but dammit I have to wait.*

That didn't stop me from kissing her like it would be our last, and it didn't stop my body from going through the motions either. My hands found her ass, then the backs of her thighs, and I lifted her. Her lithe, long legs going around my hips as I made strides over to the couch, laying her down, my body grinding against hers, my dick aching something fierce, her hands at the back of my neck pulling my mouth tightly against hers as our tongues danced and intertwined.

Fuck, I was gonna go. I was gonna come in my fucking pants like *I* was the teenager and right that second, I was like, *fuck it, I wanna.*

I wanna, and I wanna make her come too, but I couldn't, because as much as I loathed the little fucking reminder, Dragon's words were still chasing around in my head. I couldn't stop myself, though; I ground against her and ran my hand along the outside of her thigh, pushing the satin material out of my way, fingers smoothing along the silk of her skin and *fuck* I was dying. This waiting was poison, and Maren? Maren was my antidote; my only chance for survival.

"We have to stop," she uttered, her voice strained, and it was like a bucket of ice water. I stood up and retrieved the ice cream off the floor, making strides in the direction of the kitchen while she tugged the long skirt of her nightgown down over her sopping panties. God, that sight made it so hard to keep walking, but I had to. We needed a minute and we needed some distance or neither one of us was going to stop and that wasn't right, at least not by society's thinking.

Goddamnit, this was so fucking complicated, and it didn't need to be. Why couldn't people just mind their own fucking business?

"Are you mad?" she asked as I dished up two bowls of melting pralines and cream ice cream.

I looked up, and over at my beautiful woman and shook my head. She stood, hugging herself, having quickly added her bulky coat over herself, in an attempt to cover. I laughed a little.

"That coat isn't going to save you, you know. You could be wearing a burlap sack and it would probably bring on the same reaction."

She slipped up onto one of the counter stools and blushed furiously, crossing her arms and leaning forward on them to watch me with utter fascination as I finished splitting up the pint of ice cream between the two bowls.

She made me feel both powerful and sexy when she watched me like that. I didn't think it would ever get old, either. I was pretty sure it would break my fucking heart if she ever decided she was bored with me or that I was too old for her, but those were troubles I didn't want to borrow for now; not when we had so many heaped in front of us.

I slid her bowl over to her with a spoon and leaned over the counter to eat mine, keeping the expanse of whatever stone it was between us. She edged her hand out and I covered it with my own to reassure her. She'd been through so much, and we'd discovered that the bullying had had its effects; not being able to fully trust social cues being one of them. Made me wish I'd nipped that in the bud a lot sooner and made me less regretful over how it'd been handled.

"I'm not mad, Angel. I'm just frustrated, like you."

Silence pressed between us and she put a spoonful of ice cream in her mouth. She sucked on it, and it drove me fucking wild, but I held my place across the counter. Finally, she spoke, her voice solemn and a little sad, "Happy Valentine's Day."

I sighed, and nodded. "Happy Valentine's Day."

22

M aren...

I didn't think things could get worse after yesterday. I was even beginning to get my hopes up about this job interview, but now, it felt like everything was crashing down, the timbers burning, and I was utterly crushed under the weight and the rubble.

I kept listening to the phone ring as I stared through the gently falling snow at *Soul Fuel's* front door. *So close, yet so far away.*

"Yes, hi! I know that Nox, I mean Landon, is probably in with a client but it's an emergency and I really need to speak with him." I waited and stared blankly at the Ol' Ladies of The Sacred Hearts MC laughing at the counter inside, praying they wouldn't look out the window, desperate that they wouldn't see me. Not just yet.

"Maren, what's wrong?" Nox asked through the phone line and despite how hard I tried not to cry, an errant tear snuck free.

"I just got a call from Three Tree Hospital, it's an hour and a half north from here. They have Sage. I guess he left school and somehow caught a bus up there and I have this stupid interview and the school never called me, and I need this job and I don't know what to do!"

Dammit! I'd meant to hold it together, I'd meant to keep my cool and be an adult, like the adultiest adult, and here I was, crying and begging Nox for yet another fix, but honestly I was at the end of my rope and I just wanted someone, *anyone*, to tell me what to do because I just didn't know with this.

"Okay, slow down, take a deep breath," Nox murmured, and he breathed with me over the phone until I was calmer.

"Interviews don't take long, so pull it together, go in there and do what you need to do. Sage is at a hospital, baby. Nothing is going to happen to him there. I'm going to come get you and we'll go get him together, okay?"

"Okay," I said and it was a plan, it was a good plan.

"Why did he even go up there in the first place?" Nox asked, confused.

"Because our mother is there," I said miserably.

Silence on the other end of the line for several heartbeats before he said, "Okay, you know what? Doesn't matter, go in there and crush it, I'll come pick you up and we'll talk about it on the way."

"Are they going to take him away from me for this?" I asked, heartbroken.

"I don't know, but I can tell you one thing, we're going to rain some fucking fire down on that school of his."

"Yes, we are," I said, some of that fire raining down on me, finally catching in the center of my soul.

"Go to it, baby girl. You don't want to be late. Freshen up that makeup or whatever and I'll be right there."

"Okay."

"I love you," he said, and my center melted just a little in a good way.

"I love you, too, Nox."

We disconnected, and I sucked in a deep breath. He was right, I could do this. I fixed my face in the rearview mirror and squared my shoulders. A few deep breaths and I got out of the car.

Everett straightened up behind the counter and Mandy backed out of the kitchen with a cake balanced on one of those round trays with a pedestal. She smiled at me and tried to blow a stray red curl off her forehead.

"Could you get the case, Evy?" she asked, and Everett was already moving to slide it open. I went up to the opposite side and looked in from the front. Mandy set the cake down, but it wasn't showing right.

"Twist it a little that way," I said pointing the direction and Mandy smiled up at me and gave the little tray a twist. "Perfect."

I smiled and Everett and Mandy smiled back. I shifted a bit nervously and they both came around the counter.

"Right, glad you're here and that you could make it. We know how tough things are with Sage right now." Mandy was wiping her hands on her apron as she spoke.

Everett asked, "What will you have?"

I blinked and wondered if they knew for a second, but dismissed the idea pretty quickly answering, "Um, a caramel toffee mocha?"

"Coming right up," she said and went to the coffee bar to do her thing. That left just me and Mandy.

"Question for you," she said looking me over thoughtfully. I tried to smile despite my nervousness and nodded, waiting for her to ask. I mean, this was an interview after all. Finally, she leaned back in her seat, and asked, "Have you thought about what you want to do once you're out of school?"

I blinked and shook my head. "I honestly haven't thought that far ahead. I mean, I will still have Sage and there's no money for college. I'll need to work full time, I suppose." It rattled me that I hadn't thought about any of this in any kind of depth and that my senior year was almost through.

Mandy smiled gently. "Any interest in cooking?" she asked.

"I love to cook, I mean… why?"

Everett came back and handed me a paper cup with a lid, I smiled and said, "Thank you," but was really confused by this turn of events and line of questioning. Mandy smiled at me and patted my knee reassuringly.

"What Mandy is trying to say is that we have had absolute shit luck with finding anyone to help her with the chocolatier side of the business. No one that's come up has had any kind of discipline or wants to deal with the early or late hours. We feel like it might fit your schedule better, what with Sage. A few hours before school, a few hours after."

"Wouldn't I need to go to culinary school for this, I mean, after I graduate?"

"If you wanted to," Mandy said with a shrug. "If you like it enough; I guess it could be an option, but I didn't. I learned from my grandmother and I have a degree in business – not culinary arts. I figured I would teach you the same way I was taught," she said with a charmed little smile. "With love and patience."

I sat back and took a drink of my coffee, looking from one to the both of them. "You're serious," I said startled.

"I need the help with a toddler and a four-month-old at home," Mandy said slightly embarrassed, although I don't know why she would be.

"With the location here, and the location down in Florida, Mandy can't keep up production on her own. She needs help, you need a flexible job. You could even do some of the work from your own kitchen at home when it comes to the chocolates. We really need the help. The way I see it, we'd be helping each other out."

"Uh, yeah!" I said, taking in the challenge in front of me. I could do this. I certainly could give it my absolute best try.

"Is that a yeah as in you'll do it?"

"I mean, I have no idea what I'm doing, but I'll try, I'll do my very best."

Mandy looked excited, and Everett looked relieved. "Let's fill out some paperwork," Everett said and got up to go in back.

"You're sure I can do this?" I asked Mandy.

"I think you can do anything you put your mind to, Maren. You've done it so far, and I can see a lot of why Nox is so head over heels for you."

"He is?" I asked hesitantly.

Mandy smiled and nodded. "Over the moon and willing to fight anyone who disagrees, you know, with the age difference."

I blushed furiously and whispered, "Nothing's happened yet."

Mandy sighed. "I know waiting has to be hard, but it really is for the best."

"I know," I murmured.

Everett returned with the new employee papers in a manila folder just as Nox came through the door.

"Here," she said. "Take these with you and fill them out, bring me copies of these," she said pointing to a list of documents written on a post-it, "and bring it back to me as soon as you can."

"Tomorrow," I said standing up. Both of the women hugged me.

"Tomorrow would be great," Mandy said.

"Thank you both so much!"

"Absolutely, now go get your brother," Everett winked, and I blushed furiously.

"C'mon, Angel. I'll drive, and we can talk." Nox threw an arm around my shoulders and it was like instant comfort.

"Okay," I agreed and dreaded the conversation and the road ahead... although this time, for the first time in a while, it felt like I was finally on the right street. I clutched the new employee paperwork in my hands like a talisman and followed my boyfriend out into the snow.

23

N ox...

She was silent for the first ten minutes of the ride. I took us onto the freeway headed north and waited her out, rubbing the top of her thigh, massaging the muscle and wishing I could get my hands on to her shoulders to ease out the major tension riding them. Finally, when she spoke, it was in a quiet tone, almost full of defeat.

"It's a mental hospital. My mother was committed when I was seven and Sage was around one."

"What for?" I asked when she'd fallen silent again for a little too long. I kept my tone even, gentle, and most importantly, non-judgmental.

"She tried to drown him; I was there and called the police. She had post-partum depression and I guess it was really bad and led to a psychotic break and she tried to drown my little brother. She was committed for being a danger to herself or others – the 'others' in her case being her own children. My dad suddenly became a single parent, and for whatever reason, my mom just got worse instead of better. Sage doesn't know why she was committed, just that she's really sick and that we've been waiting for her to get better."

"I take it there's no getting better?" I asked softly.

Maren shook her head. "She won't take her medication, and when she does, and she gets better, it never lasts. It's really bad, Nox, and I don't know why, but after dad died, Sage got it into his head that she would try harder, and that she would come home."

"Ah." It was the best I could say. I mean, I got it to a certain extent. Rush and I languished in foster care because of our mother's drug addiction and unwillingness to kick her habit. Hell, at this point, she was probably dead. Not that Rush or I would ever know. We just took it for granted that she was. This was a bit different, though, more tragic somehow. I mean, shit, mental illness wasn't a habit you could kick, it was your own mind and body chemistry attacking you daily… and for it to be bad enough to try and kill your own kid?

"I understand why you didn't want to tell me," I said quietly when she'd been silently staring out the window for too long, "but it doesn't change the way I feel about you any."

"Doesn't it?" she asked. "I mean, things like this can be hereditary. I could have the same crazy lurking in the back of my brain waiting for the trigger to set it loose."

I chuckled lightly and said, "Angel, you forget you're your father's daughter too. Seems to me you take after him more than you do your mom. I somehow think you're gonna be okay."

"That's the problem, though, Nox. We just don't know, now do we?" she said solemnly, and I sighed.

"Doesn't matter," I said.

"It does, and that's why I've decided I'm never having kids. I don't want to go crazy, or pass this down or –"

"Seems legit," I said interrupting her with a shrug.

She turned to stare at me and I could see the wheels turning, as she was silently judging whether I was making fun of her or not. I wasn't. I'd never really banked on having kids of my own. I'd even contemplated a vasectomy in recent years to ensure I didn't have any mistakes with a random club girl or hookup. I was thirty-six. I didn't know if I could handle being a dad at forty-two like Archer, even if Noah was Grind's and not his… he'd taken on the responsibility and that was Archer for you.

Of course, I'd sort of done the same thing with Sage. Maren settled back in her seat and kept watching me. I squeezed the top of her thigh and let her gather my hand between hers, curling my fingers around it and aching to touch more of her, to comfort her better. Kind of hard when I was driving, though.

"There's a lot to all of this, baby, and we can talk about it all when the dust is settled." I raised her hand to my lips and kissed the back of it. "I ain't scared of nothing that's happened, I ain't scared of what hasn't happened yet, and I ain't going nowhere on ya either, so relax; okay?"

"One disaster at a time?" she asked, sardonically.

"Pretty much," I agreed, nodding.

She sighed heavily and resumed her sightless staring out the passenger-side window, the gears clearly turning in her head.

"What am I going to do about Sage?" she asked quietly.

"You mean 'what are we' going to do about your brother? I told you, I'm in this with you, Angel, and I'm not going anywhere."

She stared at me, her expression softening at my words and it was beautiful. The kind of beautiful that made me want to love her until the end of time. Seriously heavy shit that I wouldn't trade for anything.

"Right, what are *we* going to do about Sage?"

"The only thing we can do, really. Talk to him, for one; find out what the hell he was thinking."

"And then?" she breathed out, and her face was so solemn like she was staring at a mountain that she'd just been told she needed to climb.

"Then we go from there, figure things out; maybe we get a hold of Pam and see about scaring him straight if nothing else works; but baby, there's no way this ends where he doesn't learn the truth about your mom and what she did."

Maren hung her head and nodded in defeat.

"You aren't protecting him, not from this... you can't," I said gently.

"I know," she murmured, and I could swear it was accompanied by the pop and shatter of her heart breaking. I squeezed her hand and raised it to my lips placing a reverent kiss along its back, breathing in the earthy, herbal lavender scent that was purely Maren.

"It's going to be okay, Angel," I promised her. "It's going to be tough, but okay."

"I know, I just wish it were just tough on me. You know?" I smiled to myself a little. I did know, to a certain extent. Melody was like that with Noah, and pregnant with another now. Since Archer'd married her, he'd gotten to be a lot the same way. It was called being a parent, and Maren just seemed to have the gene. I liked it about her, her nurturing side, but I didn't dare bring it up; not now. Not after the revelation she'd just made and her stated decision about having kids.

Honestly, I didn't blame her much for making such a hardcore decision at seventeen. I mean, she'd probably been raising Sage for a while now, with her dad being so sick, and she'd be raising him for the next seven years or more. If she was still staunchly against children in the next couple of years, I'd be okay with getting snipped. That is if she hadn't outgrown me by then.

Why the hell did that thought make my stomach damn near drop out? I wondered but didn't have to for long because the answer swam right up out of the depths of my brain — *Because you really do love her, probably more than you've ever loved anyone but your brothers.*

It was a sobering thought. I hadn't meant to or realized that I'd even given that big of a chunk of my heart away, but clearly, I had and now it was gone, resting in Maren's hands. It was deep, like bottom of the ocean kind of deep level shit, and I shoved it heartily to the back of my brain for right now in an attempt to focus on the problem at hand; which was how the fuck we were going to salvage the rest of Maren's tiny broken family without it breaking some more?

We drove into the deepening gloom of sunset, and on into the dark. I followed the directions that my GPS spewed at me and held Maren's hand tightly in mine the whole way; her hurt, her fear, a palpable thing, setting me on edge. This wasn't a bully I could knock down a few pegs. This wasn't a fight I could take on and win, this was something else. Something undefinable and I hated that. I hated that a whole lot.

We made a game plan on how to best handle the situation with her brother and I took the reins for the most part. Maren was afraid she would get angry, or yell and she didn't want to drive a wedge any further between her and her little brother. The resentment he seemed to be harboring over his big sister suddenly becoming the parent was a palpable thing, and she was afraid if she came on too strong, that she'd lose him forever. It was a pretty valid fear, even if it wasn't as gloom and doom as all that. Still, pushing him further away wasn't what anyone wanted.

The hospital looked like something out of an American Gothic flick and was probably one of the oldest buildings I'd seen since moving around these parts. It looked like something out of a movie, the creepy old mental institution and I caught Maren looking at me as I looked at it. I hadn't realized I'd stopped the car to take it all in. I looked over at her and she blushed, but instead of cute or alluring, this one screamed 'shame' at me. I took my hand off the wheel and wrapped it around the back of her head, pulling her to me.

I kissed her, long and lingering deep, and hoped that if it didn't soothe her anxiety about my judging, that it would, at the very least, serve as some sort of distraction from it. She melted into me and returned it; the relief rolling off of her something else. Tangible, wrapping around me like a vapor, like something I could breathe right in like her delicate perfume.

I pulled back from her and stared into her eyes, satisfied when I found that she didn't look so far left from center. She was still worried, still a touch distraught, but who wouldn't be if their eleven-year-old brother took off from school? Disappeared for hours without your knowledge, only to find out about it when the freaking mental joint your mom was locked up in called to tell you he was there.

Yeah, one disaster, one hot mess, at a time. First, to get her brother and break the news that his mom wasn't going to get better. That life wasn't always a fairytale, and Santa Claus wasn't real. It wasn't in my nature to wreck kids, to dose 'em up with hard truths and watch them crumble. This was gonna suck for me, and for Maren even though it didn't hold a candle to what Sage was about to go through.

I parked the cage and got out, Maren slipping out into the gently falling snow, sparkling bits catching in her dark hair, the halo of light behind her making her look more like one of the solemn angel statues you'd find in a cemetery. A work of art, soul moving, but still so fuckin' sad. She was my angel, and I took a split second in my head to thank whatever fuckin' power that was bigger than us for putting me in her path, or her in mine, the day her daddy had died.

I held out my hand and she took it without hesitation as we walked up the broad, low-slung steps to the lighted glass front doors to the lobby of this place. She held my hand tightly as we dodged icy patches, my boots gritting against the salt that was meant to keep the steps from freezing but seemed like an exercise in futility.

The door opened and a man in suit pants, shirt, and a tie held it for us. We slipped past him into the linoleum entryway and he shut and locked the door behind us.

"Maren Tracy?" he asked.

"Yes, I'm her," she said holding out her hand.

The man shook it and introduced himself, "I'm Marek Greene and I'm the assistant director of the hospital."

"Nice to meet you," Maren murmured. "I'm sorry it isn't under better circumstances."

Marek nodded and shook my hand, I gave a nod and waited for him to ask, but the question never came. Instead, he looked back to Maren and said, "We've kept your brother here, away from any of the patients and especially his mother. Am I safe to speak freely in front of your... companion?" he asked.

"All of the paperwork is in order, right? I am technically my mother's guardian now that my dad has passed?"

"Yes, of course. Your mother is incapable of making sound decisions and is, technically, under your guardianship."

"It's safe to talk in front of him, Dr. Greene."

"Landon, Landon Fisher," I said sticking my hand out and shaking his once again. "I am fully aware of HIPPA and all the rules. I've run my own massage therapy practice before and am currently licensed and working."

"I see, well, we haven't allowed your brother to see your mother, she hasn't been taking her medication you see, and –"

Maren held up her hand gently. "I know the routine, she's been this way for a long, long time now."

"Yes, well, your brother seems to be fairly in the dark on the subject. You understand, his coming up here, alone like he did, we called you right away being that you are listed as his legal guardian as well."

"Yes, I understand."

"The school didn't notify you?" he asked.

"No," I said, and it came out a bit more sharply than I intended. "We'll be taking that up with them in the morning along with the state caseworker."

"Good plan," Dr. Greene said pointedly.

"Where is Sage right now?" Maren asked.

"My office, right this way." He led us down a corridor and had to unlock at least three doors with one of those fancy badges against the black box, then unlock a further two with a ring of keys. When he opened the door to the office, Sage looked up. I was the first one through after Dr. Greene and the kid all but blanched, looking around me for his sister.

"She's here, don't think it's gonna save you from some serious consequences, though."

Maren darted around me and half kneeled, half took a seat in the empty chair beside Sage's, pulling him into her arms and demanding, "What were you thinking!?".

Sage tried looking at me defiantly over his sister's shoulder and failed, his thin veneer of pre-teenage badass cracking as his own eyes welled and he blurted out, "It's not fair! She should try harder and come home so you don't have to do anything. They won't tell me anything or let me see her! I want to ask her why she won't get better, Maren! I wanna know why she left us!"

Dr. Greene and I made eye contact and he gave a nod, slipping back out the door in a bid to respect our privacy and give us some space. Once the door was firmly shut, I leaned back against it. I both was and wasn't a part of this tiny dysfunctional family at this point. Not until Maren indoctrinated me in fully. Not until she looked at me point blank and told me that she wanted me to intervene. Right now, even though it'd been a few months we'd been around each other and together, we were still on a case-by-case basis where Sage was concerned.

I tuned back in, dragging myself back out of the inside of my own head to hear what Maren was saying. "Sage, that's not your decision to make! Like it or not, I'm the adult and you're the child, and as the adult, I'm telling you right now, Mom is sicker than dad and I ever told you in a bid to protect you. She's not safe for either one of us to be around. You have to trust me on this. You have to know I wouldn't keep her away, or you from visiting, if I didn't think it was best!"

Sage pushed back from Maren and understandably demanded to know why. I let them go at it, they didn't need a referee just yet. Maren was crying and upset, but as calm as she could be given the situation. She was holding her own, and Sage? Sage just kept right on pushing.

Finally, I interjected, "Sage, I'm going to give you a very important piece of unsolicited advice, buddy." The fact I wasn't yelling, or screaming, that my voice was as calm and even as I could make it, got the little man's attention. He shut his mouth and looked at me and I imparted my wisdom, "Don't ask questions, or demand answers to questions when someone is reluctant to give them like your sister is now. Sometimes the truth is way more painful than you could expect. You need to think really long and hard on if you really want to know the truth here.

"I wanna know!" Sage said petulantly, and Maren's stricken and defeated face over his shoulder made my heart sink under the weight of the same defeat.

"Tell him," I said. "Pretty sure at this point it's the only thing that's going to work, Angel."

Maren pressed her lips together and nodded. "Could you ask Dr. Greene to bring me my mother's file?" she asked.

I nodded and slipped out into the hall to fulfill her request. It was smart. She could tell Sage, but he'd probably have a tough time believing whatever came out of her mouth now that he knew she and her dad had been lying for so long about how sick their mom was. Reading it in black and white though? A lot harder to refute.

I waited in the hall with the good doctor while Maren broke it to her brother. I didn't need to be in there for that. No telling if Sage would resent my presence or not. It gutted me leaving it all to Maren though. It was something that I solemnly vowed I would find a way to make up to her, but this went way beyond flowers or her favorite ice cream.

When the office door opened, both of their faces were tear-stained, eyes puffy and red from crying. Maren was just behind Sage, her hands on his shoulders like she was afraid he was gonna bolt or something. She addressed the good doctor, first.

"Thank you for calling me, and I am so very sorry for any inconvenience that was caused," she told him and gave Sage a little shake back and forth by his shoulders.

"Sorry," Sage muttered in the doctor's direction.

"I understand," Dr. Greene said, and went a touch further by saying, "If I may?" Maren nodded her consent to whatever unsolicited piece of advice Dr. Greene was about to impart on us all. "I know an excellent child therapist, perhaps a visit or two is in order for Sage here. Someone to talk to who is impartial to all the things going on in your lives?"

Maren nodded. "I think I would like his number," she murmured, and Sage made a sound like he was going to protest, a sound that was quickly quelled by the withering look I gave him. He shut up, Dr. Greene chuckled and pulled a business card and pen from the pocket of his slacks that were too brown to exactly be called gray.

"He's a she, but she's very good. Her name is Michelle Greene, and she's my wife." Maren smiled and took the card that the doctor hastily scribbled on with a quiet, "Thank you." "My pleasure," Dr. Greene said, and led us back through the labyrinth of locking doors to the hospital lobby.

"Wait, you aren't even going to try and see her?" Sage asked outraged and Maren's fingers tightened.

"I don't want to, Sage."

"But she's our mom!" he cried, incensed.

"Doesn't matter, buddy," I said, coming to the rescue, finally able to drop some wisdom into the mix. "If I had a choice of seeing my mom, I wouldn't either. Some things you don't come back from. What your mom did, that's one of 'em."

"I don't get it," Sage said.

"I love you more than I could ever love a mother who tried to drown her own child, Sage. She tried to kill you, and I know you don't get it, I know it doesn't make sense, but I was there. You were too young to remember... I wish I could be so lucky," Maren said, fresh tears tracking down her face.

Sage peered up at her from over his shoulder and I said gently, "This is one of those things you have to let go, kiddo. Even if you don't want to. Pretty sure you've done enough damage for one day. It's time to go home."

"Don't think there won't be any consequences for this stunt, either," Maren said, and I was proud of her for sticking to her guns. "We'll talk about it in the car that you and Nox need to get into... now," she said sharply when it looked like Sage was about to protest again.

"Thanks, Doc," I said with a quick salute, and put a hand on Sage's shoulder, leading him to the car while Maren stayed behind to talk to the doctor for a minute longer. Knowing her, to apologize some more.

Sage tried to jerk his shoulder out of my grip which only caused me to tighten it. I was a massage therapist, I knew the pressure points and was pretty unmatched when it came to my grip. Sage found that out when I just kept on marching him like a prisoner over the frozen lot to my cage. I opened the back door, and ducked his head in, to make sure he didn't hit it.

"I can take care of myself!" he barked.

"Yeah, I call bullshit," I said and shut the door on his retort.

Maren shook the doctor's hand and came toward us. I hugged her briefly and walked her to her side of the cage and opened her door for her. She didn't waste any time. "You are so grounded," she said. "In fact, you are grounded harder than you have ever been grounded in your life," she grated as I closed the door for her.

I went around and got in on my side to hear Sage's indignant shriek, "But that's not fair!"

"Woah!" I cried. "You want to talk about fair, after the shit you pulled today? Okay," I nodded, starting the cage, "let's talk about fair for a minute. Do you think it was fair for Maren to get a phone call from Dr. Greene right before she went into her job interview telling her not only did her little brother leave school without telling anyone, he made a dangerous trek all the way here unsupervised where anything could have happened? Hell, a pedophile could have gotten you!"

Sage scoffed. "Oh please, a pedophile? That's the best you can come up with?"

I tightened my hands on the wheel and backed carefully out of the space. "Okay, forget your sister and how fair it was for her to panic and worry, how about Dr. Greene? How fair was it to stop everything he was doing so he could babysit your sorry ass and wait for us to come get you? How fair is it for me to waste money on gas, time and effort to come get you? Huh? Did you think about anybody but yourself and what you wanted? What did you expect people to do? You need to get it in your head, kid. The world does not revolve around you." My tone had become hard, and Maren covered my hand with hers.

"Nox," she said gently, and I looked at her. "Go easy." She completed her request with a pleading look and fuck if I could deny her anything when she looked at me like that.

"Seems to me, Angel, that's all we've been doing when it comes to his selfish ass. Goin' easy on him doesn't really seem to be working, maybe it's time for a new tactic," I said. I tried to say it gently, take the sting out of it, but the hurt look she gave me told me it hadn't been enough. She turned to stare sightlessly out the dark passenger window and I glanced in the rearview mirror.

Sage was leaned back in his seat, head tipped back and to the side, similarly staring out his window, the gears turning behind his eyes. He was thinking hard, and he needed to. I glanced at Maren and she turned, feeling my eyes on her. I tipped my head slightly and raised my eyebrows, a silent ask for permission. She pursed her lips and nodded slightly, giving me the green light.

"You're grounded, alright," I agreed. "No games. Either I or Maren, will pick you up from school. You'll either come to work with me or with her, where you will sit quietly and do your homework until one or the other of us can take you home and stay there to make sure you're where you're supposed to be. No phone, no friends, no TV. Your life is limited to school and reading, that's it."

"You can't tell me what to do, you're not my dad. My dad's dead,." Sage said, a challenge in his eyes.

"Sage Hunter Tracy!" Maren shouted, outrage and anger coloring her voice and finally, *finally*, he'd gone and done it. "You're right, he's not your dad but I'm the parent here. The best you're going to get unless you want to go into foster care, and what I say goes! Everything Nox laid down is more than reasonable and that's exactly what we're going to do, and on top of that? I'm going to see if I can't get you in with Mrs. Dr. Greene. I can't even with you anymore."

"I don't need a shrink!"

"I don't care what you think you need! I think you do and so you're going!"

"I'll call Pam," he threatened.

"Too late! I beat you to it and texted her already. She thinks it's a fine idea and is going to sign off on you seeing a child psychologist. Something needs to happen. I don't know what to do with you anymore. I don't even know who you are." She crossed her arms and kept her back straight when it was easy to see all she wanted to do was huddle in on herself. I was proud of her. She'd just laid down the line and I could see she was going to toe it.

Sage deflated in the back seat and we pretty much made the rest of the long drive in silence.

By the time I pulled into their driveway, Sage was sullen but seemed to come to grips with the fact he wasn't weaseling his way out of this one, and Maren? Maren was settled into a sleep of the truly mentally and emotionally exhausted.

"Sage, go open up the house," I ordered quietly.

He glared at me defiantly and I turned my look that'd like to melt blacktop on him. He, predictably, backed down and opened up the cage door. He hauled his backpack out with him and slammed the door. I winced, but Maren didn't as much as stir.

I undid my seat belt, then hers, and got out myself. I closed my door gently and opened up hers. She stirred when I lifted her. Eyes heavy-lidded with sleep, sucking in a sharp breath of icy air, her arms went around my neck, so she wouldn't fall.

"I've got you, Angel," I murmured and kicked her door shut, hitting the button on my keys to chirp the alarm.

I carried her in the front door to her place, the door that Sage left standing wide open. He was seriously grinding my gears and as soon as I lay Maren in her own bed, I had every intention of stripping Junior's room of anything and everything remotely entertaining.

I set Maren on her bed and lifted one leg, easing the zipper down on her boot, sliding it gently from her foot as she struggled tiredly into a sitting position. She peeled out of her coat and scarf as I repeated the process with her other boot. She was so tired, she just let her discarded outerwear fall to the floor at the side of her bed.

I set her other boot down, and sleepily, she reached for me. I leaned over her, laying her back, kissing her gently. Her arms went around me, fingers buried in my hair, holding my face to hers, locking me tight against her lithe body, and mine? Well, mine had an immediate response, going from zero to granite in point oh three seconds flat.

I held her back, one arm behind her back, cradling her head, the other hand on her side, just above her hip. She writhed beneath me, soft little whimpers escaping her and it damn near killed me. I wanted her, I wanted inside of her, but we had to wait. I knew that *she* knew that, which is why it surprised the hell out of me when she guided my hand that was riding in the safe zone over her soft girly tee, down the front of her skin-tight jeans. She dipped it below the lace hem of her panties and I about had a heart attack from the shock.

Maren was, nine times out of ten, the more responsible one when we edged too close to the line, and dammit, I had sort of come to rely on that. I think I'd used up every last bit of adulting on dealing with her brother tonight.

I groaned into her mouth when my fingers skirted over her damp curls, and I realized how much she wanted me, too.

"Please, Nox," she begged, voice breathy. "Make me feel good, just this once."

"Fallen Angel," I observed, but I didn't deny her, I kissed her and edged my fingers down, delving between her folds, blindly searching until her hips jerked. I smiled against her mouth and teased her clit gently, with soft little strokes of the pad of my middle finger; swirling gently, teasing little circles around the engorged nub of flesh until she gasped and panted. I built her up slowly, and pushed her over the edge, swallowing her light cry, crushing my mouth over hers, stifling her moans by tangling my tongue with hers as her pussy lightly throbbed against my hand.

Fuck, she was going to ruin me. I'm pretty sure I'd just committed at least one felony, and with how hard my dick was? I needed to get out of here before I committed more. I kissed her soundly and murmured against her lips, "I love you, Angel, but I need to leave now before I can't help myself."

She groaned and let her head fall back against the pillows, her chest heaving, as I slipped my damp fingers out of her waistband.

"Shit," she muttered and covered her face with her hands.

I laughed lightly, and murmured, "I'll see you tomorrow. Consider that a preview of coming attractions," and with that parting shot, I left her room, and went downstairs, and out the front door into the brisk, winter air. I found myself wishing I had the bike then, and as much as I shouldn't torture myself further I couldn't help it. I raised my fingers to my nose and breathed her delicate perfume in.

Goddamnit! That only made the pinch of my jeans even tighter.

24

M aren…

I opened my eyes and smiled for the first time that I could remember, in a long time… It was Sunday, but more importantly? *It was my birthday,* and it was a touch bittersweet. One, I was excited to be a year older because it took the limits off of me and Nox being together, but two… never had I ever simply wanted to remain a kid before.

I missed my dad, and I wished my mom were well enough to take care of us; because taking care of Sage, it was no walk in the park, although things were getting better. He'd been to see Mrs. Dr. Greene, who had graciously taken on Sage's case at something like a quarter of her usual rate, seeing as it was really all I could afford, even with Pam helping me with the state funding for it.

He'd been angry, but the anger had grown somewhat less, even though his tight restrictions remained in place. It was typical that I picked him up from school and that he went to work with me. He got to sit on a high stool in the corner of the kitchen doing homework. The only concession I'd given him, was the ability to listen to music through his phone which he was allowed to keep. Mostly because of the potential for an emergency and so that he could reach me or Nox if need be.

If Nox could, he would pick Sage up from *Soul Fuel* and take him with him so that I could work a little later. He and Sage started regular workouts at the local YMCA, sometimes joined by Reaver and his son Connor, along with Trigger, one of the club's officers. It made me glad, because it seemed to be something Sage was really enjoying and soon we developed and fell into an easy, new routine.

As for my job? I loved it. Mandy and Everett were fantastic bosses. Patient, kind, yet firm, in Everett's case. I could understand it, though. Everett was on the cusp of expanding their business on the coffee side of things into drive up kiosks that she'd decided to name *Sacred Grounds*. It was exciting and new and required that Mandy and I expand our baking skills outside the realm of chocolate a bit to provide breakfast muffins for the three stands Everett was putting into operations.

So far, we had decided on Blueberry and Triple Chocolate muffins as well as a seasonal one, like Apple Cinnamon or Pumpkin in the fall. Right now, with spring approaching, we were thinking about a lemon variety. Even Ashton had joined in the kitchen, forsaking her job at the tattoo shop and leaving it to an apprentice that the guys had taken on.

I got up, showered and dressed, and found Sage downstairs watching TV. Despite how much we needed the money, Everett and Mandy had insisted I take the day off and Nox said he had something special planned, which meant Sage was supposed to be ready for Reaver and Hayden to pick him up. It was supposed to be so that I could have a break and so that Sage could hang out with Reaver's son, Connor, who was only two years older.

"You should be dressed," I remarked, and he snorted.

"Can't wait to get rid of me?" he demanded. I was both hurt and sick of the attitude, so I did what Nox had suggested – I called him out on his bullshit.

"Well, when you've got that attitude, can you blame me?"

Sage stared at me and blinked, slowly. I raised my eyebrows at him, and he dragged himself to his feet.

"Not the way to earn back your privileges!" I called up the stairs to his retreating back.

"Whatever," he muttered, and I sighed under my breath and went to fix myself a cup of coffee. I guess I should have considered myself lucky that I'd gotten to sleep in.

"Hey, Maren?" I turned around just as the coffee gurgled its last to see Sage standing awkwardly in the kitchen entryway, guilt painting his expression sour. His hair was getting too long in front, the dark waves were flopping into his chocolate eyes. I needed to take him to get it cut.

"What's up?" I asked softly, going a little gooey at the wrapped box in his hands, a card in a light-yellow envelope perched on top.

"Happy Birthday," he said, coming up and setting the box on the counter next to me.

I didn't care what was inside. It really was the thought that counted, especially with everything we'd been going through... especially considering that it was my first birthday without my dad.

I pulled my little brother into a tight hug, and he asked, voice muffled by my shoulder, "Aren't you going to open it?"

"When did you even go find the time to buy it?" I asked, leaving off the real burning questions of *where did you get the money?*

"Nox took me, I didn't know what you'd want. You know, Dad always used to help me, but Nox knew... it was almost like having Dad back for a second. Anyway, he helped me pay for the rest of it. I used all my allowance I had left."

I felt my eyes mist and dragged him into another hug. He struggled and pushed me off. "Geez, just open it already!" he cried, and I laughed and used the sleeve of my cardigan to dab at the moisture in my eyes.

I took up the box and shook it next to my ear, just to drive Sage nuts. He rolled his eyes at me and I laughed, and set it down, working the tape on one of the end flaps of wrapping paper free.

"Oh, my God! You're killing me, Maren," he said shaking his head.

I tore into the paper and he raised his eyebrows at me. I stopped, and asked him with a sly grin, "I thought you wanted me to open it."

"You're *always* supposed to open the card first!" he blurted and I smiled. It was something my dad had always insisted upon. Open the card first, thank the person for it and *then* open the gift, never forgetting to say yet another thank you for the gift.

I picked up the card from the counter and slid a fingernail under the flap, cutting it loose with my finger. The card was pretty, lacy with purple flowers, butterflies, and a generous amount of crystalline glitter. It read, *'To my sister...'* on the front and when I opened it, the inside made my eyes mist again.

I know we don't always see eye to eye,

I know we don't always get along,

Still, I'm lucky to have you in my life,

You're the one who keeps me strong.

I closed the card, which had been a blank one inside until my brother had taken his pen to it and set it on the kitchen counter beside the unopened box of whatever he'd gotten me. Sage hugged me almost as tight as I hugged him, and I said, "I love you, even when you are a pain in the ass, you know that, right?"

Sage sniffed. "I know," he said, voice breaking, and it didn't have anything to do with his pitching headlong into puberty, either.

I let him go and he stepped back, dashing at the moisture in his eyes, while I carefully wiped at the tears collected in my own.

"My makeup good?" I asked and he nodded.

"Yeah."

"It's my birthday, and Reaver and Hayden are about to be here any minute to pick you up. I'm going to kill you if you're lying to me," I told him and punched his shoulder lightly. He twisted away from me and laughed.

"I'm serious! It's fine."

"Waterproof everything for the win, huh?"

"I guess," he said. "You going to open that?"

I laughed and pulled the box closer to me, tearing off the paper. It was bigger than the average shoe box. The lid taped down with Scotch tape. I worked my fingernail under the satiny tape and popped it free on all four sides and lifted the lid off, setting it aside. White tissue paper blocked my view and my curiosity mounted. I lifted some of it aside and found a pair of leather gloves. Sturdy, but that would mold to my hands, and definitely made for a woman.

I set them down and lifted the paper off the rest of the way and found a pair of sturdy riding boots. They looked like typical men's boots from the front and sides, with the exception that the laces to tighten them up were located at the back of the calf, reminiscent of corset lacing and adding a decidedly feminine flair.

I looked up at Sage and asked him, "How on Earth did you...?" I left the '*afford this*' silent and felt more than a little dirty for the question escaping my mouth. It was rude and ungrateful, but with the way Sage had been acting, I couldn't be sure that a theft hadn't happened.

"Used all my allowance, Nox made up the rest. I guess it's from both of us."

"You used all of your savings? On *me?*"

"You only turn eighteen once," he said with a shrug, and it was very grown up of him. I pulled him into a hug and sat down at the kitchen table to put on my new boots, laughing with him as we figured out straps, buckles, zippers, and laces, together.

Sage had even run upstairs to bring me down an extra pair of socks, saying that Nox had told him to make sure I wore two pairs until the boots were well broken in, to prevent blisters. I was glad it was still cold enough outside that wearing two pairs of socks wouldn't be any kind of a hardship.

The doorbell rang just as I stood up and Sage and I were admiring the fit of the boots over my dark, skin-tight jeans.

"I'll get it!" he cried and went to the front door. I followed him up the hall and when he opened it, it was to a smiling Reaver and Hayden.

"Hey! Ready to go?" Reaver asked.

"Yeah, let me just run upstairs and grab my backpack."

"Hi, Maren!" Hayden greeted me.

"Hey, where's Connor?" I asked looking around them and seeing empty air.

"On our way to get him, your place came before his mom's when it came to plotting a course," Reaver said.

"Ah, I see. You guys are absolutely sure this isn't any trouble?"

"Nah, no trouble at all. I think it'll be good for the both of them."

Sage came running down the stairs at full elephant tilt and hugged me quick.

"Bye, Maren!" he quipped and I smiled, both for him and the rumble of Nox's motorcycle as he pulled up to the curb. Reaver ruffled Sage's hair and rolled his eyes over my brother's head.

"Yeah, bye, Sis!" he said, and Hayden laughed as they both stepped off the porch and went for Hayden's SUV in the driveway.

"Try to have fun tonight!" she called over her shoulder and I waved.

"I'm sure I will!"

"Oh, you will," Nox promised, coming down the path through the yard, another longer and wider box tucked under his arm. He stopped in front of me and I turned my face up to his, smiling about to say something funny when his lips crashed into mine and he very nearly devoured me from the mouth down.

I made a surprised noise, my arms twining around his leather clad shoulders as I arched into his chest. The box was set aside on the railing, his arms curving around my back as he hauled my body up tight, fitted perfectly into the curve of his own while our mouths wrought magic.

"Get me out of here," I heard my brother exclaim, and just *hearing* his eyes roll in the tone of his voice made me laugh. Nox pulled back from the kiss and laughed with me.

"That's enough out of the peanut gallery," he said, then with a wave at Reaver called out, "See you later, bro!"

"Wouldn't miss it," Reaver declared and Hayden started her lumbering giant of a vehicle and backed smoothly up the drive.

I turned back to Nox and said softly, "Hi."

"Mm, Happy Birthday, Angel," he murmured and pressed a quick kiss to my lips before letting me go and taking a half step back, retrieving his box from the railing. "Let's go inside, baby. It's chilly out here."

"I'm warm," I said, and it came out a bit breathier than I'd intended.

Nox chuckled, and I turned to go in. He gave me a slap on the ass as I went through the door and I yelped, laughing.

"That's one," he said smiling.

"One what?" I asked.

"Birthday spanking."

My mouth dropped open and I felt my eyes go wide as I rolled them dramatically, declaring, "Oh God!"

"Nope, that comes later," he said.

"What comes later?"

"You, writhing underneath me, calling me god, comes much later, Angel," he said and his tone was so serious, taking on a darker, sexier tone that made my breath still, and my heart stutter to a stop completely.

"I like the sound of that," I said quietly, and he smiled, a deliciously dark and wicked smirk that made my insides turn to liquid.

"Where do you want to open your present?" he asked, and I gave him my wide-eyed innocent look.

"The bedroom, of course," I said letting my eyes roam every delicious inch of him. He brought the box in front of him and I smiled and said, "Oh, *that* present, the kitchen, I suppose. I'm still not quite caffeinated enough, how about you?"

"I could use a cup of coffee," he said smiling, adding, "Smartass," to the end of his casual declaration.

I turned and went down the hall singing out, "Better than being a dumbass," as I passed through the archway to the kitchen.

I set about making coffee while he leaned casually against the counter, box set next to the wreckage from Sage's gift. His light eyes were fixed on my boots as they traveled across the linoleum and I smiled to myself as I poured us each a cup from the coffeemaker and added the right amounts of cream and sugar.

"They look good, Angel. Sage picked 'em out all by himself, and I couldn't argue."

"Thank you for helping him," I murmured. "Was the card you, too?"

"What card?" he asked, and I smiled to myself and handed him his cup. Once my hand was free, I slid the card Sage had given me off the counter and handed it to Nox. I sipped my coffee carefully while he read it.

"He's a good kid," he said softly, and I nodded.

"He is when he wants to be, which thankfully, is much more often now."

"I think he's just lonely."

"I don't disagree. He only gets to see his friends in school and Ian's parents are still pressuring him to stay away from Sage and not talk to him. They're so worried about their precious little snowflake and about my brother being a bad influence that they don't have a single care for how any of it is affecting Sage at all."

"Preaching to the choir on that one, Angel."

I sighed. "I know, I just wish it would start to suck less for my brother. We've all been through enough right now."

"Mm-hmm," Nox agreed. "Which is why you need to open your gift."

I smiled wryly and set my coffee down, pulling the box closer to me across the kitchen counter. I stood next to Nox, who leaned back against the counter, light eyes fixed on my face as I popped the four small pieces of tape holding the lid on the garment box. He hadn't wrapped it, just left the pristine white box to speak for itself; I liked that somehow. It felt far more grown up than Sage's wrapping paper that screamed 'Happy Birthday' with balloons and confetti.

I lifted off the lid and picked up the card lying on top of the tissue paper. Again, just a simple white fold of paper, 'Maren' written on the front and inside — 'I love you.'

"I love you, too," I murmured and smiled at the little card. I lifted the tissue paper and discovered a beautiful, black leather jacket. It was beautifully accented with silver zippers, silver buckles at the hips, and zippers at the pockets. It was fitted, the zipper to hold it closed angled and rising up one side for an asymmetrical look that worked for it, adding both edge and class to the look. I pulled it from the box as if it were made of magic and held it up.

"Look at the back," Nox said quietly and I turned the garment around, gasping at what I found on the back of the coat. There, embossed perfectly into the leather, was a pair of narrow but perfect angel wings.

I stared at them for a long minute, admiring them, finding it difficult to tear my eyes away to look at Nox who was standing quietly, patiently waiting for me to say something.

"I think this is quite possibly one of the most beautiful things I've ever been given," I said.

He smiled and reached out, lowering the zipper on the front of the coat until it opened up. He took it from me and held it out so I could turn around and slip it on.

"It's heavier than it looks," I murmured when it settled onto my shoulders.

"It has armor plates in it. Dress for the slide, Angel, not for the ride. You get me?"

"Does this mean you're taking me for a ride?" I asked, and I couldn't hide my amused smile at the double entendre.

"It's your eighteenth birthday, what better way to celebrate than with your first ride?" he asked, and I turned around to see a light I'd never seen before in his eyes. It was a look of excitement edged with a desperate hope. I felt my own enthusiasm and excitement rise in the center of my chest and laughed, throwing my arms around him and kissing him, not even caring about my coffee breath.

"Come on, baby. Let's ride."

Out at the bike, after locking up the house, my purse slung over my chest, gloves firmly on my hands and coat zipped against the cold, Nox was telling me everything he needed from me. He slipped a pair of sunglasses over my eyes as he spoke and placed a neoprene shell over the lower half of my face, something surprisingly easy to breathe through, yet enough to keep my face warm against the threat of the wind and cold.

Lastly, he buckled a helmet onto my head, one of those half-kind; black and shiny like a beetle. With a few final instructions, I was perched on the back seat, my arms around his solid body, excitement, anxiety, and a little adrenaline a heady concoction filtering through my veins, making my blood very nearly glow.

He expertly piloted us out onto my street and the feeling? The feeling was something. I don't even really know if I could begin to describe it, but I'll try... Free is a good word, something wild and barely contained. It was out of this world holding on to Nox and watching the pavement whip by beneath us. The wind was fierce, the noise incredible, but it was as if the world fell away in a blur of color and motion, yet at the same time, we became one and merged with our surroundings. The thrum of the engine beneath us, the air around us, the world whipping by as the bike carved a path down our lane of traffic. All of it was incredible, unbelievable, and I was instantly addicted.

We rode to the clubhouse, and when we pulled into the lot, it was to a noisy cheer going up from the brothers and ol' ladies who were all gathered outside and similarly dressed to ride. I got off of the bike at Nox's tapped command on my knee and pulled the face mask and glasses off. I couldn't keep from grinning.

"Well, what did you think?" Dragon asked in his deep, steady drawl.

"I want to go again," I cried, and everyone laughed.

"Well, we ain't done yet, sweetheart. Everybody, let's give this girl a birthday ride to remember!"

A loud round of cheers, whistling, and clapping went up and Nox smiled up at me. I leaned down and gave him a kiss and he laughed against my mouth, not that I could hear it. Not with all the Harleys starting up.

"Come on, Jailbait! Don't keep us waiting," Rush called over the thrum of the engines.

"Not jailbait!" I cried. "Not anymore!"

"Ah, that's where you're wrong, baby! You'll always be Jailbait to me!" he called back and held up his gloved hands in front of his chest, thumbs down, fingers curved up and over into the shape of a heart. I laughed and settled in behind Nox, excited for all the new experiences the day had to offer.

25

N ox...

It was late, and it had been an eventful day for my angel. I watched the blue light from the big screen flicker across her face where she'd drifted off against my chest and I had to smile. We'd ridden a ways out to this favorite barbecue joint of the clubs for lunch. The rest of the club who'd been able to make the ride had given Maren their gifts, which is to say the ol' ladies who had made it did. Rush surprised me and had given Maren a picture of the gift he'd made for her. A sturdy wooden chest that'd he'd carved with flowers and had stained with an antique finish.

She'd cried, and I'd held her to a course of 'aww's' from my brothers and sisters. They all liked her, I loved her, and so we'd made the day as perfect as we could for her. We'd ridden, had food, had stayed together to celebrate her special day. We'd come back to the club and had popped popcorn and let her have run of the TV; whatever she'd wanted to watch. Of course, she tortured us with romantic comedies to which the rest of the ol' ladies had cheered chanting 'One of us! One of us!' making her smile and laugh.

There had been a lot of smiling, and a lot of laughs today and now, it was way past midnight and we were all just about wore the fuck out. I sat up carefully, Cell eyeing me from the other end of the couch.

"Goin' to bed?" he asked.

"Yeah," I murmured.

"Good deal. I'll grab her boots and stuff, if you got her?"

"Thanks, man."

I picked her up carefully, balancing her in my arms. She stirred and squeaked, startled, but her arms went around me in perfect love and perfect trust and I was glad I had her to myself tonight. To take her to my bed and to sleep with her in my arms, no barriers, no bullshit, just us.

Cell followed us out the back and into the cold, both of us stopping just inside the back door to lay her coat over her for the short trek to the outbuilding my room lay in. He dropped her boots inside my door and said, "Night bro," before shutting it tightly against the outside world, leaving me alone with my girl.

I set her down gently on the bed and put her jacket aside on the chair in the corner before I went back to her, kissing her lightly, letting my hand skim up under the hem of her form-fitting, long-sleeved shirt. I lifted it over her head and she sighed in contentment, letting me take care of her.

I lost my shirt next and kicked off my boots. She laid and watched me, her breath catching when my shirt came all the way off. I was glad I still had it, and that she liked what she saw. She reached for me as I nudged her knees apart with my own, covering her mouth with mine. She tasted so damn good, salty sweet, a perfect combination. I let my hands roam over her sides and edge beneath her to go for the clasp on her bra.

I couldn't quite get it, instead, all I was getting was frustrated with my clumsy attempts as a grown ass man to get my girlfriend's bra undone. Maren didn't help my ego any by giggling. Finally, she pulled her mouth from mine and whispered, "It's a front clasp bra, lover."

I bowed my head, my forehead lightly touching her chest, above and between her breasts as we laughed together over it. A laugh I turned into a gasp and a moan when I pulled one cup aside and took her nipple into my mouth, suckling gently. *Did I ever think I could be this happy or turned on?* I thought to myself.

No. I couldn't remember a time with anyone else; no matter how hard I tried.

Maren arched pressing her breast into my mouth, her fingers twining in my hair, holding my face to her chest as she moaned, a very feral and adult sound passing between her lips. I tried like hell to think about anything and everything other than her age but for the first time since we'd met, all I kept thinking were things like *barely legal teen.* I tried not to let it deter me. Unfastening her bra and sliding it off her lithe arms, even as her legs, a mile long each, went around my hips, our jeans a tight and unwelcome barrier between us as I kissed my way back up to her mouth.

"*Nox,*" she moaned, and I ground my crotch into hers at the breathy plea in her voice. God, I wanted to give it to her. I wanted to take everything she had to give, and I wanted to make her scream my name to the heavens. *My personal angel,* defiling her in the sweetest possible way in front of man and God, until she was earthbound and tied to me forever.

"Nox, *please,*" she begged, and I smiled, a wicked, almost cruel curve of lips.

"Please, what, Angel?"

"Mm, fewer clothes."

I reached for her waistband while she writhed, rubbing herself against me as I worked them open. I peeled them down her legs, taking her socks with them, and for a second, I couldn't breathe. She was so beautiful, nude and perfect, waiting in my bed.

I kneeled between her thighs and watched her watch me as I undid my button fly; one button at a time. I didn't do boxers or briefs, so the light in her dark gaze, smoldering with raw heat as each glimpse of flesh was made, was so worth taking my time over it. Never mind that my dick was granite in my pants, so hard and straining to the point I thought it was a real possibility it was going to fall off before I got the chance to use it.

I about died and went straight to heaven when she wrapped her long, elegant fingers around the straining flesh, stroking it gently. I stopped in any efforts I had to shuck my pants off the rest of the way and watched her face as she teased my dick with her gentle little touches.

Eventually, it just wasn't enough for me and I edged my hips back, taking my cock back out of her reach. After that, it was a game of how quick I could get out of my pants without tripping over myself, and which drawer did I stash the fucking condoms in? I pulled one out of the bedside drawer and ripped open the gold foil with my teeth, extracting the rubber, slick with lube, with my fingertips.

Maren watched me, hungrily, as I rolled it down the length of my cock and reached for me once I had it settled at my throbbing base. I smiled and settled between those mile-long legs of hers and pressed myself against her opening.

I would like to have gone down on her, but I needed this; I needed inside of her before I couldn't take it anymore and went stark raving mad. I pressed gently until I slipped into her, pausing when she jumped, a little unexpected, moving again only when I was sure I hadn't hurt her.

She was unused to sex, I got that. I wasn't the clumsy little boy she'd had her first few times with. I was a man, and I was going to love her like a woman, not an inexperienced teenager. I started by making eye contact while I filled her to the brim. I moved slowly, letting her body adjust, making sure I did it right and that she was feeling nothing but good.

Her eyes were heavy-lidded, her lips parted in a way that'd like to drive me wild as she breathed deep and even, arching beneath me. She was hot, wet, and so tight; soft and slick, and being inside her was just *intense*.

I bowed my head, stilling inside of her, kissing her deeply, and loved that I could take my time with her like this, that she wasn't demanding, or in a rush either. We kissed, and I moved, she gasped, and I moaned, and we made love carefully, playing off each other, sharing like I had never shared with someone before. It was beautiful and perfect, and I could go like this all night and I planned to. Holy fuck, did I plan to.

26

Maren...

Sweet, blissful, *torture.* I wanted him, I wanted all of him, but Nox insisted on giving it to me in doses. His body moving over and inside me, taut and toned, hot and strong, loving me slowly, sweetly, until I lost my mind; my very *soul* to him. We kissed as he eased his way in and out of my body, and I almost couldn't stand how beautiful he made me feel. I closed my eyes and bit my lip, letting myself get lost in the sensations, riding the gentle current that swept us up and carried us away.

I twined my arms around his shoulders and my legs around his lean hips, which made him groan. He played his lips and tongue against the side of my neck, making me shiver as a wave of tingling bliss washed over my back and down my arm, turning my nipple into a hard kernel of pleasure. I held onto him, rocking my hips into his every thrust and did everything in my power to remain an active participant; to give him everything he gave me in return.

"*God,* Maren," he breathed, and I dragged his lips to mine, cupping his face with my hands, the light stubble on his cheeks scraping my palms.

It was everything I'd imagined and more, and I wouldn't trade it for the world.

I dragged my lips from his after a time and murmured, "I want on top." Just like that, faster than I could blink, Nox rolled, keeping himself deep inside of me and like magic, I was where I wanted to be, straddling his hips, riding him gently. The angle was deeper, somehow sharper than it had been before, and it felt like he touched parts of me that were new; igniting a fire in my soul as I rose and fell, testing the waters. Nox rested his hands on my hips, thumbs sweeping encouragingly back and forth across the hollows left in front by the curvature of bone, as I ground my body over the top of his.

I gasped his name, feeling full and so maddeningly close to the edge. A glowing, effervescent feeling lifting me, causing my head to go back and my eyes to slip closed as I rode my lover and prayed for that final catalyst to send me arching like a roman candle across the sky.

Nox gave it to me. His thumb slipping in the wetness pooled between our bodies, seeking with the pad until he found his mark. Stroking over the super-sensitive flesh there until that lick of flame turned into an inferno and I jerked, clamping my legs tightly around him, letting out a cry I could scarcely believe was formed by my lips.

He tortured me sweetly until I wrapped both hands around his wrist, laughing, attempting to stop the onslaught, overwhelmed to an extreme, limbs twitching; euphoria swirling through my veins. I didn't think I could take anymore, yet Nox wrung every last bit of pleasure and then some out of my body, until tears collected on my lashes and I very nearly had to beg him to stop.

He laughed, and it was a dark but seriously arousing sound. He guided me by my hips off of him. His cock slipping easily from my body. I followed his wordless commands, his hands guiding me where to go, as he stacked the pillows from the bed and had me lay on my stomach with them supporting my hips, raising my bottom into the air. He stroked over my skin, rubbing his hands gently over my back as I shivered with delight.

He straddled my thighs and pressed his hands into my ass cheeks, spreading me, gazing adoringly over my body as I looked over my shoulder to see what he was doing. His admiration soothed my nervousness as he rubbed his cock against my pussy, up and down, teasing, before finally sliding back in. He pressed deep, and I swear to God, that the way he had me, I could feel every single last inch of him and not just length, either.

He bottomed out, carefully, and nudged just that much further, smoothing his hands over my back, one hand creeping into the back of my hair, massaging my scalp. He fisted that hand in my hair and I gasped, arching back. It didn't hurt, but it was clear he had all the control and I was glad to cede it to him. He tugged back, and I gasped again, feeling myself twitch around him and the slow, sly grin I was rewarded with was so worth it, I tensed around him again.

"That's it, Angel, milk my cock," he breathed and closed his eyes, bowing his head as if in prayer as he rode my body.

It was the hottest fucking thing I had ever seen and I wanted to please him. I wanted to make him come, and I tensed and pressed back onto his cock and struck a counterpoint rhythm to his short strokes to achieve just that.

Nox rolled his head on his neck, his eyes closed in deep concentration over the feelings he was having, and I loved to watch it. He relinquished my hair, sliding his hands over my skin making it break out in a tingling wash, before gripping my shoulders tight. He thrust into me hard, and I cried out, it felt *so* good before he pistoned himself in and out of me at a punishing rate. The point where our bodies met reported with a slap of flesh that was punctuated by a sharp cry of pleasure from me. Nox's breathing was labored as he gasped, almost as if he were a drowning man, and perhaps he was. Perhaps, he was drowning in me, and I can't say I didn't like the sound of that.

He pulled me back onto his dick powerfully one final time with a shout of pure ecstasy, and I came with him, unable to tell where his body left off and mine began. We pulsed and twitched together, our bodies glued to one another with various fluids, sweat cooling our skins in the dim light cast by his bedside lamp. He lay over the top of me, panting; his fingers twined with mine as he kissed my shoulder between his gasps for air. I laid still, relishing the feel of him inside me and wishing we could lay like this forever.

I was mildly heartbroken when he pushed himself up, reaching between us to hold the condom on himself while he pulled out of me. I shivered, and he fell away onto his side beside me. Lying on his back, the look in his eyes glazed and dazed as he pulled me against his chest, discarding the used condom behind my back. I hadn't even seen him pull it off.

"I'm not done," I whispered and Nox gave a laugh.

"Give me a minute, Angel, I'm not as young as I used to be and need a little recovery time."

I crawled up his body and pressed my lips against his. Nox held my hair back from our faces and traced every one of my features with his gaze, lovingly.

"Well, when you put it that way…" he murmured, and reached for the bedside drawer, pulling a fresh condom from its confines and handing it to me; I smiled and ripped it open.

27

N ox...

"You are not having sex in our kitchen!" Everett cried, the doors swinging shut on her protests.

"Watch me," I muttered and pulled Maren back by the hips, the curve of her ass fitting perfectly into the front of my body. She giggled and I put my lips against the side of her neck, even as I slipped my hand beneath the hem of her tee so I could cup her breast. She gasped and bent forward, her ass grinding into the front of me, pressing against my cock which was rising to the occasion.

"At least do her in the office away from the equipment!" Mandy yelled from up front, and then exclaimed, "What? Dray does you in there all the time." Maren and I dissolved into laughter at the affronted tone Mandy used on her best friend. Everett's only retort?

"Good chocolate Christ on a cracker, Mandy-girl, we should be better bosses than this."

Maren twisted in my grasp, turning around so she could look up at me, not at all shy about pressing her body into mine as she twined her arms around my shoulders and held me back. I loved that she was comfortable with and around me, even when our age difference drew second and third looks from people. She didn't care. She loved me with a fierce fire inside and I couldn't help but love her back with my everything.

God, I would be a ruined man if she ever chose otherwise.

"Nox, what's wrong?" she asked, voice soft, her fingertips lightly touching the side of my face. I gathered them in mine and turned her hand, laying a kiss in the center of her palm.

"You just amaze me, is all," I murmured; and with a smile confessed, "I just can't wait to be back inside of you."

She smiled, and said, "Let me finish up here, and you can take me home. I have to fix dinner for Sage and make sure he's done his homework, then maybe we can quietly fool around a little?"

I laughed under my breath and nodded. "Sounds great, Angel," I said, when actually, it sounded like torture. It'd been almost a week since her birthday which had been on a Sunday. When we'd gotten up that Monday morning, it'd been to rush to get her to work, she needed the hours to make up for having to buy Sage some new shoes and jeans. As soon as she was off work, she hit school, only to put in some more hours after that. The kid had hit another growth spurt and it took everything in her to keep him in clothes that fit, even bargain shopping at discount places and thrift stores.

Tuesday, I'd picked her up in the morning outside her place to take her to school. You should have seen the look on that fucking little cock bite, Lucas' face when we'd pulled up on the bike. I'd watched his face go a whiter shade of pale when she'd kissed me goodbye. In fact, a lot of comments flew behind hands when she'd done it and I loved that she didn't care.

I'd tried to pick her up as often as I could in the mornings and drop her off when I knew I'd be off in time to pick her up. Sage and Connor had thankfully bonded pretty hard, and with the help of the child psych he was seeing, he was back to being a normal kid for the most part. I think our regular workouts and establishing some solid routines had helped out by like a lot with that. So much so, Sage had been allowed to catch the bus home on his own starting two days ago, and so far, so good.

"I'll follow you," I told Maren after she'd finished cleaning up.

We headed out of the kitchen and Everett looked up from where she was counting the till, asking, "My office the way you found it?"

"We didn't actually do anything!" Maren cried, laughing.

"Oh," Everett shrugged, "why not?"

"Uh, because I have some class?" I hazarded and was met by peals of laughter from the both of them.

"Ha, ha, ha! Laugh it up!" I mock-griped.

"Take me home and you can be as classless as you'd like after my brother has been fed and watered."

I pulled her into my arms and kissed her carefully. We hadn't really let on to her brother that we were sleeping together, and it'd pretty much been pure hell sleeping alone in my bed since. Especially considering the sheets had still smelled like my angel for a good night or two after she'd been and gone.

It was Friday, and while I still had to work tomorrow, I had every intention of sleeping well tonight in my girlfriend's bed. Maren smiled back at me after our kiss and let me lead her out the front door of *Soul Fuel* with some lingering goodbyes to Evy. While we got astride my bike, Dray pulled up on his to pick up his woman.

"Keep the shiny side up, brother!" he called over the mutual chugging of our motors and with a quick fist bump, I turned Maren and I out into the lot and went for the road. She held onto me tight, but not out of fear. My angel was fearless on the back of the bike, and I do mean fearless.

The other day on the way to her school, she'd wrapped her legs around me and when I'd glanced in the side-view mirror it was to see her leaned comfortably back against the sissy bar, texting a message to someone on her phone. When we'd stopped, I'd asked what the hell that had been about, and she'd given me a cheesy grin and had told me it was her research partner for a science project, asking a question.

I'd shook my head and had to laugh at it. I think she'd scared the hell out of me with that, but she seemed completely unfazed. The whole thing had made me not only admire her but love her even more. The fact that she loved to ride, a thing that was just so basically and fundamentally a part of me... I loved her for that so hard.

The windows of the house were all aglow when we pulled up to the curb. The light had failed a while ago out here, even though the days were getting longer; it being a Friday, Maren had worked late which is why it was fully dark when we pulled in. She got off the bike and took off her helmet, holding out her hand to me and it made my heart swell. I took it and stood, following her into the house, fingers loosely clasped together through the thick layer of our mutual gloves.

"Sage! We're home!" she called up the stairs, pulling off her gloves. When no answer immediately came, she let go of my hand and pulled the face mask off, her lithe fingers going for the buckle on her chin strap.

"Sage!" I called out, and Maren and I hit the stairs almost in unison. I stepped back and let her lead but stayed right on her heels.

We found her little brother sitting in the middle of the floor of her dad's room; boxes scattered around him, bits and bobs taking up room in some of them, a photo album sitting open in his lap. His face was stained with tears and he looked up at his sister.

"I thought I could do it, so you didn't have to but there's so much stuff here."

"Sage, what are you doing?" she asked, aghast.

"You should take Dad's room. We can't leave it like this, you know? He's gone and he's not coming back. You're dad now, and mom, and my sister and you should have his room. It's the biggest." Sage broke down, started crying, and like the lost little boy he still was, he reached for the only comfort available to him — his big sister.

Another reason I loved Maren, she went to him without the slightest hesitation. She went down on one knee and pulled him into a tight hug and let him break down. No matter all the shit he put her through, no matter how rough he treated her, she was always there for him and every time I saw it, I melted just a little bit more inside.

It was everything Rush and I had ever dreamed of having in a mother, growing up. Everything we wanted, and couldn't have, and I was man enough to admit, if I couldn't have it there, I would rather have it here, in the woman who shared my life and my bed. I just never expected that generosity and healing to come in such a young package.

Maybe I was a selfish son of a bitch being thirty-six and taking everything freely that Maren had to give at eighteen, but she was the first person I'd found this kind of selflessness and love with and I didn't want to give it up. I wanted it, and I wanted to give her everything for it.

I leaned a shoulder against the doorjamb, blown away by some of these silent revelations inside my head. Working my own issues I'd carried surrounding our age difference that'd been silently gnawing at my underbelly. I put 'em to rest right there. Let 'em go and cemented my place in Maren and Sage's lives. I went a step further by murmuring, "You guys take your time, I'll go down and get dinner started," before I stepped back and did what I knew I could to make this difficult time easier on the both of them.

I went downstairs and checked out what Maren had thawed and started making something out of it. She came down after a bit and wrapped her arms around me, snuggling up to my back. I put my hands over hers at my waist while the meat crackled in the pan on the stove and asked low and quiet, "You okay?"

"Yeah," she said, "we will be, I just had no idea he felt that way about Dad's stuff."

"I think that's what his shrink would call a breakthrough, wouldn't you?"

"Mm, he's washing his face and putting on sweats, he'll be down in a little while."

"When do you want to finish what he started up there?" I asked and took back my hands to stir the chicken in the skillet.

"I don't know, maybe some here and there until it's done?"

"Sounds fair."

"I don't know how I feel about taking Dad's room," she said.

I turned around, twisting in her arms to pull her close, tucking her head under my chin and pressing a kiss to the top of her hair.

"Let me ask you something, knowing you as I do... Does it matter? Angel, we both know you're gonna do whatever it takes to make your brother happy. It's who you are. It's what you do... my question is — what can I do to make this transition easier on you?"

She leaned back and looked up at me, searching my face. "What do you mean?"

"Well, would it help if we painted or something? Moved your dad's furniture out, changed up the room, before moving yours in? Make it your space?" She stared, her gaze a fragile one on the verge of tears of her own. Tears that I could tell she just refused to let fall. She nodded once, carefully, and I smiled gently down at her.

"Okay, then. We've got this," I murmured and she smiled, charmed.

"Yes, *we* do."

I kissed her then, carefully, and we broke apart when Sage came into the kitchen, clearing his throat. Maren blushed with something akin to guilt and Sage stared at her blankly.

"If Nox is moving in, you need Dad's room," he said flatly.

"Woah, hey," I said letting his sister go, even though it pained me. "We're nowhere near anything like that, buddy."

"I think it's cool, you know," he said matter-of-factly, and Maren and I exchanged a look like we had both just entered the *Twilight Zone*.

"Sage, let's not try to take on the world," Maren said tiredly, rubbing her temples.

"Sorry," he said. "It's true, though. I like Nox, he takes care of you. You need someone to take care of you, too." Sage dropped into one of the seats at the kitchen table and I chuckled, sparing a glance at the chair with my jacket and cut hanging on it.

"It's sort of what we do when we consider someone family," I said jutting my chin toward my colors.

Maren brought down plates and listened to Sage and I talk about club life in the most PG to the PG-13 way I could muster. It was a good way to get us out of the heavier topics, and, as far as I could tell, one of the safer options we all had in common at this point that we had to choose from.

We strayed back into dangerous waters a few more times but managed to navigate our way back out again. It was a pretty surreal evening as far as evenings went, and overall, one of the better ones we'd had in a minute.

Eventually, Sage went up to bed after helping clear the plates and loading them into the dishwasher. He'd made pretty fast friends with Connor and I guess they'd traded some Xbox shit so they could play together. It was one of the reasons Maren had relented on giving his game system back earlier than she'd planned, but it wasn't out of pocket; both Reave and Doll had nothing but good things to say about Sage and his recent overnight.

His good behavior had earned him back quite a few privileges at once. Not just his freedom but his game system, too. Like I said before, so far, so good, and I think that Reave had a lot to do with that. Sage had come from his overnight at my club brother's place with almost a brand-new attitude. Come to think of it though, it could have had more to do with Doll. In fact, the more I thought about it, the more the changes out of Sage seemed to have the woman's gentle touch to it than my brother's. The women of the club were typically something else. Like Maren was to me.

I went up behind her in the bathroom upstairs and pulled her back into me while her hands were occupied in the sink, rinsing them. She laughed and it quickly turned to a gasp when I locked my fist in her dark hair, drawing her throat taut beneath my lips as I kissed the side of it, attacking it with lips and teeth, watching her reaction in the mirror.

She swooned and I held her up, pinning her between myself and the bathroom counter, my other arm locking her tight against my body.

"Oh, Nox…" she moaned and I chuckled darkly beside her ear.

"Finish up, Angel," I ordered softly. "I want to take you to bed."

"I'll be right there," she said, a sly smile in her voice. "Hope you brought enough condoms."

"Oh, I brought enough," I said, giving her a sharp slap on her shapely ass, leaving the restroom to cross the hall into her bedroom.

I stripped down, quietly but efficiently, leaving a small dragon's hoard of gold-wrapped condoms within easy reach on her bedside table. We would have to be quiet, with Sage just across and down the hall, but it was doable. Besides, I didn't think Maren and I could hold off another minute.

I lay in her bed, hands behind my head, blankets pooled at my waist and waited. The little minx one-upped me by sliding into her room in that black satin number of hers, that clung to every plane, curve, and angle of her figure. I had already been halfway hard just thinking about her skin under my lips, now, at the sight of her, I was all the way there.

"I have something to ask you," she murmured, shutting her door silently but tightly.

"Take that off, climb on my dick, and you can ask me anything you want."

"You have to promise not to laugh," she said, "and you have to promise you will really think about it. Not just say yes or no, but really consider it before you pick either way."

"Maren," I chuckled. "What do you want to ask me?" Her seriousness had caught me off guard.

She came over to the bed, gathering the long skirt of her nightgown in her hands. She planted a knee on the edge of the bed and awkwardly walked on them until she could straddle my hips. I made sure to shove the blankets down before she settled and had to smile appreciatively at the lack of panties she had going on. She settled her silken flesh against the heat of mine. I wasn't going to slip inside her, not without a condom on, but this felt too good. Good enough, I might be willing to agree to anything that came from her parted lips.

"Come here," I gasped and slid my hands over the satin enclosing her warm skin. She leaned down and we kissed, my arms wrapping around her, holding her tightly against my body as I thrust, sliding my cock against the lips of her pussy, teasing us both.

She tore her mouth from mine with an impassioned gasp and pushed against my chest, straining against my arms to sit up; reluctantly, I let her.

"I'm being serious," she murmured.

"I can see that, Angel, and like I said, you can ask me anything... just do me a favor and reach for one of those condoms while you do it." I bounced my eyebrows and she laughed at me, but obliged, leaning over and capturing one of the small packets off the pile. She shifted back and moved her nightgown so she could stroke me and get me ready. I left my hands on her hips and watched her, dark eyes alight with love and lust, a mirror for my own.

"I was wondering..." she said and smiled mischievously.

"Yeah?" I asked, drawing out the word.

She tore open the condom and picked up my cock, rolling it on with her deft fingers and I smiled, saying, "You really don't want me to say 'no' to whatever it is you're gonna ask me, do you?"

"I really want you to say yes," she murmured, making sure the rubber was secure at my base. I squeezed her hips gently with my hands.

"You're doing a great job of convincing me, baby."

She kneeled up, holding her nightgown out of the way enough to put myself at her entrance, she slid down me, throwing her head back with a passionate gasp, her long hair tickling the tops of my thighs before the cool satin of her nightgown fell back into place.

I gasped right along with her, massaging her hips through the satin as she placed her hands on my chest to give herself enough leverage to fuck me.

She fucked *me*, and I loved that about her. The fact that she was so bold, and took the reins, especially with the gap in experience. She let go when she was with me and it was beautiful.

"God, Maren!" I closed my eyes for a second, and the image of her riding me wantonly was seared into my vision so hard, I could still see her there in the dark behind my closed lids. She felt amazing; warm and wet, silken soft around me, gliding up and down my cock with what felt like minimal effort. She was so beautiful, so fierce, I couldn't stand it any longer.

I rolled toward the empty half of the bed, taking her with me, staying with her, staying inside her, as I put her on her back and loomed over the top of her. She gasped, hips rising off the bed to meet my slow, hard, deliberate thrust into her.

I made love to her slow, raining butterfly kisses all over her face and neck, gathering her tightly under my body, caging her with my arms and pressing into her as deeply as I could go. She panted softly, keeping her moans to quiet whimpers that made the lust already rushing through my body nearly double. I covered her mouth with mine and drank those small sounds down, amazed at how much they satiated me.

She was so wet, so aroused, and I couldn't torture her forever because while my being inside her was clearly doing something for her, it wasn't quite enough. I reared up, and put some space between our bodies, changing angles, driving into her with short little thrusts as I dipped the pad of my thumb between our bodies; seeking out that small nub to push her over the edge.

She was laid out flat beneath me, her legs spread to accommodate me between them. The straps of her nightgown had fallen gracefully off her shoulders, her chest rising and falling, the tops of her breasts neatly displayed by the lace and black satin of the gown. Her long hair fanned out behind her head, and her dark eyes aglow, I took my time committing all of it to memory; knowing that no matter what life dealt us, no matter how things wrinkled or eventually started to sag, that this right here would be how I would always see my beautiful angel.

Her eyes closed, and her back arched. She clasped one of her hands over her mouth to stifle any sounds that escaped and shuddered as if electrified, her pussy clamping around my dick in rhythmic pulses that touched off a fire in my soul.

I threw back my head and let go, the tight, tingling at the base of my spine causing my cock to jerk inside her as bursts and waves of pleasure swept out through my skin. I emptied myself into the condom inside her and rode the high she gave me, pressing into her tight and tighter, gasping for breath.

I looked down at her and smoothed my hands over the satin encasing her body and said, "You wanted to ask me something?"

She gasped, taking a moment to catch her breath and murmured, "I want you to take me to prom."

I laughed. "All you ever have to do is ask, Angel. I can't deny you anything…" and it was true.

28

Maren...

Spring break felt like a long time coming. We were starting it a little early by taking off the Friday before our official week off from school was supposed to begin. It was Nox's club's annual club-only spring lake run. Nox had convinced me that Sage and I should go, that it would be good for us to get away for a bit. With Evy and Mandy all but closing *Soul Fuel* down for it, it wasn't like I had anywhere else to be.

Sage was excited, although a little less so when he found out he was riding in the van behind everyone with Mandy, Melody, and their babies. Melody couldn't ride anyway with how pregnant she was. She had three or so months to go. Due in the summer sometime, I think July or August. I hadn't asked and couldn't remember if it'd been mentioned.

"Ready?" Nox asked from behind me, his hands smoothing over my denim clad hips, pulling me back against his chest. I rolled my head back against his shoulder and reached up, cupping the side of his face and standing on tiptoe. He bent down and kissed me softly, cheers, whistles, and a few catcalls going up around us. I laughed lightly, and his hands slid around me, causing me to shiver with anticipation.

"Gross," Sage muttered and walked past us to the van. Reaver's son, Connor, laughed and got into the last row of seating behind my brother, sitting down next to him.

"I don't need to remind you to behave for Mandy and Mel, do I?" I asked and Sage rolled his eyes.

"You just did," he said and Connor elbowed him lightly.

"She's a parent now, they've assimilated her into their evil cabal. She has to say shit like that it's in their rulebook."

"Connor!" Hayden barked and Connor grinned wide.

"Yes, Stepmother dearest?" he said, a comedic twinkle in his blue eyes, just like his father's.

"Eighteen, remember that," she said coolly.

"If you can't remember that," Reaver said, "then at least remember you're near Noah and Eden, and they're at that age they can pick that shit up."

Hayden elbowed Reaver with a scowl and he yelped. "Ow! Hey, what'd I say?" he asked.

I laughed lightly and cuddled back into Nox who kissed the side of my neck. He asked me, "You all set?" and I smiled, feeling lighter than air, loved and in love; and totally excited to get on the road.

"I can't wait," I said, and he chuckled darkly, the sound making me shiver.

"I can't wait for it either," he murmured into my ear and I closed my eyes.

Life wasn't exactly perfect. When I say that, I mean, with being responsible for Sage, and both Nox and my work schedules, sex and intimacy didn't exactly get to happen often or spontaneously. It was hard for us to hook up. We'd only managed to a couple of times so far, and I realized that adulting, and being an adult, seriously wasn't all it was cracked up to be.

Though I wouldn't trade having my brother with me for the world, it gave me even more serious pause before making any decision regarding having kids of my own. Not only when it came to the genetics, but because as selfish as it sounded, I really wanted to have a chance at a life of my own for a minute without having someone totally dependent on me.

I looked back to Sage, sitting in the backseat laughing and talking with Connor and an overwhelming sense of guilt and resentment flooded me. It was a hard combination of emotions to deal with and so I did what I did best in those moments when they came up – I shoved them down and ignored them as hard as I could. Because, you know, bottling everything up was totally healthy.

Nox had let me go and was setting about doing last checks on gear and making sure everything was lashed down and strapped tightly before we set off on our weekend adventure with the club. I was so focused on how the denim of his jeans hugged his ass, I completely missed Dani slide up beside me.

"You okay?" she asked, half hiding behind a sweep of her black hair. I nodded and plastered on my fake-it-'til-you-make-it smile. She tilted her head curiously to one side and it made her man, Red-Thirteen, stop what he was doing by his classic bike to look over.

"You good, baby?"

"I'm fine," she called back over her shoulder, but her eyes never left mine.

"She doesn't believe you," a soft male voice said from my other side and I looked over to Blue, who gave me his boyish grin. I blinked, I couldn't remember ever hearing him speak before, but he did it again, when he said, "I don't believe you either." He took the sting out of his words by smiling wider and punctuating them with a wink of his light gray eyes, several shades lighter than Nox's steel-gray ones.

"If you need to talk about any of it, you know we're here." Dani said, and I turned my attention back to her.

I was completely unnerved by the two of them at this point and just managed a feeble, "Yeah, sure… okay."

Dani smiled apologetically. "I don't mean to creep you out," she said. "I just see it, you know?"

"See what?" I asked.

"The adults in your life are so worried about Sage and his development, they've completely forgotten about you, haven't they?" she asked.

I nearly startled and found myself nodding before I could stop myself. She'd gotten right to the heart of my resentment. Sometimes I simply felt so taken for granted, I couldn't even… I didn't think anyone but Nox knew, and while he tried his very best – for the most part — he was right in the trenches with me when it came to Sage. It was less lonely for sure, but not something we talked about.

"Come find me sometime this weekend, I think you need to vent," she said and gave me a quick hug before going over to Thirteen. The look he gave her was the same look Nox gave me, and it warmed me down to my toes to see it.

I had no doubt that I was loved, and that meant so very much to me. Another unsettling stab of guilt pierced my heart, only this time, for a different reason. I suddenly felt bad for any resentment that I harbored knowing how incredibly lucky I was to be so loved and by such a good man.

"Maren, you good, Angel?" I looked up, smiled, and felt like I had absolutely zero handle on my emotions lately. I hid it by nodding and went to Nox, wrapping my arms around his waist and hugging myself tightly against his chest. His arms went around me, and he tossed my long braid over my shoulder to lay down the leather covering my back.

"I love you," he said suddenly, and I smiled with nothing forced about it this time.

"I love you, too. What was that for?" I asked.

"Just something in your eyes, it looked like you needed to hear it," he murmured.

"I did," I confessed and went up on tiptoe, pressing my lips to his. He smiled against my mouth and gave the guys making comments about his display of affection the finger. I laughed and we all turned to listen as Dragon's voice boomed over the small crowd of bikers and bikes.

"Listen up!" he shouted, and we did, with rapt attention. Dragon was just that kind of man and leader.

"HEY." I looked up from where I was washing my hands in the small bathroom's sink, just off our room in the great lodge.

"What's up?" I asked and felt a shiver of anticipation as Nox let his eyes roam over the back of my body. I stared at him in the mirror above the sink while he shuddered as if being released from a dream.

"Dinner's not for a few hours," he drawled, and I smiled.

"I should hope not, we just ate at the diner not too long ago."

"Meh, usually us guys are hungry by the time we get from there to here and dinner is being served up, but something delayed the lodge getting on the food…"

I turned, and he stopped talking, letting his beautiful gray eyes give the front of my body the same treatment they'd given the back a moment before. I felt my chest squeeze down tight with want, making it hard to draw air, and asked, "What do you want to do to kill time?"

"I thought…" he said, taking my hands in his, drawing me closer, into the protective curve of his body, hands finding my hips, sliding around to my lower back, delving beneath the hem of my shirt.

I closed my eyes, the light, lingering touch of his long fingers against the warm skin of my lower back like heaven as he finished his sentence… "We could talk about what was bugging you before we hit the road."

It wasn't what I expected, and it startled me out of my enjoyment, putting me slightly on the defensive.

"I don't know what you mean," I murmured and Nox sighed softly.

"You can't bullshit a bullshitter, baby. Dani saw it, and when she did, I did. I just feel bad I didn't pick up on it sooner. It's okay, you can talk to me… what's up?"

He stared into my eyes, his expression so intent and sincere, it made me swallow hard. I both ached to tell him, to let it out and to feel better, and feared what his reaction would be. If it were anyone else, anywhere else, it would likely be yet another minimization of my feelings. Like at school, whenever I complained about the bullying and abuse… I was told I needed to get a thicker skin, I was told that 'boys will be boys' and to 'lighten up', or that I was too sensitive.

Nox closed his eyes and rested his forehead against mine, patiently waiting me out. I licked my suddenly dry lips and made my confession. "I feel guilty," I whispered.

"For what?" his voice gentle.

"I… I don't want kids," I said.

"We talked about this, babes. I'm okay with that."

"I know, I know, but I feel guilty because I don't want kids because… because…"

"Because why?" he asked when I was silent too long.

"Because I want to have a life of my own," I whimpered, sniffling, my eyes welling up with tears. "I know that sounds incredibly selfish, and I love Sage, I really do, but it's harder than I expected, you know? I feel like I am missing out on so much and I know it isn't fair to think like that –"

"Shh." He slipped his hands out from the back of my shirt and brought them to cup my cheeks, smoothing the moisture out from under my eyes with his thumbs. "It's totally okay to think like that, Angel. You're human, and in the grand scheme of things, you've been dealt a seriously shitty hand. You've been cheated, and you're making the best of it, baby. You're allowed to have all of these feelings and more about it and that doesn't make you selfish. If anyone is selfish, I'll tell you who is; it's these fucking people who expect you to do all of the things and don't even bother to check in with you to make sure *you're* doing okay."

He pulled me tight against his chest and rested his chin on top of my head. I sniffed and cuddled in closer, taking the comfort he was offering even as he sighed and said, "I should have seen this coming. I should have asked, but I figured you were doing okay with it, you know? That we've been in it together. I forget how good you are at hiding feelings that might make other people upset."

I jerked back and looked at him. "Why would you say that?"

His shoulders dropped and he smiled sadly. "Been around the block more than a few times, Angel. Had enough state shrinks and been around enough 'troubled youth' councilors to know what's what. How long your ex-boy-toy been fucking with you? How long was your dad sick? It all amounts to the same thing, 'cept worse because you're a woman."

"Worse? Why worse?" I asked, suspicious that I already knew the answer, yet still surprised he would give it voice.

"Shit, Angel, look at the world today. As a girl, you get pissed off and all dudes do is go right to 'oh, what're you on the rag or something?' Never mind if you have a valid reason to be pissed off. Look at you, your dad sick… how many times did Sage irritate you or piss you off and you just let it slide, stuffed it down, so you wouldn't upset your pops?" he asked.

I felt my body relax as I listened to him and smiled a bit wryly. "A feminist biker, isn't that an oxymoron or something?" I asked.

"It's just common fucking sense, Angel. Ain't nothin' special about it, plus you think I give a fuck about whatever stereotypes citizens put on me?"

I laughed a little and shook my head. "No."

"Listen," he took me gently by the shoulders and pushed me back just enough to make eye contact with me. "don't you ever try to validate your feelings with me, you get me? You feel something, you feel it. You don't have to justify it. It's fucked up, and a citizen thing and you don't have to be a part of that world if you don't want to. Our world is right here, waiting for you with open arms if you want it."

"Are you asking me to marry you or something?" I asked incredulous because this was starting to sound bizarrely like a proposal of some kind.

"No, not yet," he said with a smile and I think my heart skipped a beat.

"Yet? You've thought about it?"

"You're too young, Angel, but I'm serious; my offer is a real one if you want it."

"What are you asking me, Nox?"

He stared at me intently and licked his lips. "I was going to wait, but now is as good a time as any." He stepped away from me and back into the room, and I was drawn as if by strings, compelled to follow.

He went and kneeled by the saddlebags he'd leaned against the luggage rack by the distressed wooden dresser. I leaned a shoulder against the bathroom door frame and watched as he unpacked it neatly on the floor, stacking everything off to the side as he went for, seemingly, the very bottom of the bag.

He pulled out a fabric-wrapped bundle, the material wrapped gently around something soft. He stood up and turned, considering the bundle in his hands for a long minute before looking up, eyes locking with mine. He held it out to me and I swallowed hard, my mouth suddenly dry.

Nox had never looked so serious and I felt the gravity of what was about to transpire. That if I took that bundle, whatever decision lay inside would change things. I took it, and turned, laying it on the bed with a mixture of reverence and fear. I didn't know what lay inside, the Ark of the Covenant or a viper poised to strike; either or seemed just as likely at this point.

"Are you okay?" he asked, voice deep, falling into the moment like a stone into a deep well.

"A little scared, you?"

"Yeah, me too."

"It's going to change everything, isn't it?" I asked.

"Do you know what it is?" he asked.

"I have an idea," I murmured, and it was true, I did.

I stared down at the light cloth, a wrap of some kind, and with a hard swallow to get past the lump in my throat, lifted the thin fabric aside. Leather, black as pitch, kissed my gaze first and I felt my eyes well. I knew what it was, and I knew what it meant.

I touched the embroidered name patch on the breast that read *'Angel'* and with trembling fingers, lifted the vest, turning it so I could see the back. Sure enough, there they were the rockers that proclaimed 'Property of Nox' just like the rest of the Ol' Ladies of the Sacred Hearts Motorcycle Club.

Nox was asking me to be his, and I wanted it. I wanted him so badly. This was a proposal, albeit one with far more weight and importance than just a mere ring could convey. I wasn't a stupid girl. He'd explained it once, what property meant to these men, and it was a lesson deeply ingrained. This meant far more to a man of the club than any civilian or citizen could fathom.

"Yes," I murmured, the word falling from my lips on an exhale of pure relief.

"Yes?" he asked.

I turned my head and looked up at him. "Yes," I repeated and let the happy tears fall.

He smiled, the happiest, most relieved smile I'd ever seen him make and then his mouth was on mine, his hands back beneath the hem of my shirt, caressing my heated skin.

I held his face to mine between my hands and returned his kiss with every bit of fire I held in my veins. He turned me and lifted, setting me on top of the dresser, pulling my legs around his waist which I clamped tightly around him. He pulled his shirt from the back and we broke apart with a gasp, so he could get it over his head.

I stared, letting my gaze drink him in. Every inch of corded muscle, every hill and valley, the dark colors inked under the skin of his left arm, the crows and roses so lifelike, as if the birds would burst into flight from beneath his skin at any moment. I loved it, I loved him, every bit of him, from the sight of him to the smell of him, to how his voice sent shivers down my spine.

I couldn't fathom ever wanting to belong to anyone else, and I had no doubt in any part of me that this was both real and permanent. Nox had indelibly marked my very soul with his brand and I was proud to wear the mark of such a kind and generous man. He pushed my jacket off my shoulders, smoothing his hands down my arms until it was free, letting it carelessly fall to the dresser and slide to the floor.

We lifted my shirt together, and he laughed a little when my fingers immediately went to his belt as he awkwardly kicked off his boots. He lifted one of my legs and braced the sole of one of my boots against the top of his thigh, working the knots in the laces free. He repeated the process on the other side until my feet were free of the leather. His fingers going for the waistband of my jeans.

We undressed each other, and with each article of clothing we managed to discard, the hungrier, the more desperate and savage we became in our endeavors to fit into one another.

Finally, the both of us nude, I pressed my body up against his, both in a bid to be close and to warm myself against him. He bent at the knees slightly, kissing me fiercely, his long, strong fingers kneading my ass.

He lifted me again, and I again wrapped my legs around his waist. The hard length of him throbbing against my body turned me on like no other as I buried my hands in the softness of the back of his hair. He set my ass on the cool wood of the dresser which was the perfect height for this and tore away from my mouth just long enough to tear open the wrapper of the condom we needed to make this happen.

I watched him roll it on and found there was nothing more erotic to me than watching this man make himself ready to penetrate me. I spread my legs and reached for him, digging my nails into his ass to pull him closer. He swiped his dick against my clit a few times, building my anticipation before slowly sinking into my body.

I wrapped my arms around him, pulling him close, edging my butt closer to the edge of the dresser to make sure I took all of him inside me. We both bowed our heads, breath coming in passionate moans, watching him slip in and out of my wet, waiting, pussy until I gave myself over to simply feeling, planting my hands behind me and arching back. Letting my head fall loosely on my neck, my long hair sweeping down my back as I gave myself up like an offering to Nox's skilled hands and lips.

He gently leaned closer, lips sliding against the side of my neck, my breath falling from my lips in a shuddering sigh, as his hands trailed softly against my skin. He was exciting me, winding me up so that he could watch me go, and I loved it when he was like this. Taking care of me before meeting his own needs.

He caressed my ribs, letting his left hand, the one he was dominant with, slip between my thighs. He leaned back to look at what he was doing, slipping his thumb through my wetness, teasing my clitoris gently with the pad until I gasped, my pussy throbbing and twitching around him.

"Oh yeah, baby, like that... Come for me, Angel," he whispered in silken undertones. I sat up straight and wrapped my arms around his shoulders, my place on the dresser for once, giving me a height advantage.

I did to Nox what he did to me, threading my fingers through the back of his hair, pulling his head back so I could kiss him with every ounce of fierce passion I felt for him. He moaned into my mouth, making a sound like I was the best, most satisfying thing he'd ever tasted, and pressed his cock and his thumb into me just a little bit more.

I cried out into his mouth, the pressure building in my womb, my pussy tightening around him to the point he gasped, as the starlight of orgasm filled me slowly in steady increments. I wanted it, I wanted him so badly, my body tight and ready, crying out and begging for that sweet release with every fiber of my being. He rocked his hips forward, questing, looking for that spot inside of me even as his thumb kept up the exquisite, gentle torture from the outside and it was as if the world snapped right out of focus.

I tore my mouth from his and cried out, arching, body writhing in counter rhythm to his. He thrust forward, and I matched him until we crashed together with the sharp report of flesh meeting flesh. His fingers dug tightly into my hips, with near bruising force as we left love making behind. My orgasm seemingly unleashed a primal need in him, pushing him into the response to fuck me. I was okay with that. I wanted that. I wanted every part of him. His love, his trust, and in that moment, his intensity and even that edge of violence that made Nox fall firmly into the category of 'bad boy.'

He pulled me off the dresser and set me on my feet, turning me around, his fist finding the back of my hair and gripping it in that way that screamed that he had all the control. It made me melt, I loved it; I loved when he bent me over the dresser and pressed my breasts and stomach flat against the scarred wooden surface, his necklace, the one with the dog tags bearing his twin's name, brushing coolly along my spine.

He shoved into my dripping cunt from behind and went all the way in, in one smooth, demanding stroke. My hip bones cracked painfully into the edge of the dresser top at first, until I shoved myself forward, planting my palms against the wall, bracing myself to take him and every dominating stroke he had to give me.

He fucked me hard, breathing labored, my pussy wet and wanting, another orgasm threatening from my depths, lurking and waiting, as he dragged it to the surface with every impatient hard thrust of his hips. He smoothed his hands over my ass, and I yelped when one of them came down on one cheek, crashing into the flesh with a sharp snap of sound. I could feel his handprint, pink and angry, raising to the surface with a delicious sting.

"Nox, oh please! Do that again!"

He obliged, with a deep, dark, chuckle and I yowled, shoving myself back harder, clenching down with my pelvic muscles, forcing him to slow just a bit as it became harder to enter and withdraw from me.

"Oh yeah, like that Angel, just like that," he murmured, and I redoubled my effort to do what he commanded.

He cried out and shoved into me once, twice, a third and fourth final time, collapsing over my back, his teeth gently setting into the back of my shoulder in a light and loving bite that sent a wash of tingles down my spine. My pussy gently throbbed and pleasurable little pulses shook me, and I realized that I'd come again, with him; it'd just been such a perfect, shining moment I had a delayed reaction of the euphoria sliding around me.

"I love you, Angel," he gasped between my shoulder blades and I forced myself back onto him just a little bit more, loving how he touched the deepest parts of me. He cried out softly with the unexpectedness of it and I smiled.

"I love you, too."

We made love on the bed, the next time. Carefully relocating my property vest to the dresser top. The next round far more languid, and the round after that, lazy by comparison to the first two.

I almost wished that we could stay like this all weekend long. Lying in bed together, making love over and over until the afterglow just became glow and the lines of reality softened and blurred until we simply had no responsibilities left but what we owed to each other; making one another feel good.

29

Nox...

She laughed and smiled and loaded some more food onto her plate. Our sex-fueled rampage over one another's bodies had worked up a massive appetite between the both of us, and I found myself wishing that cardio was always so much fun.

"What's that secret smile for, yo?" my twin asked, dropping onto the bench beside me.

"Just madly in love," I told him.

He looked over to Maren who was laughing at something Reaver was saying and shook his head. "Yeah, until she decides the novelty of it has worn off."

"Dude, why you gotta be like that?" I asked, irritated. Rush stared me down with his caramel brown eyes, his golden-brown eyebrows raising.

"What? She's *seventeen*, bro –"

"Eighteen," I cut him off and gave him a murderous look, a warning look, like if he didn't want to get his ass beat, he'd better shut the fuck up, right fucking now. He glared back and shook his head.

"Whatever man, same difference. She's a barely legal teen, but she's a fucking *teen*... When you gonna wake up? She's just gonna use you until something younger and prettier comes along and –"

"Rush, knock it off." Archer, our older brother, dropped onto the bench at my back and stared my twin down.

Rush pushed his hands off his knees and stood. "Whatever man, y'all motherfuckers are blind."

He walked away from us and went over to sit with Red-Thirteen, Data, and Zeb. Archer grunted, and I turned to meet his discerning gaze.

"What, not you too?"

"No, not me too, jackass. I wanted to know what you did to make little miss over there so fuckin' happy. There's give her some great dick kind of happy then there's this. What did you do?"

I bowed my head and shook it, sure this was going to hurt some kind of way but having zero fucks to give. Maren was happy, I was happy, and despite what a lot of these motherfuckers wanted to think, she and I were solid. So I told him, "Gave her my rag, bro. She's my ol' lady."

"No shit?" Archer asked surprised, his mouth turning down at the corners like he was some kind of impressed. "Rush is gonna shit, but good on you, bro."

"Really?" I asked.

"Yeah, really," he said. I nodded slowly... that was Archer, a man of few words but when he did put in his say, it was something like sixty/forty you were gonna get ripped to shreds by whatever came out of his mouth. I was surprised to land in the forty percentile this go around so I had to ask,

"What makes you say that?"

He gave me a wicked grin like he knew I would ask, and I probably wouldn't like the answer, but then surprised me again by saying, "I got a good feeling about her. For being so young, she's been through some shit, and she really seems to have her head on straight about it all. Don't worry about Rush, he'll come around. I think he likes to forget he wasn't the only one with the same kind of intensity at her age."

I nodded carefully. "He get at you about Melody cheating yet?" I asked.

Archer snorted. "Nah, he and Mel are in the same boat on a kind of how Grind treated her. Kindred spirits or some shit. Think there were a couple times back in Arizona they ended up drinking buddies over their respective partners lack of fidelity if you know what I mean."

"Yeah, I do." I shook my head. My twin sure knew how to pick bitches. We never got exactly why he went for the mouthy, disrespectful cunts with no loyalty, but more often than not, he hooked up with a bitch and fell hard – unfortunately they always seemed to have other ideas. His bitterness at the injustice of it was showing. I could take it, but he was fucked if he ever brought it up to Maren. I'd throw down over her, with my own twin, I loved her that much.

"Unca Nox!" I jerked my attention to the toddling slap of my nephew's little Velcro sneakers against the deck we were all on, getting our grub on.

"Hey, little man!" I swept him up as he threw himself at me, wrapping his little arms around my neck.

I caught Maren's uncertain gaze over his little shoulder and smiled at her reassuringly, giving her a wink. She smiled back, and whatever she saw on my face made her relax. She said her goodbyes to Mandy and Everett and slipped over to us, slinging one of her long legs that went on for days over the bench on the side of me my twin had vacated.

"Hi, Noah!" she said smiling for the benefit of my nephew.

Archer grunted. "Thought you didn't like kids," he said, and Maren frowned at him slightly.

"I never said that," she said, and waved back at Noah who decided he was being shy and would only curl his little fingers at Maren in a toddler's wave.

"You don't want any," Archer said succinctly, and I wanted to smack him. The only problem was, he hit a fuck of a lot harder than me, and I needed my hands for work, by like a lot.

Maren though? Maren handled her own. "Just because I don't want any of my own doesn't mean I hate kids, and even if I didn't like them, that doesn't give me the right to be a jerk to them."

Archer grunted and tilted his head to the side as if thinking in the way that was purely typical of him before finally giving an absent-minded nod. His gaze remained fixed on Noah, his stepson, and nephew by marriage and birth, but don't tell Arch that. He'd claimed Noah as his own and would fucking kill you if you suggested he was anything other than one hundred percent his boy.

"There you are!" Melody cried, laughing. Her stomach was getting big, swollen with Archer's legitimate child, and Archer smiled up at his wife.

"Yeah, I got him."

"Oh really?" she asked coolly. "Looks like Uncle Nox is the one in charge, here. Huh, baby boy?"

"Whoa!" I cried, as Noah pitched himself headlong toward his mother. Archer grabbed for him, caught him, and lifted him squealing and laughing into the air. I laughed with them both and even Maren cracked a wide smile.

No, my girl didn't hate kids, she loved them, she just didn't want to have any of her own and it was a sad reality that no one in this day and age had the couth to be respectful of a woman's reproductive rights.

Everyone had their questions and opinions about it, when really, it was none of their fucking business.

Of course, god forbid I say my opinion on the matter out loud. Then I was just pussy whipped, or my masculinity was called into question when the truth was, men needed a little feminism too.

On the flip side, me being me, I could give a fuck less what anybody thought. I did what I did and damn it anyhow.

"You cool, Angel?" I asked when Archer and Mel were distracted by Noah and their banter enough that I could ask.

"Fine," she said with a genuine smile and I felt my heart lift in the center of my chest.

"That's my girl," I murmured, and I felt my chest squeeze with joy at how she flushed with pleasure at what I'd said.

We ate together in companionable silence for a little bit until the conversation at our table with Archer and Mel, Evy and Dray, drew us out to participate. It was a good dinner, and a relief to look over at Sage and Connor getting along across the deck. The carefree smile plastered to the kid's face worth the trip already.

We finished up our food, the sun starting to set, and took our time wandering along the lake, talking and holding hands. With the fading light, the chill started to rise, and Maren hugged herself. We hadn't needed our coats, opting instead to just be out in the sunshine in our long sleeves which had been fine during the day. Not so much with the fading sunlight.

"I'll go in and get our coats," I said and pulled her close, kissing her gently.

"I'll go with you."

"Nah, no need for that, I'll drop you off at the fire with the others. You relax, I'll be back in a couple of minutes."

She smiled. "Okay."

I took her hand and led her over by the fire. Trigger was leaned up against the log everyone used as a back rest, Sunshine cradled against his chest.

"Hey, man, look after my best girl for a minute while I run and get our coats?"

"Sure thing, man. Hey, Maren." He inclined his golden head and smiled up at my woman who smiled back down at him, settling on her jean clad butt on the plaid blanket next to him.

"Hey." She settled in and I left off, heading back up toward the lodge, digging in my hip pocket for our room key. I met Sage and Connor on their way down, arms loaded with boxes of graham crackers and chocolate bars.

"Woah, hey, where are the marshmallows?" I asked.

"My dad's got 'em," Connor said and I nodded.

"Good deal, can't do s'mores without 'em."

"Ever had one with a peanut butter cup instead of just plain choco-late?" Sage asked, and I put my hands over my heart in mock indignation.

"Sounds like sacrilege to me!"

"No, it's hella good! Ask Maren, it's her favorite."

I laughed. "She's been holding out on me! Not sure we can date anymore."

"Then pretend I didn't say anything!" Sage called, and I grinned at him as he marched backward down the trail. I do believe I just got the kid's official, unequivocal, stamp of approval, and that felt damn good.

I let myself into our room and pulled my cut off from over my shirt, laying it on the bed. I swung into my jacket and got it settled comfortably before I put my cut back on over it. When I took up Maren's coat, I spied my rag, folded neatly on the dresser we'd fucked on earlier. I picked it up and slid her sleeves through the arm holes. If my twin had anything to say about it, he could take it up with me.

Her jacket and my rag slung over my arm, I left out of our room shutting and locking the door tight behind me. It wasn't that I didn't trust my brother's locking it up like this, it was more the lodge itself. It had staff that wasn't club, and so it was better safe than sorry – for them, not us.

I found Maren and Sage by the fire getting their marshmallows done up on long roasting skewers and laughing. She handed her skewer to Sunshine when she saw me and got up. The air was crisper than even when I'd left, and she looked grateful for her coat. I held it open for her and she slipped her arms into the sleeves. I took a brief moment to smile over my name against her back, a little disappointed I'd had to cover up her wings.

"Thank you," she murmured.

"What's *that* supposed to mean?" Sage demanded, and I sat down next to him, between him and his sister.

"It means I love your sister, and if anyone tries anything, I'll hurt them," I said.

"Like you did Luke?" he asked.

"What do you know about that?" I asked as Maren settled in next to me, her fingers threading through mine as she took up her marshmallow from Ashton on her other side.

"Nothing, just that he was hurting my sister, then you went over there, and he stopped."

I nodded, and said, "That's all you need to know."

"Why?"

"Because, boy. That's the way it is among our kind," Dragon said. He had his legs stretched out, the soles of his boots nearly smoking with how close they were to the fire. He had his hands folded across his belly and the tops of his shoulders leaned against one of the other logs, the picture of his namesake guarding his horde. He sucked on his cigarette, the coal flaring bright, and let out a stream of smoke through his nose.

"And how do I become one?" he asked, and Maren turned her head.

"Sage," she said, a warning in her tone.

"What? I'm not trying to be rude! For real, I'm just asking. I've never asked before."

Dray chuckled. "You gotta be eighteen for one," he said.

"And have a bike," Duracell chimed in.

"What else?" he asked curiously.

"You have to prove yourself," Connor said, staring into the flames with a level of resolve out of character for his thirteen years. Reaver stared over at his son, pride shining in his icy blue eyes and it made me smile. Connor was definitely a kid he could be proud of. Despite his batshit crazy mother, he was somehow turning out right.

Maren lifted my arm and put it over her shoulders, I hugged her into my side and listened as my club brothers and my family explained to Sage everything involved with what it was to be one of us. Family, honor, and loyalty being just the tip of the iceberg.

Maren made us s'mores and when I bit into mine it was with surprise. She smiled, laughing, and I shook my head and chewed. Salty sweet, I'd already forgotten about the conversation Sage and I had about using peanut butter cups rather than straight chocolate in his sister's s'mores.

"Told you they were good," he said, laughing, and he had me there. They really were. It was a perfect first night so far.

30

M aren...

Music and laughter. Zeb played his guitar by the fire and sang songs from New Zealand that were beautiful, even though they were in his native tongue and we couldn't understand a word. The guys drank beer, the women drank wine, except for Melody, who couldn't. She sipped iced tea along with me. Everyone said I could drink around them, but I wanted to set a good example for Sage.

Unfortunately, that good example now led to my bladder crying out for relief when I was comfortably, and languidly, lounging against Nox with no desire whatsoever to actually move. I sighed piteously and stirred which caused Nox to kiss my temple and ask, "What's wrong?"

"Have to pee," I whispered. He chuckled and relinquished his hold on me. I sat up, out from underneath the blanket we had covering us and stretched.

"Be right back," I said and got up.

"Inside the back door, follow the signs to the ballroom, and take a right down the little hall just before the doors. It's the closest one, sweetheart."

I smiled. "Thanks, Dragon."

"No sweat."

I followed his directions and took care of things quickly, washing my hands and drying them, running the damp paper towel over my face which was tight from the heat of the campfire. I slipped back out and went back the way I came.

I slipped out the back door into the cool night air and very nearly smacked right into Rush.

"Oh, geez! I'm sorry," I stammered. He looked over my zipped-up jacket and vest with distaste and I leaned back, surprised.

"You have no idea what that really means," he mumbled. "You're too young. You're just gonna get bored and break his fuckin' heart and I don't want that for him. Why don't you stop using him and just leave him alone?" He slammed his shoulder into mine on the way past me, knocking me off balance. I stood there, stunned, and blinked once, long and slow.

I had no idea that Rush thought that way of me, and I found it both distressing and depressing. I looked down the trail, speechless, and locked eyes with Nox, who instantly scowled and waved me toward him.

I couldn't make my feet move right away, turning Rush's words around in my mind. I was worried, I mean, *was it true?* It was as if he had flipped a switch and the whole perfect day shattered around me, like some kind of illusion.

I felt like I had just been sucked down into a black morass of these awful feelings, sadness, anger, bitterness, worry, concern, fear; all of them twisted into a Gordian knot of awful in the center of my chest. I didn't know what was happening.

Nox stood up and I just stood there and stared, my eyes welling up with tears. *No, it wasn't true!* I loved Nox more than I had ever loved anything in my life. I not only loved him, I relied on him... but *did I rely on him too much*? Was I indeed using him?

Panic welled up, sharp and fierce. The serrated edges tearing me up from the inside even as Nox's hands landed gently on my shoulders.

"Angel, baby, what's wrong?" he murmured, cupping my chin and raising my face to look at him.

His eyes locked onto mine and some order was restored, the panic ebbing just long enough for me to burst out, "You don't think I rely on you too much, do you? That I'm using you?"

"Aw fuck. No, Angel, not at all; those are Rush's issues. You're having an anxiety attack. Just breathe, baby." He pulled me tight against his chest, his arms going around me, and murmured, "I'm gonna beat his fucking ass."

"I'm sorry!" I whined, fear rising like a bubble off the surface and when it popped, I cried. I shook, and the tears slipped free and I gripped the lapels of Nox's coat and sobbed.

"Maren?" Sage called and Nox fixed it like he fixed everything.

"It's okay, Sage. Your sister's just having a little panic attack, that's all."

"Why?" my brother demanded, and I took in several deep breaths and tried valiantly to calm down. It'd been a while since I'd had one.

"It's okay, baby. Three things you can see," Nox said and I tried to focus.

"You, the trees, and my brother."

"Good, two things you can hear."

I closed my eyes and said, "Frogs, and the fire crackling."

"Good girl, that's it, one thing you can smell."

"Campfire," I muttered, and he held me a little back from him. I opened my eyes, feeling a little calmer, a little more centered, and I apologized again.

"No need to apologize," he murmured, and I reached for Sage, hugging my brother tightly who looked like he was on the verge of tears himself.

"How much has this been happening?" he demanded.

"It just happens sometimes," I said. "It's okay, I don't need you to worry about it. Everything is fine."

"No, it's not!" he cried, and then he started to cry.

I hugged my brother tightly, but by now we had the attention of the whole fireside, and Archer called out, "Nox, what's going on?"

"Rush needs his fuckin' ass beat," Nox called back. "But first, I need someone to take Maren and Sage inside."

"Right here," Everett said and just sort of appeared, then Sunshine and Doll showed up right behind her.

"We've got just the thing for you, sister-mom, just as soon as we get little brother squared away," Evy said, and then called out, "Reaver, Dray, and Connor. Could use you too!"

"Anything for you, baby," Dray called and heaved himself to his feet.

"Whipped," Duracell said, laughing.

"I ain't got a problem with that," Dray uttered, secure in his masculinity, but then ruined it by shooting over at our club brother, "At least I got pussy to fuck." Duracell laughed and even Blue hazarded a smile, even if it was secretive like he knew something the lot of us didn't.

"Come on, honey," Everett said and took me and Sage from Nox. Sage, I was guessing by now was having his own issues. Distressed to find out I wasn't as infallible as he thought I was and honestly, I was a bit crestfallen that he had to find out this way. I'd always prided myself on keeping it together around him.

I looked back over my shoulder at Nox who smiled and gave a nod. "Be right there, Angel. Just as soon as I have a talk with my twin."

Apprehension made me want to stay, but practicality told me there was something much deeper at play here, and so I let Everett and the other ol' ladies take me inside. It wasn't missed by me that the rest ghosted to their feet and began to follow, leaving just the men outside.

31

Nox...

When Rush came out, it was to my fist right in his fucking mouth. He grunted and staggered back, his hands going to his lips while I shook out my aching left hand. Fuck, I needed to watch that shit, or I was going to miss work.

"What the *fuck*, Nox?"

"You need to keep your fucking mouth shut around my woman," I grated.

"What the hell are you talking about? She go cryin' about it to you or something? Fuck, man! She's seventeen! She don't know what she wants and she's gonna wreck you!"

I swung on him, but Rush had always been the better fighter. He side-stepped and swung on me, but he was drunk to my sober so I dodged pretty easily.

"Shit, boys, I can't tell if this is twin business or club business," I heard Archer say.

Dragon harrumphed. "A little a both I'd say, but the result's the same. Disrespect is an ass whoopin' and bein' that it's Nox's ol' lady? That makes it Nox's huckleberry."

"We should let them sort it out then?" Trig asked as sergeant-at-arms. I was focused on Rush, who had his hands up now and got myself into a traditional boxer's stance.

"Yup," Dragon said, and it was all I really needed to hear. I swung on my brother again and this time, I clocked him, cracking him a good one on his cheekbone.

"Ow! Motherfucker!"

"That's what you get for being a fucking douche!"

"You know I'm fucking right, you assclown," he grated and came at me.

We danced, trading blow for blow with me landing more than him only by the grace of his fuckin' drunk over my sober. Unfortunately, his drunk meant he didn't really feel half the blows I landed, while my sober meant I felt every one, which sucked hard. My brother hit like a motherfucker, and that shit hurt.

He got in a lucky shot, right in my mouth and I tasted blood. I grunted and let fly, tackling him to the ground and laying into his gut with four or five well-placed blows.

"God damn motherfucking son of a bitch!"

"She was your fucking mother too!" I pointed out and caught off guard, he laughed, which pissed me off more.

I drew back to really fuck him up and was pulled off of him. I struggled for a fraction of a second, Revelator and Trig on either side of me, while Archer and Dragon hauled Rush to his feet.

"You're gonna fucking apologize to Maren after you admit that your punk ass is just fuckin' jealous!" I spit at him.

The outdoors got real fuckin' quiet, my twin's eyes growing stormy before he jerked out of Dragon and Archer's hold.

"Man, fuck you!" he shouted and spun, marching off past the fire into the dark.

"Think you might have hit a lot closer to home than Rush'd like to admit, little brother," Archer said quietly. I sniffed and wiped at the blood under my nose.

"Yeah."

I went to go inside, after my woman, after what was now my family to watch over, to hold close and to guide and heard my brother Archer behind me.

"Heh, don't worry about 'em, they ain't done it quite like this before, but they always kiss and make up in the end."

I raised my middle finger up over my shoulder at him and dragged the back door to the lodge open, letting the wooden screen door crash closed behind me. I went to the nearest bathroom first to clean up. Maren and Sage were both either freaked or freaking out, and the last thing they needed was to see me bloodied.

I turned on the tap to cold and let the water run, bracing my hands on the edge of the sink and staring into the mirror above it.

It was eating at me, fighting with my twin. It always did until we resolved it somehow, but this one was one of the bigger divides we'd encountered yet. I didn't like that but knowing Rush, he didn't like it either.

I splashed cold water onto my face several times over and ignored it when the bathroom door swung open and shut. When I looked, I wasn't too surprised to see Archer in the mirror above the sink. Used to be Grinder who carried out all the peace talks. It was kind of outside Archer's realm of responsibility. Grind had always been the peacemaker among us. This just twisted the knife of missing him even harder.

"You're pretty serious about this bitch, eh?"

"Don't call her a bitch," I said and scowled. Archer raised his hands in surrender.

"Didn't mean nothin' by it, you know that, kid."

"Yeah, still, don't do it, okay? That's my ol' lady."

"I noticed. About that… you sure? On a kind of Rush and all?"

"Yeah. She and I are solid, bro. More solid than anything I've ever had before. I feel it in my bones. She's young, but she's got an old soul… you know?"

Archer shook his head, smiling, his long hair dragging across the patches on his cut. "Don't start with that meta-whatsit, magic, mumbo-jumbo, new age bullshit."

I laughed lightly. "'Scuse the fuck out of me for being more spiritually enlightened that you sorry fucks."

"Whatever you say, kid."

Worry crossed his face, flickering through his eyes for a moment that was clear as day, and it knocked me off my reservation. I straightened and went for the paper towels, pulling some and squashing them against my face to soak off some of the water trying to drip off it before I completely straightened up.

"This ain't a catastrophic divide between you two fucks that I'm dealing with, is it? Because I ain't suited to try and fix that shit. I ain't Grind."

I shook my head. "No. He's my twin, Archer."

"Never seen you go at him like that before. Not for anything."

"I will, and I did, for her. Doesn't that tell you something?"

Archer was quiet for some long minutes before he finally nodded. "It does," he said quietly, and something passed between us. I could see it then, in my brother from another mother.

"You'd do the same for Mel, now wouldn't you?"

"Yeah, I would," he said without missing a beat.

I tipped my head back and rolled it on my neck, sighing out. "Never thought I'd see the day, man."

"That makes two of us," he said staring at the toes of his boots. He heaved a sigh and fixed me with his considering, calculating stare. "Welcome to the club, I guess."

"What club?" I asked with a reckless grin.

"Club pussy whipped," he said, and I laughed.

"Nah, man, this is just welcome to what it's like to love and be loved. As far as clubs go, it ain't half bad, is it?"

"No two I'd rather belong to," he confessed, and I nodded.

"It's different," I admitted.

"It is that."

"Just hope our brother gets to join it soon."

"That makes two of us, maybe then he'll pull his head out of his fuckin' ass."

"Amen to that," I muttered.

I sighed and looked up at the ceiling. Archer grunted, and asked, "She do that epic freak-out shit often?"

"Used to, but it's been a while."

"Didn't I always tell you not to stick your dick in crazy?"

"Sure did, but it's not that kind of crazy. Just got to her a little too late when it came to that school of hers."

"Ah, that little problem you cleared up left a mark, huh?"

"That it did."

"Well, it looks like you got instant family, just add relationship, so you got some responsibilities now. Best get back out there and live up to 'em."

"Think I've been doing pretty well so far," I said.

"Weren't no accusations comin' out my mouth otherwise, kid. You been doin' alright, for all I ain't been paying much attention on account of my own thing going on over here." He frowned, and I held up a hand.

"Family looks good on you, Brother. I'm glad things are working out for you and Mel."

"Thanks," he said and dragged open the bathroom door.

"No problem," I muttered and went on through.

We found our ol' ladies and the boys in the lodge's main room, parked in front of a big screen TV just getting started on a movie. Sage had bounced back, smiling and laughing with Connor at one end of the couch, while Maren sat huddled in one of the recliners. Her eyes traveled over my face and came to rest on the scraped and bloodied knuckles of my left hand. Sorrow passed through her eyes which she tried to cover with a brave smile.

"Work things out?" she asked softly, and Archer answered before I could.

"Not yet, but trust me, they will. They always do."

I appreciated Archer's attempt at comfort. I knew it wasn't his strong suit, and I had to give Melody a wink. She was changing my hard-assed older brother, and the changes were good.

I went to the recliner and held out a hand. Maren took it and stood, and I sat down in her place, pulling her into my lap, kissing the top of her head.

"What're we watching?" I asked and Sage piped up.

"Night of the Living Dead!"

Zombie apocalypse. Cool.

ABOUT THREE OR four torturous days after the lake run, I finally went out to Rush's shop to see if peace could be had. I hated being at odds with my twin. It fucking sucked massive dick, and truthfully it sucked the balls too that he hadn't reached out to me.

He sat at his workbench, hand carving a service tray with flowers and vines, and I leaned a hip against the edge of the bench, arms crossed over my chest.

"What's that?" I asked, just to break the ice and get the conversation going.

"You wanted me to fucking apologize, what's it look like?"

"That's for Maren?" I asked.

"Yeah."

A long silence stretched out between us, and I sighed.

"Look –" I started but he shook his head.

"No need. You were right... I am jealous, I guess. It's like you and Arch have both got just about everything I've wanted and are leaving me in the dust, and it sucks."

I blinked, stupefied, and it was out of my mouth before I could stop myself, "Seriously? That's what you think? That I'm trying to shut you out? Dude, Rush… Maren and Sage are basically my family now and as cool as it is, it scares the fuck out of me too."

He looked up at me and scowled. "Why? You fuckin' got this."

I raised my eyebrows. "Glad you fuckin' think so douche nozzle! Shit. Feels like I'm flyin' by the seat of my pants and seriously feels like you're shoving me away over it. You're my goddamn fuckin' *twin*, Rush. I ain't interested in gaining over there while I'm losing over here."

He crossed his arms over his chest and chewed his split lip. "You ain't losing shit over here, you greedy fuck."

"Fuckin' straight! You heard that right, I want my cake and I'm gonna eat it too."

Rush smirked and pressed his mouth shut, trying not to laugh and I felt my face split into a fuckin' mile-wide grin.

"Just fuckin' say it you perverted fuck. We shared a goddamn womb for nine months and I know what you're thinkin'."

"Why the fuck you want cake when you can eat barely legal teen pie?" he demanded, and I bowed my head and shook it.

He held out his hand and I put mine in it, pulling each other into it to bump shoulders. Peace made, squabble in the rearview… thank fuck.

32

M aren...

I texted Nox, dying to know.

Me: Did you work things out with Rush?

It felt like forever before the phone buzzed through with an answer, and when it did, it made me smile.

Nox: Yes Angel. U worry too much. Told u it was going to b fine.

I smiled and tapped out another message to him, a question this time.

Me: When can I see you again?

A few seconds later...

Nox: Knock knock

I looked up, just as a knock came at the front door. Sage slammed down the stairs as I moved through the kitchen. He beat me to the door and flung it open.

Nox smiled and laughed. "Hey, buddy!" I paused in the kitchen archway, smiling but a little unsure. His twin, Rush, stood behind him on the front porch.

"Hey, Nox! I didn't think you were coming."

"What, and miss out on Taco Tuesday? You kidding me?"

"Can I come in?" Rush called out from behind Nox and I forced a brave smile, his words still cutting from the lake.

I called back, "Sure, there's plenty for everyone."

Rush smiled, and the two men came into the house, closing the door behind them and hanging their jackets and cuts on the hooks set into the wooden plaque on the wall by the door.

"You miss me?" Nox asked, coming to me for a kiss. I smiled up into his face.

"Always," I murmured.

"How was work?" he asked, and Sage scoffed.

"Boring!" he declared.

"She make you go with her?" Rush asked and Sage nodded.

"I didn't want him here playing video games all day. We still have some spring break left. I told him I'd let him do it one day, but today wasn't it." Sage rolled his eyes and passed me going into the kitchen, taking a seat at one of the kitchen counter stools.

Nox and I went to work cooking dinner, as we all laughed and talked, ignoring the elephant in the room for the time being. After dinner, Sage helped clean up along with Nox and Rush, giving me a break. Though truthfully, it was actually Rush's idea.

I could sense he wanted to speak but was graciously waiting on Sage to leave the room. I had some mixed feelings about it. While I was grateful to keep the grown-up stuff between the grownups, there were times, like this one, that I felt like I was doing Sage a disservice.

Rush kept giving me sidelong looks, and then trading yet more side-long looks with his brother until, eventually, Nox sighed and said, "Hey Sage, do me a favor and sit back at the table for a minute before you go upstairs."

"Am I in trouble?" Sage asked, hesitating.

"No, little man... I am," Rush said with a tired smile.

I perked up a bit, and the three of them joined me at the table. I took a fortifying sip of my tea and waited Rush out patiently.

He addressed Sage first. "So, you know, part of being in the club is having your brother's backs and holding them accountable, right?" he asked.

"I guess so," Sage said slowly, his face guarded.

"Well, the same is true in reverse," Nox said. "Part of being in the club is that your brothers have your back, but that they hold you account-able when you f-fudge up."

I bit my bottom lip and tried to hide my smile at Nox's last second correction.

"Okay, did I screw up?" Sage asked.

"No, man. I screwed up, at the lake, and I need to apologize to your sister," Rush said.

"It's okay," I said softly, shifting uncomfortably in my seat.

"It's not, and I'm really sorry for what I said to you, Maren. It was unfair. I fucked up; it came out of my own bad history and insecurities. I upset you, and your brother by default, for no reason and it wasn't cool. I hope you can forgive me."

The silence stretched between us for a moment as I tried to find words. "Of course I forgive you. I'm sorry I reacted badly —"

"See, you ain't gotta apologize for that —"

"No, in some ways I do. It came from a similar place, out of my own bad history and insecurities."

Nox was staring at Sage who was ping-ponging between me and Rush as we spoke. He nudged my brother and said gently, "See, this is what real men do. We apologize when we screw up, and we own it. We don't try to hide it, or pretend whatever we did, didn't happen. That's called honor and if you don't have honor, you have nothing."

"You are nothing," Rush added. "It's okay to make mistakes. We all do. I did. It's what we do after we make them, how we handle them, that matters. You get me?"

I smiled then, eyes growing wet with tears as my heart swelled to ten times its size with both gratitude and pride. I could see it in my brother's face that he was really thinking about this. Filing it away for future reference and that what Rush and Nox had just done was making quite the impression and I couldn't even begin to tell them just how grateful I was for it.

Sage looked over to me and asked, "Think this calls for ice cream?" a hopeful edge to his voice and the two men laughed with me.

"I think that's a fine idea," I said.

We had ice cream and talked until way past mine and Sage's bedtime, but it was worth it. When I saw Nox and Rush to the door, it was with a bittersweet longing for them both to stay. I wasn't quite ready for the magic captured that evening to end.

It'd felt like a family around our little dining room table. For a moment or two, it had felt like when my dad was alive and I missed him, so, so, much. While it hadn't been exactly as when he'd been alive, it had been close enough, and I wanted to hold on to that feeling.

Nox kissed me goodnight, and whispered, "Goodnight, Angel," against my lips.

I smiled and had the thought that he had it wrong… if anything, Nox was my angel.

"Can you come back?" I whispered.

"After Sage is asleep?"

"Yeah."

He smiled. "I think that can be arranged. Let me ride to the club and grab a change of clothes for work in the morning. Sound good?"

"Sounds good."

I let him go and set about getting ready for bed along with Sage who surprised me when he said, "Nox should move in with us."

I spit out my toothpaste, holding my hair aside, and asked, "What makes you say that?"

He shrugged. "He's family now. I like him, and you don't think I know he sneaks back here and stays the night?" My brother rolled his eyes at me. "I'm eleven. I'm not a baby anymore, and I'm not stupid."

I made an incredulous sound, my mouth falling open as he headed out the bathroom door and went to make the turn into his bedroom.

"Don't worry," he said, smirking. "It's not like I hear you having sex. You guys are really good at being quiet."

"Sage!" I shouted indignantly, but it was met by the sound of his bedroom door closing. I stood, shocked, face flaming with my tooth-brush forgotten in my hand for a full minute before I got back with it.

When Nox returned, slipping quietly into my room, I told him what happened. My cheeks flamed further when he couldn't stop laughing. Loud peals of laughter that became infectious, until before long I was laughing, too.

"You're not helping!" I declared, and he dropped onto the edge of the bed beside me.

"I think we should finish the room swap with your dad's old room, how about you? Put some more distance between yours and your brother's and while you're at it, officially claim the title of 'parent' of the household."

I searched his face. He wasn't wrong, and my father's room was essentially gutted now. All of his belongings in storage in the attic or donated to *Goodwill*, accordingly. We had no reason to keep his clothes and it had been a painful thing to take them away, but Sage and I had done it together.

"I can get some of the guys to help, maybe in the next weekend or two? I think it's time, baby."

I nodded mutely, and wondered, not for the first time and probably not for the last, how I would ever do any of this without Nox there to hold my hand.

I must have said it out loud because he smiled at me, and it held the warmth of the sun despite the night pressing against the window glass.

"You never have to find out, Angel, because I'm here."

I melted. He gathered me into his arms, and I fit so wonderfully against his chest. Like two jigsaw puzzles, we just fit, and I was really beginning to think that God intended us that way. I felt equal parts blessed that I had found Nox so early in life and saddened that it had taken poor Nox so long.

"Babe?" he asked as I slipped from the bed and onto my knees in front of him.

He held his hands out to the sides as I undid his belt. A gleam of deep, dark desire moving behind his eyes, and he made no move to stop me.

Permission granted, I thought to myself, and undid his jeans, lifting him out of the front and wrapping my lips around the head of his cock. He was soft but wasn't staying that way. He grew in my mouth and down my throat and I closed my eyes, relaxing and swallowing, concentrating so I wouldn't choke. I took him deep into my mouth, so far, my lips touched his body and listened with satisfaction at his, *"Oh, God, fuck yes, Angel!"*

I took my time with this, slow and patient, a serenity filling me that I could do this. Give him pleasure, and that he not only was letting me have my way with him, that he was genuinely enjoying it. It gave me a sense of power, made me feel almost invincible, and on top of that; sexy, and alluring.

His moans and heavy breathing made me bolder in my explorations, and I took my time, rolling my eyes to look up his body and take in every subtle reaction. He gathered my hair and held it back for me as I bobbed my mouth up and down, slicking his cock with my saliva, teasing the underside with my tongue, velvet against the satin flesh of his erection.

I grew wet. I wasn't wearing any panties under my nightgown, which I was happy for, because I knew just about any second he was going to grab the condom I had waiting off my bedside table and would put it to good use. He fisted his hand in the back of my hair in that controlling way that turned my insides to liquid fire and I pressed my thighs together, body trembling finely as he pulled my mouth off his cock and bent, shoving his mouth against mine.

He kissed me long and lingering deep, even as he stood, gently pulling me up by a combination of my hair and an arm around my body. I shivered with want and anticipation as he tore his mouth from mine and growled at me, "Lose the nightgown."

I slid the straps off my shoulders slowly, making eye contact the entire time, and let the material inch down my body, a slow, sexy reveal that left Nox's gaze heated and hungry. He tugged gently at my scalp and I sank down onto the mattress, sitting at his wordless command. He nudged my knees apart with one of his and surprised me when he relinquished my hair and went to his knees between mine.

"Lay back and relax, Angel," he murmured, his breath hot and tantalizing against my skin. He placed a gentle, chaste kiss against my right inner thigh and I shivered, laying back even as he used the breadth of his shoulders to keep my legs open for him. He wrapped his arms around my outer thighs and with one strong motion, pulled me, sliding me bodily against the bed, until my ass barely rested at the edge. I squeaked in surprise which Nox quickly turned to a moan as he lapped at me, his tongue hot and wet against my sex, splitting the lips of my pussy until he reached the pearl at the top. He teased my clit with a gentle probing of his tongue and I stuffed both my hands against my mouth to stifle the moans and cries trying to escape.

His finger slid inside me with hardly any effort at all, my arousal peaked as it was. I writhed at the feeling as he teased my walls, and his response was to use his other arm as a barrier across my hips, pinning me down so that he could have his way. I'd never had anyone do this before and I was amazed at just how good it felt. His lips and tongue were sweet and considerate, as was he, listening for my cues and trying new things accordingly.

I yipped when he found a particularly sensitive spot inside me and he chuckled, the sound dark and rich like fine chocolate as he pinned me down harder with his arm and began to exploit the spot with gentle probes of his finger even as he began a new assault with his tongue on the outside.

Oh. My. God.

I collapsed back onto the bed and felt like I had both died and gone to heaven. I gripped the covers in my fists and panted as he wound me up, my body tightening in response to what his lips, tongue, and fingers did to me. I closed my eyes, breath coming in heavy pants as that warm glow of champagne bubbles zephyred through my body, brushing every last nerve ending with pleasure.

He grabbed for the condom off the bedside table as I lay panting and spent, my hands over my mouth, looking at him. He loomed above me, standing between my legs, kicking off his boots and out of his pants the rest of the way. He put the condom on carefully, and stared down at me for a full second, sweeping me with his hungry gaze, before he pulled his tee over his head.

I drank the sight of his hard, nude body in, and reached my hands out to him. He smiled and it held a light that was beautiful, as he once again wrapped his arms powerfully around my legs above my knees and jerked me, dragging me back to the edge of the bed from where I'd squirmed away from it. He lifted me, back arching sharply, and fitted himself inside me. I put my legs around him and he stroked a few times before lowering himself to his knees and me back down to the bed.

He ravished me. He pushed inside me and followed through with his thrusts until I thought for sure that he would either come out the other side or split me in two. It took me a little while to adjust, while I liked it when he gave it to me hard like this, it sometimes started off with an edge of pain to it as he nudged so deep inside of me, my body was cranky about yielding to the invasion.

The orgasm first had helped, and he helped things along by straddling one of my legs on the bed. He raised my other one against his chest, hugging it, massaging my thigh, before unknotting one of my hands from its death grip in my quilt and leading it, skimming across my skin, to my pussy.

"Touch yourself, Angel. I want to watch." As an afterthought, he took my hand away from my body and put those fingers in his mouth, sucking them, teasing them with his tongue, and lubing them up with his saliva. He guided them, wet and ready, to my waiting clit, and I closed my eyes and arched, doing as he asked, touching myself.

It was such a sense of power and beauty he gave me with the request, I don't know, it's hard to explain. Still, whatever the case may be, it was both hard for me and a long time for me to come but *God* did it feel good in the meantime. I lay as his strokes went from punishing and fast to long and lazy as he attempted to find what worked that would work me into another orgasm.

He was so patient, and I found myself apologizing for taking so long to reach one. He laughed and shoved himself all the way deep, holding himself there.

"Don't you ever apologize for taking too long to come, baby; you take as long as you take. It's no hardship for me, believe me. Now touch that clit, breathe for me and relax."

I closed my eyes, concentrating on the feeling of him and did as he ordered, sliding my fingers through my wetness and around that sensitive bundle of nerves. He made short, deep, strokes, and I gasped, the tide of pleasure rising. I kept at it, finding what worked until I felt full to the very top.

"That's it, baby, tighter," he murmured and I let the tide roll me and sweep me under, the whole time Nox held me tight, my anchor to reality and my rock to shelter against. He drove into me, through my spasms and with a subtle 'oh God' and a final thrust, he let my leg off to the side and collapsed over me, sealing his mouth to mine and burying his fingers in my hair, holding it back from our faces.

This was heaven. This is where my happiness lay, and this was where I was safe. With Nox, in his arms.

33

N**ox...**

My brother Archer was on the floor, melting the fuck down like I had never in my fucking life seen before. I swallowed hard and exchanged a look with Rush who's face said just as loudly as my thundering heart – *this was scary. No, terrifying.*

How many times had Archer been there for us? How many times had he shouldered the burden, so we didn't have to? And now, here he was, the most vulnerable I had ever seen him, his newborn son being taken from his arms, openly weeping and all I wanted to do was hide from it.

Not going to happen.

I stood shoulder to shoulder with my oldest brother, even as Rush took his other side. We watched through the glass set in the operating room's doors as Doc did his thing. All of us, our eyes glued to the monitor. The line went flat, and Archer wailed, turning, slamming his back against the wall by the doors sliding to the floor.

Rush and I braced him and let him weep. What else could we do?

I felt hollow. I'd held a fondness for Melody, ever since she'd been with Grind. She was sweet, and everything Grind, God love him, didn't deserve. When she'd come here with Noah is when I discovered that I'd loved her like a sister, and now, too soon, she was gone? After everything Arch had done to protect us, to protect and become a better man for her, and it was over like this?

No. It couldn't be.

"Please, God, don't you take her from me," Archer said through his tears and I was struck low. I had never, once ever, heard my brother pray and it did something to me. Sent me into a state of numb fear... and I felt *myself* start to spiral and lose strength and will.

It was the weirdest fucking thing as if Archer's weakness over the situation threw my world off its axis, and out of its spin.

This wasn't how things were supposed to be.

Numbness took over, and duty. I had a duty to my brother and my sister-in-law both, to shore him up as best I could, to have faith that she was going to pull through, and above all, be there for their sons.

Rush and I helped Archer to the waiting room for two of the most agonizing hours of our lives.

Doc finally came and found us, all of us, the whole club, waiting for him. He pulled the mask off his face and said, "She lost a lot of blood, we had to perform an emergency partial hysterectomy, but she's still with us. She's sleepin' now. Come on back, Papa."

Archer lurched to his feet and hugged Doc, while several of us were laid low with relief. Most of the ol' ladies had tears in their eyes. Some of the rest of the men, myself included, were doing their best to hold theirs back.

I exchanged a look with Rush and he gave me a nod. He got it. Too many people. Too much all at once. I needed space. I needed to go.

Archer looked back at me and Rush and said, "Thanks, I got it from here," and it was all the absolution I fuckin' needed.

I left, didn't look back, went straight out to my bike and straight to the one person I knew could fix this with her kindness, understanding, and grace… this war of fucked up emotions, this scared, lost little boy inside me.

I went to Maren's and stood on her front stoop knocking, *pounding* on the front door until she opened it.

"Nox! What's wrong?" she asked, but I was already on my knees, arms around her, face buried in her stomach and sobbing like a child.

"Oh my, God…" she gasped and wrapped her arms around me, taking me in, kissing the top of my hair and giving me a place to shelter from this shit storm of emotions I had absolutely no fucking control over.

"What happened?" she asked me gently, sometime later. I was huddled miserably on her couch, head in her lap staring at the fire I'd gotten going in the fireplace. Maren sat stoically, gently running her fingertips through my hair.

"Mel had her baby," I said and shifted uncomfortably.

"Oh, oh no… did he die?"

"No, Mel almost did."

She stilled, and I closed my eyes and told her everything. She kept up with the soothing little touches, and it did a lot to keep me calm. She sighed gently and bent over me, placing a kiss on my temple.

"I don't know what happened," I said and rubbed my eyes.

She was quiet for a time, lending me back the strength I'd poured into her time and again and I thought to myself, *this is what partnership should be,* before she spoke again.

"Could it be, watching Archer, the always strong and solid one, break down... could it be that it triggered a panic attack or a flashback of some kind?" she asked quietly.

I nodded. "I think you might be right," I said, thinking back to how I'd felt thrown back in time. How I'd felt like that fucking helpless little boy with Duncan bearing down on me. How I felt like my only defense against anything in this world had crumbled and I was suddenly on my own.

"Maren?"

We both turned, startled, at Sage's voice. He sat on the stairs, peering at us through the spindles holding the railing together and I recognized that look. It was the same one that I'd seen on Rush, Grind's and even Archer's face a thousand times and more coming up.

"It's okay, Sage," Maren said, beating me to it.

"What happened?" he asked, and I sat up and sniffed, realizing that what Archer was to me, a defense, a big brother and someone I could always count on — I was that to Sage now. It was a huge responsibility and one I never fully appreciated until now.

I owed Archer one hell of an expensive bottle of scotch, and it still wasn't even close to expressing the gratitude I had for him in that moment.

"Come on down here, buddy."

Sage came down the stairs and sat next to me on the couch. The three of us talked and worked on some of our issues. Sage's distress at my distress diminished and even he asked if Melody was okay, and what was going to happen.

"I don't know, buddy. She stays in the hospital. I know Archer is gonna stay with her until she gets better. I guess it means I'll be hanging out with Noah a little bit more for a while until they can all come home as a family."

"Can I help?" he asked, and I huffed a bit of a laugh.

"We'll see," I said.

"I thought you said that brothers helped each other when sh- things went sideways," he corrected.

"They do," I said, blinking in surprise.

"Then I want to help," he said, mouth thinned down in a line of grim determination.

I exchanged a look with Maren, whose expression was a mix of pride and wistfulness. She said, "Good, I'm going to need you to help because I still have to work."

She put out her hand and Sage put his on top, without hesitation. He looked at me expectantly and as cheesy as it was, it felt good and I felt like it was our own thing, so I put my hand on top of the pile. We raised them and dropped them with some finality and stayed on the couch, all of us staring into the fire for long minutes until we all agreed the following day wasn't going to wait for us, and we needed sleep.

I stayed, cradling Maren in the curve of my body, pulling her back against me tightly and swearing on whatever powers that fucking be, that I was never letting go and that no matter what life threw at us, it was going to be me before her.

If it wasn't, it was going to be me, not long after. I couldn't fathom a life without her, but she never had to know. No one did. That was just inviting trouble and shrinks and what have you. Just another thing my fucked-up childhood had taught me early on.

34

M aren...

"You look beautiful," Shelly said, leaning back with the mascara wand.

"Pictures, we need pictures!" Evy cried and then there was Melody, her camera in her hands, clicking away. Dazzling flashbulbs going off in my face until I raised my hand laughing at all of them.

We were at the club, and all of the ol' ladies had taken over one of the guy's rooms to get me ready for my prom date with Nox.

The club was having a huge laugh at my boyfriend's — excuse me, my ol' man's —expense and I felt very lucky that he not only was taking it in stride, he seemed to revel in it.

All because it makes you *happy,* I thought. I smiled and stood up, the white dress Dani, Ashton, and Hayden had helped me pick was gorgeous. It was a solid opaque with spaghetti straps to hold it up. It clung to every curve and angle and made me look feminine, but that wasn't the coolest part.

Overlaying everything was a gauzy, ethereal material, long bell sleeves of it off my shoulders and draping finely, millions of little crystal jewels glued to it so no matter where I stepped or how I moved it sparkled and flashed like I was something out of a fantasy movie.

I'd tried it on for laughs, the price tag way exceeding my modest budget, but when I had stepped out of the dressing room? No one had laughed, and Ashton had declared she was buying it for me. No 'buts' and no arguments.

I'd tried anyway, but Hayden and Dani had good-naturedly bullied me into accepting the expensive dress as a gift. Dani had even pulled a sketchpad out of her back pocket, a little notepad kind, and had started drawing in it before we even reached the register.

She'd made jewelry to go with it. Beautiful white gold drop earrings and drop pendant that rested in the hollow of my throat. Shelly had expertly done my makeup and standing in front of the mirror, I looked much closer to twenty-eight than eighteen. I wondered what Nox would think, as Everett fussed with my hair a few more times, getting the light, loose curls to lay over my shoulder just so before giving me the okay to go out and be seen.

"I think you're gorgeous," she declared.

"You're really beautiful," Melody said, sniffing.

"Oh, don't cry!" I said and felt my own eyes tear up. "You do and I'll ruin my makeup!"

We laughed, and she moved slowly, still sore and not fully healed from her ordeal of only a couple of weeks before. It would take four to six more for her to be fully at one hundred percent, but she'd insisted on being here with everyone else for my special night. She came towards me and hugged me saying, "I'm so proud of you."

I sniffed and said back, "Okay, really now, stop it or I'm gonna cry."

There was laughter, several of us choking up, and then Mandy clapped her hands together. "Well, as much as I thank you for the early practice before Eden gets to be this age," more laughter, "I think we should go see what your ol' man looks like, yeah?"

I smiled bravely and nodded, nervous for the first time in a long time about seeing Nox. I followed the rest of the club women out toward the club's common room and bar. Holding my breath slightly as they parted and let me through to see Nox.

He straightened from tying one of his black and white wing-tip shoes and I forgot to breathe for a moment. He wore black slacks and a deep, blood red shirt that had a vaguely metallic sheen to it. A narrow black satin tie looked smart against the red, and his dark hair was slicked back. He looked dashing and daring and was probably more attractive than I had ever found him. We stood several paces apart, just looking at each other, speechless.

Rush ruined the spell by slapping his twin brother in the arm, holding out his leather jacket and cut to him. I smiled and didn't have a single complaint. It was so much a part of him, a suit jacket would have seemed... weird. Nox shook his head and held his hands out to Trigger who handed him a plastic clamshell box; a white orchid corsage inside of it.

Nox opened it up carefully and came to me, holding the band for my wrist. I slid my hand through and he breathed, "You're so beautiful. My angel fell to earth, didn't she?"

I blushed furiously, and smiled mischievously, asking "With the color scheme, does that make you the devil tonight?"

"Only when the music stops, and I have you to myself," he murmured.

My breath caught again, and I pressed my thighs together unconsciously against the sudden tingle of want between them. He leaned down, cupping my cheek and carefully kissed me, a slight brush of lips so as not to ruin my lip gloss.

The camera went off, and some catcalls and whistles went up and I smiled.

"Come on you two," Archer said. "Up against the mural and let Mel get some real good shots of you."

We obliged and smiled, standing in some traditional prom photo poses in front of the Sacred Heart's mural behind the pool table, which had mysteriously moved to allow Mel the space she needed to get all of us in the photo without hassle.

"Like to think you planned this or something," I said to some laughs and chuckles.

Archer held his new son, Chandler, and stared dotingly after Mel while Dragon had a hold of a sleeping Noah. The little guy was completely racked out against the president's shoulder.

"Okay, family, both club and not, let's let these two get to dinner and their dance," he said and some of the guys started cracking up at Nox's expense.

"Yeah, yeah, y'all are just jealous you can't recapture your youth," he said and I smiled.

"Hey Nox, think fast," Rev called and threw something at us. I flinched but Nox caught the flashing object, the ring of keys slapping his palm reaching my ears.

He looked down. "The Chevelle? Really?"

Rev shrugged. "You only go to prom once…" He frowned. "Except for you."

"Hey, this is my first prom too. I skipped out on my first one."

"You did? I didn't know that."

Nox smiled at me. "I did, and I'll tell you over dinner."

We left, and when we stepped out front, it was to a classic red and white muscle car waiting for us. It was beautiful, and worth it to see the light in Nox's eyes over it. He opened my door for me and I got in, murmuring my thanks.

"Anything for you, Angel. You should know that by now."

He closed the door on me and went around to the front, getting in on his side. He started the engine with a feisty growl that settled into a dangerous rumbling purr and with a lot of cheering and applause, we pulled down the club's driveway and onto the street.

"Are you going to tell me where we're going for dinner now?" I asked, curiosity killing me. He smiled, and it held such love and so many secrets. I laughed. "You're going to drive me insane," I told him.

"Every intention of it, baby. Just like I have every intention of pulling that dress off with my teeth."

I felt my mouth drop open as he chuckled and accelerated, and I found myself laughing with him. I perked up when we turned down some familiar streets and a smile painted itself from ear to ear.

"It's Filiberto's, isn't it?" I asked and he smiled.

"First place we had dinner out together and it's your favorite. I thought it was as good a place as any." He pulled us up smoothly to the curb.

"I love you so much for not putting me through the torture of some ridiculously fancy and stupid restaurant we'd need to go to McDonald's for after."

He laughed and said, "Filiberto's is pretty fancy as far as places that I frequent go; but yeah, at least we know the food is good and there's enough of it to be satisfied. Don't go anywhere, let me get your door."

He came around and opened up my door and held out his hand to me, gallant, like the gentleman his rough exterior hid. I took it and stepped out onto the curb and he shut and locked up the car. He held out his arm and we strolled up the sidewalk to the restaurant.

We exchanged a look inside the door and had to laugh. We weren't the only well-dressed couple waiting to see the hostess. It seemed that this may be a favorite spot for more than a couple of high schools having their prom tonight, because while I recognized a few of my classmates, the majority of the students here were complete strangers.

"I love your dress," a blonde girl in royal blue murmured and hers was pretty, too, with her coloring. I smiled and complimented her while her date stared wide-eyed at Nox and his colors.

"Is that your dad?" she asked quietly and I laughed and smiled, used to it by now.

"No, he's my boyfriend," I responded, and she colored lightly.

"I'm so sorry," she stammered when her boyfriend elbowed her.

"Don't be, it happens all the time," Nox said and gave her one of his best, disarming smiles.

"Comes with the territory," I assured her.

"Anyone with a reservation?" the hostess asked above the slight crowd and Nox raised his finger.

"Name?"

"Nox," he said and she looked. He smiled and said, "It might be under Landon Fisher."

"Ah! Thank you, here it is… right this way, Nox," she said and when we looked back at the touchscreen at the hostess station, we both laughed.

Displayed was 'Reservation for two, second level, table nineteen, Mr. Landon Fisher – call him 'Nox' whatever you do.'

"What was that?"

Nox laughed a little and told me, "When I made the reservation, they kept asking for my name and I'd tell her 'Nox', she asked for my first name and I told her 'Nox', she asked for my last name and I said 'no last name.' She said she didn't understand, so I finally said 'Fine, Landon Fisher but call me Nox, dammit!' I must have scared her."

I laughed. "If they only knew how absolutely amazing you are, Mr. Nox," I whispered and leaned up to kiss him on his cheek. He laughed and smiled and pulled out my chair for me, and I had to smile even wider... it was our table, the one on the second floor in the back.

We had a fine meal and being seated where we were, we had the illusion of privacy. Nox twined his fingers with mine and we spoke of the future. Of the plans I had for working at *Soul Fuel* and the possibility of further education. We slipped back to the conversation of making my dad's old room my own, which I still hadn't done, but had been slowly chipping away at storing things and getting comfortable with the idea of it.

It was a lovely dinner and I found myself both sated and relaxed without being overly full. I fixed my lip gloss in my small compact and stashed both items in the small clutch purse I carried with me.

He got my door for me once more, and we drove to my school. One of the very last times for me. Graduation was just days away, our prom late this year. He pulled into a space and we walked across the parking lot hand in hand toward the main doors.

The prom was held in the cafeteria in my school. Much preferable to the gym, as well as much easier to transform. When we went through the doors it was into another world. The theme this year was 'Happily Ever After' which wasn't that ironic? Mine was guiding me with a hand on my lower back in front of a fairy tale themed backdrop for yet more photos of us.

The photographer tried to take Nox's coat to which he snapped, "Hands off my colors." The photographer froze and Nox added, "Please," at my gentle reminding look that these people just didn't understand.

The photographer let it go and Nox took off his jacket and cut, hanging them close by, just out of the camera's view but within reach, on the back of a chair Mr. Hunter set out. Nox gave Mr. Hunter a nod which Mr. Hunter returned, and we had our photos taken, Nox remaining polite, even nice to the photographer who really hadn't known any better.

We slipped off to the side and Mr. Hunter suggested, "Perhaps it would be best if we locked it in my office?"

Nox smiled, thinly and shook his head. "Maren, Angel, I'm going to run this outside, maybe have one of my brothers pick it up. You cool to wait here for a minute?"

"Absolutely," I agreed, and he left to take care of things.

"I don't believe I will ever fully understand that culture," Mr. Hunter remarked, and I smiled at him.

"You would be amazed at how fiercely loyal and protective they are," I murmured.

"Of their property, yes... treating women as property... Maren, I would be remiss if I didn't say I worry about you."

"I appreciate the concern, Mr. Hunter, I really do, but I can't explain things to you. Just believe me when I say, part of why they are so misunderstood is because of how intensely private they are. The other side of the coin is that they have no desire whatsoever to compromise that privacy in order to explain or reveal their views to what they perceive as the idly curious."

Mr. Hunter chuckled. "Ever the scholar, Ms. Tracy."

I blushed. "They're good people; they just do things very differently to us. It's simpler in some ways and vastly more complicated in others."

Mr. Hunter chuckled. "You were so very adult long before you ever turned eighteen. I suppose no one should be surprised at an older part-ner, but a Sacred Heart?"

I laughed lightly and shifted a bit uncomfortably. "I suppose I've always marched to the beat of my own drum." I gripped Mr. Hunter's hand subtly and gave it a squeeze. "Thank you for letting me have this... my prom, I mean... with Nox."

Mr. Hunter smiled and nodded, crossing his arms over his chest, "You've always been truthful with me; always been a stellar student despite this school's inability to protect you. I didn't mind going to bat for you for this. There's nothing against school policy that dictates the age of your partner or where they come from... simply that they are here by invitation of a currently enrolled student. I simply reminded Mr. Barber of that."

Mr. Barber was the school principal, and not exactly known for his patience, leniency, or forgiving nature. I nodded, and said, "Thank you, anyway."

"You're welcome, Maren. Just whatever you do? Do well in life for me."

"She will," Nox said from behind me, drawing me back against him. "My angel can do anything she puts her mind to."

I leaned my head back against his shoulder and smiled, and he smiled down at me. Mr. Hunter gave a nod with a smile of his own, and spoke with Nox briefly, before shaking his hand and moving off. I turned and caught Lucas staring in our direction, his expression clearly unhappy. Oh, well.

Nox led me around and we spoke to a few classmates of mine that were mostly outcasts like me. Their curiosity evident, but their attitudes about it refreshingly cool. It didn't hurt that Nox was gorgeous.

Chelsea Day had her nose in the air, but Nox laughed at her and her expression hardened in her best, glacial, ice princess fashion, but Nox wasn't even phased. He put his lips near my ear and murmured, "If someone fucked her like I give it to you, you think she'd mellow out some?"

I smiled and tucked myself closer into his body and murmured, "She'd never have it so good, and I'd honestly feel sorry for the poor chump that had to stick his dick in her."

Nox laughed and pulled me into his arms for a slow song on the dance floor. We skipped the faster-paced songs, opting for a little punch and light conversation with Hillary Womack and her boyfriend Jack Schilling. They were both extremely intelligent and honors students. We'd shared some of the honors classes together and had done some group projects.

"I'll be back," I murmured to Nox. "Restroom."

"Okay, baby. No problem."

He let me go and continued to listen with genuine, as far as I could tell, interest to Jack's theory about the latest sci-fi movie's plot line. I slipped out of the cafeteria and down the hall to the nearest ladie's room and freshened up a touch.

I slipped back out into the hallway and was stopped by a familiar voice asking, "Maren, can I talk to you?"

I looked up and bit my bottom lip, shaking my head. "Luke, I don't think that's a good idea."

"Please," he said, taking a few more steps into the hall. "It'll only take a minute. You have to know, I feel really bad—"

"Look," I said holding up my hand with a sigh. For the last couple of months, the closer we got to the end of the year, the more his attempts at holding doors for me and more attempts at actual conversation, were being made. The problem was, I just wasn't interested in anything Luke had to say.

Whatever apology he had that he wanted to make was all well and good, but it couldn't and wouldn't change things. As upset as I was about Nox doing whatever he did to scare Lucas into leaving me alone, I just couldn't bring myself to feel all that bad about it. I had prayed so many times for the cruelty to stop, the hurtful words, the pranks, the rumors… just all of it to stop that when it was finally lessened by such a great degree? I was so relieved, I couldn't bring myself to be angry about it. Not with Nox, no matter how bad it had been for Luke or his dad. It was Karma. I'd made peace with that.

"I'm really sorry, Luke, but nothing you could possibly say could fix things between us."

"I know," he said rushing up to me. I backed up out of habit and slid sideways, along the bathroom door until I was stuck, backed up against the side of the lockers; Luke invading my personal space.

"I know there's nothing I could say or do to fix things. I was an asshole. I was trying to impress my dad, and it was wrong, but, Maren —" I yipped when I tried to side step him and he grabbed me by my shoulders to bring me back in line with his gaze.

"Maren, no, you have to listen to me!" he grated and gave me a rough shake.

All I could think was, *oh my God, he's lost it.*

"Okay! Okay, Lucas, I'm listening."

"Okay, okay, sorry, I'm sorry," he said rubbing up and down my arms, but it hurt with the intensity of his grip. It wasn't at all like when Nox touched me to comfort me.

"I'm listening," I said, swallowing hard, afraid.

Luke leaned in and whispered harshly, "He's bad news, Maren. He hurts people. His club hurts people and you need to get away from him."

"Nox isn't like that, Luke. I promise," I stammered. When he'd breathed on me, I could smell it, the alcohol on his breath.

"He is like that, Maren!" he whisper-shouted. He placed his hands on the side of my neck, stroking my jawline with his thumbs. I'd used to love when he'd called me his girl, when he'd stroke along my jaw and pull me in for a kiss. Now I strained backward away from him.

"Luke, let me go, please, you're starting to scare me."

"He came to our house, him and two of his buddies; they hurt my dad; you have to believe me. You'd be much better off with me, you should come back."

"I-I don't think so, I can't do that," I said, tears slipping free. I took a deep breath to scream and he *squeezed*, my air was cut off and I felt my eyes go wide as he tried to get me to be quiet.

"Shh, shh, shh, I'm not going to hurt you, Maren. Not like you hurt me. You hurt me when you broke up with me, you know that right? It's okay, though, I forgive you."

I clawed at Luke's hands and wrists, trying to get him to let me go, but he was too drunk to realize he was even hurting me. I choked and tried to get air, starbursts of color and light that wasn't really there going off in my vision.

A blur of crimson and suddenly I could breathe, my hearing tuned into shouting. Hands on my shoulders propping me up; I screamed or tried to, but I was too busy sucking in much-needed air. I blinked and looked up to Mr. Hunter, and over to Nox, who was kneeing Lucas in the face, a good portion of the student body gathered in the doorway to the gym behind us.

Luke was down, Mrs. Cox leaning over him and shouting at the students to go back in the cafeteria while Mr. Hunter was trying to take me toward the offices. I reached for Nox who pulled me into his arms and away from Mr. Hunter and it was the only place I wanted to be.

I sobbed, and he held me; safety, warmth, and comfort wrapping around me tight. Nox made soothing sounds and put us in motion. We followed Mr. Hunter down the hall and left Lucas behind.

I hoped I would never see him again.

35

N ox…

I was pretty much hating every minute of this prom thing, but I'd promised Maren and she was so happy that it almost made it worth it. I had been talking to her geeky friends for a minute and was beginning to wonder what was up. She was taking way longer than was typical of her, and I was half worried one of the bitches that had kept it up with the bullying and bullshit had cornered her in the bathroom. After five minutes more, I decided to find out.

"Mr. Fisher, what seems to be the problem?" her vice principal, Hunter, fell into step beside me.

"Maren's been in the restroom a little too long for my liking, I figured I'd go check on her."

"Well, yes, I could understand your concern, but it being the ladie's room…" he waved Ms. Cox over to us.

"Is there a problem?" she asked.

"Yeah, a big problem," I said, filled with pure fucking rage at the flip of a switch.

Her fuck nugget ex-boy-toy had her up against the lockers and was choking the living shit out of her.

"Hey!" I shouted and reached in, pulling him off of her. Mr. Hunter went for Maren while Ms. Cox stood off to the side shrieking about God.

He wasn't here, but I was pretty sure the devil himself was and he was in me. I slammed Lucas up against the lockers and fed him a left hook right into his fucking mouth. I buried my other fist in his gut, and when he bent over, kneed him right in the fucking face. I hit him and he hit the floor, it was over that fast.

Maren was sobbing, terrified and reaching for me and I took her off her vice principal and pulled her in tight against me.

"You saw that, right?"

"I most certainly did," Mr. Hunter said and took me by the elbow leading me toward the front.

"Let's go to my office."

We went with him, through the front office and into his, where he picked up the phone. I sat down on the couch he had against one wall and pulled Maren into my lap, moving her hair back from her throat, hissing at the bruises already coming up on her skin.

"You okay, Angel?"

She sniffed and opened her mouth and tried to speak, but wasn't very effective at it, her voice coming at a hoarse squeak.

"Don't let me go."

"Never, baby, never. I've got you."

I looked over to Mr. Hunter who was saying, "Yes, I believe he is still unconscious. I was more concerned about his victim. Yes, two ambulances and police. The attack was unconscionable."

He hung up the phone and Maren looked up at him like a deer in the headlights, her makeup-streaked face heartbreaking.

"I don't care what Mr. Barber says this time. There's no denying what I just saw. Maren, I'm so sorry."

"I need to get my coat, she's shivering," I said and she turned her attention back to me eyes too wide with panic.

"If you can trust me to get it for you, I will."

I let him have the keys to Rev's Chevelle and told him, "It's in the trunk, don't fuck me."

"Wouldn't dream of it," he said and went out. He returned moments later with my jacket and cut, which I wrapped around Maren's shoulders. I tucked her head under my chin and rocked her, even as Mr. Hunter set my keys on the edge of his desk.

A minute or two later, we heard approaching sirens. This was going to be a fucking bitch.

"Tell me again, just what fuckin' happened that you thought it would be a good idea to call *these two* in, first thing?" Dragon ordered and didn't look at all happy about it.

We'd ended up taking Maren to Doc's ER, but Doc wasn't on duty. She was sedated and resting in my room at the moment, Doc had come in and was hanging with her to watch for any problems. I guess near strangulation was a serious thing way beyond a raspy voice for a bit.

She'd filed charges on Luke, and with Mr. Hunter's help, I'd managed to avoid any for the beatdown I'd put on his drunk ass; despite the principal, Mr. Barber's, bitching about that fact.

Still, didn't mean we were out of the woods because Luke been awfully vocal about our visit some months back when he'd come out of it. Now I was sitting down with Dragon, Dray, and Trig and coming clean before any LEO's came knocking. Reaver and Cell had just come through the door, and everyone else was either in their own room or the media room.

Cell and Reave exchanged a look and pulled out chairs, Cell asking, "What's up?"

"You, going 'own fucking program,' again," Dray said bitterly.

Dragon shook his head. "Jesus H. Christ, Nox. You had to know takin' these two was like using a thermonuclear device to kill ants. That shit's just sheer overkill."

"I wanted to make my point clear," I said flatly.

Trigger shook his head and said, "You were at my place, with me," he said flatly to Reaver. "That was the night my Sunshine and Doll went out and had a ladies' night, remember?"

"Yes, I do," Reaver said with a shit-eating grin.

"I was with my twin, out in his shop."

"I was with Blue, watching TV."

"And I was here and saw you and Nox both," Dragon said with a sigh. "Weren't the first time I would hafta lie to law enforcement. Probably won't be the last, but just what the fuck was you thinkin' pulling a stunt like that?" he demanded of Cell.

"I have a rule — you're gonna threaten something, seems to me you ought to know exactly what it's like, yeah?"

"This have anything to do with that waitress Blue's hung up on?" Trig asked, and I leaned back, antsy, wanting to get back to Maren.

"Ask Blue," Cell said with a shrug, but it was the first time I'd seen him look even remotely uncomfortable.

"You all put the club in trouble, and there needs to be some consequences for that. It'll get discussed at the next church meeting. For now, get you gone, motherfuckers. I don't even want to look at you let alone think about what you done." Dragon crossed his arms over his chest and I felt my heart bottom out.

I got up without a word after the rest of the guys left out and Dragon said to my back, "I get what you was trying to do, but takin' Cell was a mistake. Don't make it again. You feel me?"

I nodded, and said, "Trust me, I wasn't keen on it and I was there." I shuddered, but it wasn't for effect. What'd been done that night had seriously disturbed me.

"Get back to yer ol' lady. Shit ain't deep," he said and I nodded and went to my room. Doc looked up from the book he was reading when I came through the door. He leaned forward and put his forearms on his knees, looking at me plainly over his half-moon specs.

"She's gonna sleep like the dead. Ain't nothin' broken according to her x-rays, but she's gonna be bruised, prolly be raspy for a while, and it's gonna hurt to swallow. She'll need to take it easy for a bit."

I nodded. "Thanks, Doc."

"It's good you got to her when you did."

"Yeah," I murmured.

"Hold her tight," he suggested dragging himself to his feet. He clapped me on the shoulder a couple of times and left out of my room.

I stripped down and got into bed with my woman, pulling her into the curve of my body and closing my eyes, just listening to her breathe.

36

M aren...

I wanted to skip my graduation, but the club wouldn't let me. They'd gone with me, had filled up two entire rows and had spilled into a third in the gallery, waiting for my name to be called and for me to walk across the stage and accept my diploma. Sage was with them, had been inseparable from me ever since he'd seen the bruises. I traced a finger along the fading but still very much so visible marks as Mr. Barber called out, "Maren Tracy."

A loud cheer went up behind me as I made my march, stepping up onto the stage and crossing. I took my diploma from Mr. Barber, looked him right in the eye and said, "You're despicable," refused to shake his hand, and went on to Mr. Hunter whose hand I did shake.

The cheers behind me got loud and louder when I passed him up. He had tried to stop me from pressing charges against Lucas, had told me it wasn't worth ruining a boy's life over a misunderstanding; that I was being dramatic.

It had taken everything in me not to hit him. When I'd told Nox what had happened, he did hit something... a door, which Rush had then had to come and replace. I had no regrets about it. It was just a door and knowing how much Nox loved me was hardly something to get angry about.

I reached the end of the stage and began my descent down the other staircase. Nox was waiting for me with a dozen red roses, which he handed me. He kissed me long and deep to more cheers from the club and even quite a few from the student body. He held my hand all the way back to our seats. I refused to go back to my seat with the rest of the student body. I wasn't one of them anymore. I hadn't been since that night, and I never would be again.

I was okay with that, glad for it, and overjoyed to belong here with Nox, Rush, Archer, Mel and their family and the extended chosen family that was The Sacred Hearts MC.

I shifted uncomfortably in my seat, fidgeting between Sage and Nox until Nox had enough. He stood up and took my hand, and the rest of the club followed suit. We left, as they were still calling out names, and I felt slightly bad for ruining some of the student's moments, but not bad enough to actually stay in my seat.

Out in the parking lot, I unpinned my graduation cap off my hair and dropped it on the ground after saving the tassel. I unzipped and left the gown in a heap next to it. Nox shook out my jacket and his rag, and I slid into them, relief settling on my shoulders with it. I hugged Sage who hugged me back and jogged over to Sunshine's Jeep to ride with her, Hayden and Connor.

"Go for a ride?" Nox asked, and I nodded.

"Wind therapy sounds really good right now."

"Hey, D!" he called out. I wasn't really listening, my mind whirling and twisting over all the events that led up to nearly being strangled to death, instead.

I stuffed the tassel from my cap into my pocket while Nox stowed my diploma in one of his saddlebags. Climbing on behind him instantly made me feel better, the thrum of the bike stripping more anxiety away, and then we were moving.

Becoming one with man and machine as we took corners in sweeps and curves, riding just for the sake of riding, just the two of us, taking the long route back to the club. It was like a balm to my wounded soul. I wrapped arms and legs around Nox and cuddled against his back. I heard him laugh, and he took us on the highway for wind and speed.

We couldn't dally too long, I mean, there was a party waiting for me back at the club, but I needed this. I needed to unwind and relax, and if I couldn't do it beneath Nox's body and his careful attentions, then this was the next best thing. Except when we got back to the club, he skipped the front drive in favor of riding around to the back, stopping on the asphalt loop in front of the building that housed his room.

"Do we have time?" I asked, and he gave me a flat look.

"Babe, we're gonna make time. They can wait five or ten more goddamn minutes."

I laughed and took his hand following him into the building and down the long hall. We were barely inside the door and the clothes started coming off, dropping to the floor in a frenzy. I didn't even bother with the boots, I got my pants and panties down and bent over the dresser, Nox more than happy to oblige me.

He got himself out of his pants, got a condom rolled on in record time, and with a fist wound in my hair, shoved into me hilt deep.

I moaned, thrusting my body back onto his straining cock and meeting him stroke for thrust. The pressure built quickly, my emotions tangling with the physical build of his body moving with mine, and I let them.

I craved release, I wanted to feel good after the last couple of weeks of feeling so awful, and I let Nox do that for me. His body bent over mine, his fingers finding my clit and teasing me higher, euphoria swirling in my veins, a taste of things to come.

"You like that?" he asked and I whined, a whimpering, begging, wordless moan escaping my lips. He gently bit the side of my neck where it met my shoulder and thrust into me as far as he could go, teasing me from the outside.

"Oh God! Like that, just like that," I gasped and then I was pressed flat against the dresser's top, Nox riding my body through my orgasm and sucking in a breath between his teeth.

"Oh shit, Angel, that feels so good," he moaned as I came around him, and I smiled to myself.

He stroked lazily a few times, in and out of me, before chuckling, withdrawing his hand from my hair carefully, so that he could hold the condom on and pull out of my pussy. He massaged my ass and admired the view a second before letting me straighten and I'd be lying if I said I hated that. I loved every minute of how he looked at me. He made me feel beautiful just by virtue of his looks and that was something special.

"I love you," I murmured as I pulled my panties and jeans back into place. Nox smiled, tucking himself back into his pants.

"I love you, too, Angel. You alright?"

I was. Completely relaxed and languid. The release I had craved delivered two-fold. I gave him a cheeky grin and said, "Be better if you promised a more thorough round later tonight."

He smiled. "Anything for you, babe."

He pulled me close, our clothes set to rights and kissed me long, slow and lingering deep and I laughed. "Why do I feel like I just had a prison sentence commuted?" I asked.

"Because with the way shit was heavy and going down at that school, you're not far off. You're out of there, Angel, done and graduated with honors. Real life starts now."

I touched the side of his face, and felt my expression soften, sighing out and asked, "Does real life include you in it?" I asked.

He cocked his head to the side and considered me. "You know it does."

"Then move in with us," I said and kissed his mouth. He kissed me back, his hands curving around the back of my neck in the barest of touches, thumbs gently caressing my jaw, and I felt the last of the tension I'd carried ease out of me. It should have scared me after Luke and nearly being strangled, but this was Nox, and I trusted him implicitly.

"All you had to do was ask, Angel," he said softly.

"I think I would feel better about taking over my dad's old room if we did it together," I whispered and Nox smiled.

"Think Sage'll be alright with me moving in?"

"He's the one that suggested it first."

Nox smiled harder and put his mouth to mine again. We kissed, long, slow and lingering deep, his hands delving beneath the hem of my shirt to caress my skin.

We had to do a more thorough round of lovemaking before joining the party. One with fewer clothes and more touches.

EPILOGUE

N ox...

I went up behind her and pulled her back into my arms, as Rush and Archer set the trunk Rush had made for Maren's birthday down at the foot of our new bed. She looked drawn and a bit pinched, and I knew she had so many mixed emotions about moving into her dad's room, but overall it really was the best idea.

"It looks really cool," Sage said, looking over everything. We'd overhauled the entire thing from the paint to the carpet, to the furniture which had been made by Rush and had been meticulously picked out of his dusting collection in storage lockers. Rush straightened and looked around, a shine of pride in his eyes.

"Mind if I get Mel up here to take pictures of it like this?" he asked.

Maren frowned. "Why?"

"Uh, because you guys did a bang-up job and my furniture looks great as a result?"

Maren snorted. "Get your pictures, but your furniture is what makes the room gorgeous, retard."

"Whatever, nerd-girl." He raised his fist and Maren grinned and bumped it.

"I'm out," Sage said to Archer and Rush. "They're going to start making out."

"Shit," Archer grunted and was the first one out the door.

"Right behind you, kid. Don't get come stains on anything until after Mel gets those shots for me," Rush called over his shoulder, guiding Sage in front of him by his.

He propelled Maren's little brother out of the room and I gave the lot of them the finger over my shoulder. My angel giggled as I covered her mouth with mine and kissed her. My girl, my woman, forever.

"I love you," she murmured and I smiled.

"Time to break in that new bed," I said back.

ALSO BY A.J. DOWNEY

Indigo Knights

1. Her Thin Blue Lifeline

2. His Cold Blue Command

3. A Low Blue Flame

4. His Wild Blue Rose

5. Her Pained Blue Silence

6. A Cold Blue Call

7. Her Reluctant Blue Cavalier

8. Forged Under Fire

9. Under A Blue Moon

10. Sound of Blue Thunder

Sacred Hearts MC Pacific Northwest

1. Over the High Side

2. Wind Therapy

3. Apex of the Curve

4. Low Sided

5. Eating Asphalt

6. Hammer Down

7. Only Fool Riding

The Voodoo Bastards MC

1. Bourbon & Blood

2. Whiskey Shivers

3. Moonshine Lullabies

4. Cognac Secrets

5. Tequila Damnation

Iron Wraiths MC

1. Original Syn

2. Love & Fear

3. The Hangman's Rope

Royal Bastard MC: St. Augustine Chapter

1. Iron Hearts

Paranormal Romance (with Ryan Kells)

1. I Am The Alpha

2. Omega's Run

3. Hunter's End

Indigo City Darker (with Jared KingPacal Lain)

1. Triple Threat

2. Double Shot

Standalones

Synchronicity

ABOUT A.J. DOWNEY

A.J. Downey is a Pacific Northwest girl living in an East Tennessee world who finds inspiration from her surroundings, through the people she meets, and likely as a byproduct of way too much caffeine. She specializes in real and relatable romance stories featuring that real-life kind of love that everyone craves.

Stalker Information:

Website
www.ajdowney.com